Acclaim for Lee Goldberg's previous mysteries

"A nifty creative take on the tradition of great amateur sleuths with a cast of quirky characters."
—Stuart M. Kaminsky

"A clever, high-octane whodunit that moves like a bullet train." —Janet Evanovich

"Well plotted and beautifully rendered."
—Margaret Maron, Edgar, Agatha, and Macavity Award–winning author of the Deborah Knott mysteries

"Elegant writing, wry humor, a suspenseful premise, [and] a fast-paced plot."
—Aimee and David Thurlo, authors of the Ella Clah, Sister Agatha, and Lee Nez mystery series

"A clever, twisting tale." —Lisa Gardner

"A riveting mystery . . . wonderful stuff!"
—Paul Bishop, two-time LAPD Detective of the Year and head of the West Los Angeles Sex Crimes and Major Assault Crimes Units, and author of *Twice Dead*, *Chalk*, and *Whispers*

continued . . .

MR. MONK
GOES TO HAWAII

A Novel by
Lee Goldberg

Based on the television series created by
Andy Breckman

A SIGNET BOOK

SIGNET
Published by New American Library, a division of
Penguin Group (USA) Inc., 375 Hudson Street,
New York, New York 10014, USA
Penguin Group (Canada), 90 Eglinton Avenue East, Suite 700, Toronto,
Ontario M4P 2Y3, Canada (a division of Pearson Penguin Canada Inc.)
Penguin Books Ltd., 80 Strand, London WC2R 0RL, England
Penguin Ireland, 25 St. Stephen's Green, Dublin 2,
Ireland (a division of Penguin Books Ltd.)
Penguin Group (Australia), 250 Camberwell Road, Camberwell, Victoria 3124,
Australia (a division of Pearson Australia Group Pty. Ltd.)
Penguin Books India Pvt. Ltd., 11 Community Centre, Panchsheel Park,
New Delhi - 110 017, India
Penguin Group (NZ), cnr Airborne and Rosedale Roads, Albany,
Auckland 1310, New Zealand (a division of Pearson New Zealand Ltd.)
Penguin Books (South Africa) (Pty.) Ltd., 24 Sturdee Avenue,
Rosebank, Johannesburg 2196, South Africa

Penguin Books Ltd., Registered Offices:
80 Strand, London WC2R 0RL, England

First published by Signet, an imprint of New American Library,
a division of Penguin Group (USA) Inc.

First Printing, July 2006
10 9 8 7 6 5 4 3 2 1

To Valerie and Madison,
who take very good care of me.

ACKNOWLEDGMENTS

I would like to thank Cynthia Chow of the Kaneohe Public Library for her help on all things Hawaiian, but any mistakes are entirely my fault (particularly my attempts at pidgin). I am also indebted to Dr. D. P. Lyle, Wayne Aronsohn, Steve Wurzel, William Rabkin, Tod Goldberg, Kathleen Kay, Anne Tomlin, Christine King, and A. Lyn Bell for their assistance. And, finally, this book would not have been possible without the inspiration and enthusiasm of my friend Andy Breckman, the creator of Adrian Monk.

1

Mr. Monk and the Perfect Murder

Here's the thing about brilliant detectives. They're all nuts.

Take Nero Wolfe, for instance.

He was this incredibly fat detective who wouldn't leave his New York brownstone. He stayed inside the house tending his orchids, drinking five quarts of beer a day, and devouring gourmet meals prepared by his live-in chef. So he hired Archie Goodwin to screen clients, run investigative errands, chase down clues, and drag people back to the brownstone to be rudely interrogated. Archie was an ex-cop or an ex-soldier or something like that, so he was well suited for the job.

Then there's Sherlock Holmes, an eccentric, wound-up cocaine addict who played his violin all night and conducted chemical experiments in his living room. He probably would have been committed if it weren't for Dr. Watson. The doctor retired from the army with a war injury, rented a room from Holmes, and ended up being the detective's assistant and official chronicler. His medical degree and experience serving in the war gave Watson the skills and temperament he needed to deal with Holmes.

At least I didn't live with Adrian Monk, another brilliant detective, the way Archie and Dr. Watson did with their employers, but I'd still argue that the job was a lot harder for me than it was for them. For one thing, I didn't have any of their qualifications.

My name is Natalie Teeger. I've had a lot of odd jobs, but I'm not an ex–FBI agent or a promising criminology student or an aspiring paramedic, one of which I'd be if this were a book or a TV series instead of my life. I was bartending before I met Monk, so I suppose I could have mixed myself a nice, strong drink after work if I wanted to. But I didn't, because I was also a widowed single mother trying to raise a twelve-year-old daughter, and it's a good idea to do that sober.

If I'd done my research into brilliant detectives *before* working for Adrian Monk instead of *after*, I might not have taken the job.

I know what you're thinking. Nero Wolfe and Sherlock Holmes are fictional characters, so what could I possibly learn from their assistants? The thing is, I couldn't find any real detectives who were anything like Monk, and I was desperate for guidance. They were the only sources of information I could turn to.

Here's what I learned from them: When it comes to assisting a great detective, you can be an ex-cop or a doctor or have other qualifications and it's not going to make a difference. Because whatever makes your boss a genius at solving murders is going to make life impossible for everybody around him, especially you. And no matter how hard you try, that's never going to change.

That's especially true with Adrian Monk, who has a smorgasbord of obsessive-compulsive disorders. You can't truly grasp the magnitude of his anxieties and phobias unless you experience them every single day like, God help me, I did.

Everything in his life has to be in order, following some arcane rules that make sense only to Monk. For instance, I've seen him at breakfast remove every bran flake and raisin from a bowl of Kellogg's Raisin Bran and count them to be sure there's a four-flake-to-one-raisin ratio in his bowl before he starts eating. How did he come up with that ratio? How did he determine that anything else "violated the natural laws of the universe?" I don't know. I don't *want* to know.

He's also got a thing about germs, though not to the extent that he won't go outside or interact with people, but he doesn't make it easy.

Monk brings his own silverware and dishes to restaurants. He takes a folding lawn chair with him to the movies because he can't bear the thought of sitting in a seat a thousand other people have sat in. When a bird crapped on my windshield, he called 911. I could go on, but I think you get the picture.

Dealing with all of his quirks and acting as the middleman between him and the civilized world was very stressful stuff. It was wearing me down to the point of total exhaustion. So I turned to the books about Nero Wolfe and Sherlock Holmes hoping to glean from them some helpful advice that might make my job a little easier.

I didn't find any.

I finally realized that my only hope was to escape, to get far away from Monk. Not forever, because as difficult as he was, I liked him, and the job was flexible enough to allow me to be there for my daughter. All I really needed were a few peaceful days off to go someplace where he couldn't reach me and I could get some rest. The problem was, I couldn't afford to go anywhere.

But then Lady Luck took pity on me.

I went to my mailbox one day and found a round-trip ticket to Hawaii, courtesy of my best friend, Candace. She was getting married on the island of Kauai and wanted me there as her maid of honor. She knew how strapped I was for money, so she paid for everything, booking me for seven days and six nights at the fanciest resort on the island, the Grand Kiahuna Poipu, where the wedding was going to be held.

The easy part was talking my mom into coming up from Monterey to take care of Julie for a week. The hard part was finding someone to take care of Monk.

I called a temporary staffing agency. I told them the job required basic secretarial work, some transportation, and strong "interpersonal skills." They said they had just the right people. I was sure Monk would go through all of them before the week was over and that I would never be able to call that temp agency again. I didn't care, because I could already feel the sand between my toes, smell the coconut lotion on my skin, and hear Don Ho singing "Tiny Bubbles" to me.

All I had to do then was break the news to Monk.

I kept putting it off until finally it was the day before I was leaving. Even then, I couldn't seem to find the right moment. I still hadn't found it when Monk got a call from Capt. Leland Stottlemeyer, his former partner on the SFPD, asking for his help.

That made my predicament even worse. Stottlemeyer brought Monk in to consult whenever they had a particularly tricky homicide to solve. If I left Monk in the middle of an investigation, it would make him crazy (or crazier than usual, to be precise). And Stottlemeyer wouldn't be thrilled either, especially if it meant his case would drag on without a solution because Monk was distracted.

I cursed myself for not telling Monk before and prayed the case would turn out to be a simple one.

It wasn't.

Somebody poisoned Dr. Lyle Douglas, the world-famous heart surgeon, while he was performing a quadruple bypass operation on Stella Picaro, his forty-four-year-old former nurse, at the hospital where she worked.

Dr. Douglas was midway through the delicate procedure, which was being observed by a dozen doctors and medical students, when he had a violent seizure and dropped dead. Another surgeon, Dr. Troy Clark, had to jump in and save the patient from dying. He succeeded.

Nobody realized Dr. Douglas had been murdered until the autopsy was completed the following day. By then, all the evidence that might have been left at the crime scene was gone. The operating room had been thoroughly cleaned, the instruments disinfected, the linens washed, and everything else discarded as biohazardous waste immediately after the surgery was over.

There might not have been any evidence, but there

were plenty of suspects. The main one, of course, was Dr. Clark, the surgeon who saved Stella Picaro on the operating table and was being treated as a hero. He also happened to be Dr. Douglas's major rival.

Dr. Douglas had a lot of other enemies. He was a manipulative egomaniac who'd hurt a lot of people, including just about everybody on his surgical team, many of the doctors observing the operation, and even the patient he was cutting open when he died.

But neither Stottlemeyer nor his assistant, Lt. Randy Disher, could figure out how Dr. Douglas was poisoned in front of so many witnesses without anybody seeing a thing. They were stumped. So they called Monk.

They briefed Monk at the station and afterward he wanted to visit the scene of the crime. I could have told him about my trip on the way to the hospital, but I knew if I did that, he wouldn't be able to concentrate on anything else all day.

When we got there, he insisted on wearing surgical scrubs over his clothes, a cap on his head, a mask and goggles on his face, plastic gloves on his hands, and even paper booties over his shoes before going inside the OR.

"Are you trying to get into the mind of the surgeon?" I teased him as the two of us stood outside the operating room doors.

"I'm trying to avoid infection," Monk said.

"Heart disease isn't contagious."

"This building is filled with sick people. The air is thick with deadly germs. The only thing more dangerous than visiting a hospital is drinking out of a water fountain," Monk said. "It's a good thing there are a lot of doctors around."

"There's nothing dangerous about drinking from a water fountain, Mr. Monk. I've been drinking from them all my life."

"You probably enjoy playing Russian roulette, too."

Monk stepped into the OR, and I watched as he carefully surveyed every corner of the room and each piece of equipment. His investigation of the crime scene resembled an improvised dance with an invisible partner. He repeatedly circled the room, making sudden pirouettes, gliding back and forth, and dipping every so often to peer under something. He stopped at the stainless-steel table where the surgery was performed and gazed down at it as if imagining the patient in front of him.

He rolled his shoulders and tilted his head as if he were working a kink out in his neck. But I knew that wasn't it. What was irritating him was a detail, some fact that didn't fit where it was supposed to. Nothing bothered Monk more than disorder. And what's a mystery, after all, but a situation in disarray, crying out for organization—an imbalance that needs to be set right?

"Where's the patient Dr. Douglas was operating on?" Monk asked.

"She's upstairs," I said. "In the ICU."

Monk nodded. "Call the captain and ask him to meet us there."

There's something really creepy about intensive care units to me. I've been in only a couple of them and, while I know they exist to save lives, they scare me. The patients connected to all those machines don't look like people to me anymore, but like corpses some mad scientist is trying to reanimate.

That was the way Stella Picaro looked, even though she was wide-awake. There were all kinds of tubes and wires connecting her to an EKG, a respirator, and a toaster oven, for all I knew. Machines beeped and lights blinked and she was alive, so I guess it was all for the best. Still, I tried not to look at her. It made me too uncomfortable.

Monk and I were standing next to the nurses' station. He was still in his surgical garb and he was breathing funny, almost gasping.

"Are you feeling all right, Mr. Monk?" I asked.

"Fine."

"Then why are you gasping?"

"I'm trying to limit my breathing," Monk said.

I thought about it for a second. "The fewer breaths, the fewer chances you have of inhaling some virus."

"You should try it," he said. "It could save your life."

It was scary how good I was getting at understanding his peculiar way of thinking, his Monkology. That in itself was a pretty strong argument for me to get away from him for a while.

I was about to tell him about the Hawaii trip right then and there, when Stottlemeyer sauntered in, holding a latte from Starbucks in his hand. There was a little bit of foam in his bushy mustache and a fresh stain on his wide, striped tie. I found his disheveled appearance endearing, but I knew it drove Monk insane. Sometimes I wondered if the captain did it on purpose.

Lieutenant Disher was, as usual, right at Captain Stottlemeyer's side. He reminded me of a golden retriever, always bounding around happily, blissfully unaware of all the things he was destroying with his wagging tail.

Stottlemeyer grinned at Monk. "You know it's against the law to impersonate a doctor."

"I'm not," Monk said. "I'm wearing this for my own protection."

"You ought to wear it all the time."

"I'm seriously considering it."

"I bet you are," Stottlemeyer said.

"You have foam in your mustache," Monk said, pointing.

"Do I?" Stottlemeyer casually dabbed at his mustache with a napkin. "Is that better?"

Monk nodded. "Your tie is stained."

Stottlemeyer lifted it up and looked down at it. "So it is."

"You should change it," Monk said.

"I don't have another tie with me, Monk. It will have to wait."

"You could buy one," Monk said.

"I'm not going to buy one."

"You could borrow one from a doctor," Monk said.

"You can borrow mine," Disher said.

"I don't want your tie, Randy," Stottlemeyer said, then turned to Monk. "What if I just take mine off and put it in my pocket?"

"I'd know it's there," Monk said.

"Pretend it isn't," Stottlemeyer said.

"I don't know how to pretend," Monk said. "I never got the hang of it."

Stottlemeyer handed his latte to Disher, took off his tie, and stuffed it into a biohazard container.

"Is that better?" Stottlemeyer asked, taking back his latte from Disher.

"I think we all appreciate it," Monk said, looking at Disher and me. "Don't we?"

"So what have you got for me that was worth chucking my tie for?" Stottlemeyer asked.

"The killer."

Stottlemeyer and Disher both glanced around the room. So did I.

"Where?" Stottlemeyer said. "I don't see any of our suspects."

Monk tipped his head toward Stella Picaro. Just seeing the breathing tube down her throat nearly triggered my gag reflex.

"You're talking about *her*?" Disher said.

Monk nodded.

"*She* did it?" Stottlemeyer said incredulously.

Monk nodded.

"Are you sure?" Stottlemeyer said.

Monk nodded. I looked back at Stella Picaro. She seemed to be trying to shake her head.

"Maybe you forgot this part," Stottlemeyer said, "but when Dr. Douglas died, that lady was unconscious on an operating table, her chest cut wide-open, her beating heart held in his hands."

"And based on that flimsy alibi, you wrote her off as a suspect?" Monk said.

"Yeah, I did," Stottlemeyer said.

"Even though you told me she was his surgical nurse and his mistress for five years?"

"That's right."

"Even though when Dr. Douglas finally left his wife, it wasn't for her but for a twenty-two-year-old swimsuit model?"

"Look at her, Monk. She was having a quadruple bypass when the murder was committed. She nearly died on the operating table."

"That was all part of her cunning plan."

We all looked at her. She stared back at us wide-eyed, not making a sound. All we heard was the beeping of her EKG—which sounded kind of erratic to me, but I wasn't a doctor.

Stottlemeyer sighed. It was a sigh that conveyed weariness and defeat. It was tiring dealing with Monk, and futile arguing with him about murder. When it comes to homicide, Monk is almost always right.

"How could she possibly have done it?" Stottlemeyer asked.

I was wondering the same thing.

Disher snapped his fingers. "I've got it. Astral projection!"

"You're saying her spirit left her body and poisoned him," Stottlemeyer said.

Disher nodded. "That's the only explanation."

"I sure hope not. I'd like to keep this badge for a few more years." Stottlemeyer faced Monk again. "Tell me it's not astral projection."

"It's not," Monk said. "There's no such thing: Her body was the murder weapon."

"I don't get it," Disher said.

"When Stella discovered she needed heart surgery, she realized it was an opportunity to commit the perfect murder," Monk said, shooting a glance at Stella. "Isn't that right?"

She tried again to shake her head.

"You appealed to Dr. Douglas's ego by begging him to save your life and then talked him into performing the surgery here, at the hospital where you work."

"What difference did it make where the surgery was done?" Stottlemeyer asked.

"Because here she had access to the operating room, the supplies, and the equipment before the surgery and could doctor them, no pun intended," Monk said. "The iodine Dr. Douglas applied to her skin before making his incision was laced with poison."

"Wouldn't that have poisoned her, too?" Stottlemeyer said.

"It did, but she was getting the antidote in her IV," Monk said. "Take a look at her chart. It shows higher than normal levels of atropine."

Stottlemeyer took the chart that was hanging from the end of her bed, opened it, and stared at it for a long moment before closing it again.

"Who am I kidding?" he said as he put the chart back. "I don't know how to read a medical chart."

"Neither do I," Monk said.

"Then how do you know what is or isn't in her blood?"

"Because she's alive," Monk said. "And Dr. Douglas isn't."

"But what about the other doctors who were working on her?" Disher said. "How come they weren't poisoned, too?"

"Because they weren't wearing the same gloves as Dr. Douglas," Monk said. "He used only Conway gloves; the other brands gave him a skin rash. Before the surgery Stella put tiny pinpricks, invisible to the naked eye, in all the gloves in his box, so he would absorb the poison through his skin."

Stottlemeyer looked at Disher. "Contact the crime lab, Randy, and make sure they hold on to the box of gloves Dr. Douglas used. Have them examine the gloves for perforations."

Disher nodded and scribbled something in his notebook.

I looked at Stella. She was so pale and weak, she

seemed to be melting into her bed. Her eyes were filling with tears. I remembered hearing how Dr. Clark had to reach into her open chest and save her life after Dr. Douglas collapsed.

"But Mr. Monk," I said, "even with the antidote in the IV, it would have been suicidal for Stella to kill her surgeon while he was operating on her heart."

"It was a risk she was willing to take," Monk said. "It was poetic justice. She used her heart to kill the man who broke it."

Stella closed her eyes and tears rolled down her cheeks. I couldn't tell whether they were tears of sadness or anger. They might have been both.

Stottlemeyer shook his head in amazement. "I never would have caught her, Monk."

"You would have, sir," Disher said. "It might have taken longer, that's all."

"No, Randy, I wouldn't have. Not ever." Stottlemeyer regarded Monk with genuine appreciation. "How did you figure it out?"

"It was obvious," Monk said.

"Go ahead, rub it in," Stottlemeyer said. "Don't let my remaining shreds of self-respect stop you."

"There is no way any of the doctors or other medical personnel could have poisoned Dr. Douglas without being seen," Monk said. "That left only one possible suspect."

Stottlemeyer frowned. "Makes sense. I wonder why I couldn't see it."

The captain turned toward Stella, so he didn't notice Monk studying him, regarding his friend as if he were a complex painting.

Disher marched over to Stella's bedside. "You have the right to remain silent—"

"Randy," Stottlemeyer interrupted. "She's got a breathing tube down her throat. She couldn't say anything even if she wanted to."

"Oh," Disher said, then dangled the handcuffs he was holding. "Should I secure her to the bed?"

"I don't think that will be necessary," Stottlemeyer said.

"Captain," Monk said, "I could never drink out of a water fountain."

"Is that so?" Stottlemeyer seemed a little confused by the non sequitur.

"Not if my life depended on it," Monk said. "You probably do it without a second thought."

Stottlemeyer looked at Monk for a long moment. "All the time."

Monk shrugged.

Stottlemeyer nodded.

I guess what Monk was getting at is that life has a way of balancing out. It figured Monk would notice that more clearly than the rest of us.

2

Mr. Monk Gets the News

Monk has a standing appointment every Tuesday afternoon with his psychiatrist, Dr. Kroger. I've known this for over a year, and yet it somehow slipped my mind that his appointment fell on the day before my trip until it was time for me to drive him to Dr. Kroger's office.

That's when I came up with a scheme so evil and so perfect, it's amazing that I didn't think of it before. I decided to tell Monk about my trip as we were walking into Dr. Kroger's office; that way the shrink could deal with Monk's meltdown while I enjoyed a cup of coffee and flipped through the latest issue of *Esquire* in the waiting room.

It was such a brilliant scheme that anybody looking at it in retrospect, especially Monk, would be convinced I had planned it that way from the start. Not that it mattered when I came up with it. What mattered was that I did it.

I parked my Cherokee on Jackson Street in Pacific Heights and we started walking down the steep hill to Dr. Kroger's office, a recently constructed two-story concrete-and-glass building in the aerodynamic Streamline Moderne style that fit poorly amidst a row of stately Victorians.

The sky was a cloudless, dazzling blue, and a cool breeze was sweeping up off the Pacific and through the trees of the Presidio, carrying the scent of sea salt and pine. In front of us we could see the Marina District, the Golden Gate Bridge and clear across the bay to the wooded hills of Marin County.

We were halfway down the block, both of us admiring the view, when I told Monk, in an offhand sort of way, that I was leaving the next day for seven days in Kauai to be maid of honor at my best friend's wedding.

Monk blinked hard, but otherwise kept right on walking without changing his expression.

"You can't go," he said. I noticed he was still limiting his breathing.

"Why not?"

"You don't have any vacation days."

"Of course I do," I said. "I haven't used any yet."

"Because you don't have any," Monk said. "I thought you were aware that this is a full-time job."

"Full-time doesn't mean all the time," I said. "Everybody gets a vacation."

"Working for me is a vacation."

"No offense, Mr. Monk, but it's not."

"I'm a fun guy, aren't I?"

"Yes, of course you are," I said. "But I have a life outside of my job."

"I think not," Monk said between gasps. "So we're agreed. You'll stay."

"Mr. Monk, I'm going to Hawaii, even if it means

you'll fire me," I said. "Candace has been my best friend since we were kids. She was there for me on my wedding day. She was there for me when Julie was born. And she was there for me after Mitch was killed in Kosovo. I'm going to be there for her."

Monk gave me a forlorn look. "But who is going to be here for me?"

"I've contacted a temp agency and they're sending someone."

Monk let out another deep, rasping gasp and then sucked in a lungful of air. It was really beginning to get on my nerves.

"We're not in the hospital, Mr. Monk. You don't have to limit your breathing anymore."

"I'm not."

"Then what are you doing?"

"I'm having a stroke," Monk said, and fell against me. I grabbed him under the arm, opened the door to Kroger's building and half dragged him into the empty waiting room.

Dr. Kroger emerged from his office at that same moment, no doubt alarmed by Monk's histrionics.

Monk's psychiatrist is a fit and trim man in his fifties, the kind of guy who doesn't try to hide his age because he's proud that the years look so good on him. I found his presence naturally calming, but I could see how it could become irritating if you had to live with him. I'd be tempted to do horrible things just to get a rise out of him and maintain my own sanity. Does that make me a crazy person?

"What's wrong, Adrian?" Dr. Kroger asked in a gentle voice, taking Monk's other arm and helping me lead him to an armchair in his office.

"Massive. Heart. Attack," Monk said as he collapsed into the armchair in front of the window, which looked out over a concrete-walled courtyard and a burbling fountain.

"I thought you said it was a stroke," I said.

"And a stroke," Monk said. "I can feel my internal organs shutting down one by one."

Dr. Kroger turned from Monk and focused his intense shrink gaze upon me. "What happened, Mrs. Teeger?"

"I informed Mr. Monk that I'm leaving town tomorrow and that I won't be back for a week," I said, wondering if Dr. Kroger's even tan came from the sun, a salon, or a spray can.

"I see," he said, squinting into my eyes. "And you told him just now, outside my door."

I knew what he was thinking—no, *insinuating*—and I didn't care. I figured that dealing with stuff like this was what he got paid for anyway. And he must have liked doing it or he wouldn't have made it his profession.

So I nodded and smiled.

"You got it," I said. "Has the new issue of *Esquire* come in this week?"

What I liked best about Monk's appointments was that Dr. Kroger subscribed to a wide array of magazines and I got to thumb through stuff I wouldn't ordinarily read. Over the next forty-five minutes, I browsed *Maxim, GQ,* and *FHM* and learned that all women have a "secret button" that, when touched, triggers uncontrollable multiple orgasms. I also discovered there's a pickup line that all women are incapable of resisting. It's not so much a line as it is a

little story that's full of powerful psychological triggers that will subliminally spark in a woman an instinctive need to copulate immediately.

All you've got to do is tell her about this amazing
roller-coaster ride you went on, how it started with
a slow, steady climb that made every muscle in your
body tense up with excitement and anticipation.

And that the coaster crested at the top of an incredible peak, where it teetered for one tantalizing moment before plunging over the edge, taking your
breath away. You've never felt anything more exhila-
rating in your life and were shocked to hear yourself
screaming with wild abandon with each breathtaking curve.

And when it was over, your entire body tingled
and all you could think about was how much you
wanted to experience it again . . . and again.

I set the magazine aside and sat there for a moment, waiting to see if I felt an overwhelming desire
to find that special button of mine.

I was still waiting when Monk came out of Dr. Kroger's office. Monk seemed unusually subdued. Come
to think of it, so was I, considering I was supposed to
be foaming at the mouth with uncontrollable lust and
two men were there for the taking.

"Is everything okay?" I asked.

"Peachy," Monk said, and walked past me out the
door. I glanced at Dr. Kroger.

"You didn't give him a tranquilizer, did you?"

Dr. Kroger shook his head. "Adrian has simply
accepted the situation."

"He has?"

"He's in a good place emotionally right now."

"How long do you think he'll stay there?"

"Adrian knows how to reach me if he finds himself in crisis," Dr. Kroger said.

"Every day is a crisis. Mr. Monk couldn't sleep after watching Alfred Hitchcock's *The 39 Steps* on TV the other night. He spent the next day on the phone with the studio trying to convince them to add another step to the title."

"Don't worry about Adrian. He'll be fine." Dr. Kroger smiled and patted me on the back. "Have a nice vacation."

Monk lived in an apartment building on Pine, just a few blocks south of Dr. Kroger's office, in a homey neighborhood that had somehow avoided being stripped of its natural charm and upscaled beyond affordability like the rest of the city.

Since he lived so close by, Monk didn't wait for me to drive him home. Instead he gave me a dismissive little wave and started trudging sadly up the hill on his own.

Fine, I thought. *Be that way. Walk home. Be a petulant child. I don't care.*

But the truth was, I *did* care. I felt a deep stab of guilt and cursed myself for it. I refused to feel bad about needing some time to myself or for supporting my best friend on her wedding day.

And what did I have to feel guilty about anyway? I was Monk's employee and his friend, but that was it. I wasn't responsible for him.

I wasn't taking my daughter with me, and she wasn't upset. Julie was happy for me, and for Candace, and while she would have liked to visit Hawaii, she didn't want to get behind on her schoolwork.

And there was another reason she didn't mind my going.

"We're together all the time, Mom," Julie said with a weariness only a put-upon adolescent can convey. "I love you, but sometimes it's a little much. I really need a break."

I'm sure there was some truth to that. Hey, I was a kid once myself. I knew how she felt. But there was more to it than that. She was looking forward to spending a week with her grandmother. Not only does my mom let Julie stay up late and eat whatever she wants, but they love to go shopping together. Mom doesn't get up to San Francisco very often and has a notorious open-checkbook policy where her only granddaughter is concerned. I was sure I'd come back to find a closetful of new clothes in Julie's room. Maybe even a pony.

I figured if my twelve-year-old daughter could handle my going away for a few days, Adrian Monk certainly could. He was a grown man. He'd survive without me around to hand him disinfectant wipes.

Well, he might survive, but could he *function*?

Sure he could, I told myself. He'd functioned for a long time before he met me.

Of course, those were different times—at least, that was what Stottlemeyer explained to me.

Although Monk has always had obsessive-compulsive tendencies, he was once able to control them enough so that he could get a job on the SFPD and rise from a patrolman to homicide detective.

But then Monk's wife, Trudy, a freelance reporter, was killed by a car bomb. She was the most stabilizing influence in his life. Without her, he was lost. His grief, combined with his inability to solve her murder, ate away at him. His phobias and compulsions took over his life. That cost him his badge, which was as dear to him, and as vital to his mental stability, as his wife.

I didn't have compulsive tendencies, but I certainly knew how losing a spouse could tear you apart in ways you never thought possible. What saved me when Mitch was killed was my daughter. I focused entirely on the fact that I was the only parent she had left. That knowledge, that commitment, kept me firmly centered when the gale-force winds of grief threatened to sweep me away.

There were two things that saved Monk: Stottlemeyer threw some consulting work his way and, at Dr. Kroger's insistence, Monk hired a full-time nurse to help him get back into the world again.

After a few years, his nurse abruptly moved to New Jersey one day and remarried her ex-husband. Monk had recovered enough by then to know he didn't need a nurse anymore but that he still could use some help.

That was when he met me, but that's a whole different story.

I didn't do anything for him that anybody else with a lot of patience couldn't do just as well. Or that he couldn't do for himself if he put his mind to it.

I was convinced that Monk didn't really need an assistant anymore; he just liked having someone there to talk to and to deal with the little things in life that might otherwise distract him from what he did best, which was solve murders.

So was I really messing up his life that much by leaving for a week?

No, I reassured myself, of course not. It wasn't as if he were all alone in the world. He had Dr. Kroger and Captain Stottlemeyer and the temp worker to turn to for help.

That was more than enough.

At least I hoped so.

And I hoped that I'd stop feeling guilty long enough to enjoy my trip.

3

Mr. Monk and the Pill

I had to leave the house at five A.M. to make my eight-o'clock flight to Honolulu. I drove to the airport, stowed my car in long-term parking, and took the shuttle to the terminal. I stood in a long line at check-in and waited in another at security and still got to the gate with twenty minutes to spare before boarding.

Adrian Monk was the furthest thing from my mind as I settled into my narrow economy-class seat for the five-hour trip.

The flight attendants were all Hawaiian or Polynesian women wearing floral aloha shirts and red hibiscus flowers in their hair.

A video of palm trees, waterfalls, and pristine Hawaiian beaches screened on all the plane's TV monitors. Hawaiian music—that gentle rhythm of ukulele, ukeke, steel guitar, and native chants flowing like the tide, lapping at the white sand—played softly throughout the cabin.

I closed my eyes and sighed. The plane was still

on the tarmac at LAX, but mentally and emotionally I was already more relaxed than I'd been in weeks. The clatter of passengers getting settled, the murmur of conversation, the wail of babies crying, the hum of the engines, and even the sweet Hawaiian music all faded away.

And before I knew it, I was sound asleep.

I was awakened seemingly an instant later by the gentle nudge of a flight attendant asking me if I wanted breakfast.

"You have a choice between a cheese-and-mushroom omelet, macadamia-nut pancakes, or a fruit platter," she said, pulling out trays from her cart and showing me the entrées.

All of the choices looked gross to me. Even the fruit looked as if it had been soaked in grease.

"No, thanks," I said. I glanced at my watch and was surprised to discover I'd actually slept through takeoff and had been snoozing away for forty-five minutes.

"If she's not going to have it, I'll take it," a man said. I knew the voice, but I had to be wrong. It couldn't possibly be who it sounded like.

"You already have a meal, sir," the flight attendant said. I tried to see who she was talking to, but I couldn't see past her cart.

"But I'm almost finished with my omelet, I'm still hungry, and I'd like to sample the pancakes," he said. "If she's not going to eat her meal, what difference does it make who does?"

No, it wasn't him. He'd never say what I'd just heard. He'd never get on a plane. And he'd certainly never sit in an odd-numbered seat in row thirty-one.

What I was hearing was my guilt tormenting me. Yes, that had to be it.

The stewardess forced a smile, took a tray of pancakes and handed it to the passenger on the other side of the cart.

"Mmmm," the familiar voice purred. "Looks mighty tasty. Thank you, sweetheart."

It can't be.

She pushed her cart along, and Monk smiled at me from across the aisle, his mouth full of pancakes.

"You don't know what you're missing," he said. "This is delicious."

I blinked hard. He was still there.

"Mr. Monk?"

"Hey, we're off the clock, sister. The Monk says, let's keep it casual."

"The Monk?"

"You're right, still too formal. Call me Chad."

"Chad?"

This was too much, too fast. I was either still asleep and dreaming this whole encounter, or, worse, I was awake and delirious.

Monk leaned into the aisle and whispered, "Chad is more tropical than Adrian, don't you think?"

"What are you doing here?" I whispered back.

"Going to Hawaii, of course," he said.

"But you hate to fly."

He ignored me and nudged the heavyset man sitting beside him. The passenger was wearing a too-tight bowling shirt and plaid Bermuda shorts.

Monk motioned to the man's breakfast plate. "Are you going to finish that sausage?"

The man shook his head. "It's too salty and I'm on a restricted diet."

Monk speared the half-eaten sausage with his fork. "Thanks."

The man stared at Monk in shock and so did I.

"You're not going to eat that," I said in disbelief.

He sniffed the sausage. "It smells good. I think it's smoked."

And with that, he chomped half the sausage and offered the remainder to me across the aisle.

"Want the rest?"

I shook my head and pushed his hand away. The sausage fell off the fork and landed on the floor. Monk snatched it up.

"Two-second rule," he said before plunking it into his mouth.

Now I was convinced that this couldn't really be happening. I turned to the child in the seat beside me. She was about ten years old and was listening to her iPod.

"Excuse me," I said.

She pulled out her earphones. "Yes, ma'am?"

"Do you see a man in the seat across the aisle from me?"

She nodded.

"Could you describe him?"

"He's a white guy wearing a dress shirt that's buttoned up to his neck and a sport coat," she said. "Isn't he going to be awfully hot in Hawaii?"

"What's he doing?"

She looked past me and giggled. "Sticking his tongue out at me."

I turned and looked at Monk, who was pulling his mouth open wide with his fingers, wiggling his tongue, and rolling his eyes at the girl.

I swatted him.

"What is the matter with you?" I asked.

I was relieved to know I wasn't nuts. But that

didn't explain Monk's bizarre behavior, or what he was doing on my flight to Hawaii.

He licked his lips and smacked them a couple of times.

"My mouth is dry," Monk said, and turned to the passenger beside him. "You're right; that was a salty sausage. I need a drink. You mind?"

He picked up his tray and held it out to the passenger to hold for him. The man took it.

"Thanks." Monk lifted up his tray table and went down the aisle toward the back of the plane. I looked over my shoulder and saw him filling a paper cup with water from the plane's dispenser. Before I could say anything, he drank it all.

I bolted out of my seat and hurried down the aisle after him. "Are you insane, Mr. Monk? That's the deadliest water you can drink."

"People drink out of water fountains every day."

"Drinking airplane water is like drinking out of a toilet."

"Dogs do it without a problem," Monk said. "Doesn't kill them. Chill out, hotcakes."

Hotcakes?

"Mr. Monk," I said firmly, hoping to get his complete attention. "Are you on something?"

"I thought we agreed you were going to call me Chad."

"You *are* on something."

"It's a prescription Dr. Kroger gave me once to relieve my symptoms in extreme circumstances."

"What symptoms?"

"All of them," he said. "As long as I'm up, I think I'll use the restroom."

"You're kidding," I said. Wherever we were in San

Francisco, he always made me drive him home to go to the bathroom.

"Where else would you suggest I relieve myself?"

He edged past me, opened the restroom door, and went inside. Monk was using a public lavatory. I would never have believed it could happen.

I continued back to the galley and asked the flight attendant for a drink.

"What would you like?" she asked.

"A scotch," I said.

Monk emerged from the bathroom a moment later, not caring at all that he was trailing a piece of toilet paper from his shoe.

"Better make it two," I said.

The rest of the flight was a living hell.

Although Monk wasn't obsessing about how things were organized (or, more accurately, disorganized) or freaking out about little stuff that normal people would take in stride, he was irritating in an entirely new way. He was like a restless child.

What did he do? Let's see, where should I start?

He led a *Hawaii Five-O* singalong with everybody making up their own lyrics to the theme. His lyrics went like this:

> *If you get in trouble, call the Monk, that's me.*
> *If you find a dead body, I'm the guy to see-eee.*
> *Stop! In the name of the law.*
> *Stop! Murder sticks in my craw.*
> *I'll find the killer. Call the Monk, that's me. . . .*

There were more lyrics, but those are bad enough. I couldn't get them out of my head for the entire flight. It was a crime against humanity, since I certainly wasn't the only one suffering. (Even now, when I least expect it, those lyrics will come back and torment me for hours.)

He took off his shoes and roamed barefoot up and down the aisles, striking up conversations with startled passengers.

"I'm the Monk," he said to one woman. "That looks like an interesting book you're reading. Can I read a chapter? I know—let's read it aloud."

And he did.

He also went to the galley and hounded the flight attendants for their macadamia-nut-pancake recipe and refused to believe them when they insisted they simply reheated frozen food.

"But they taste so fluffy and fresh," he said.

And he ate twenty-one bags of roasted peanuts, leaving the wrappers all over the plane.

"Everything should be dry-roasted," he proclaimed to one and all. "Has anyone here ever tried dry-roasted chicken? Or dry-roasted granola? The possibilities are limitless!"

I thought the flight would never end. Finally we made our descent into Oahu. It says something about the beauty of Hawaii that the moment I glimpsed the island out the window, all my frustration with Monk disappeared.

Our approach to Honolulu International Airport took us over Pearl Harbor and gave me a terrific view of Waikiki and Diamond Head. The colors were so bright, the mountains so lush, and the water so blue, it didn't seem real. It didn't help that I was seeing it through a tiny porthole. I was separate from it. It was too much like seeing it on TV.

Television was my entire frame of reference for Hawaii anyway. I couldn't look at the Waikiki shoreline without thinking of that shot from the *Hawaii Five-O* main titles, the camera zooming up from the water to the rooftop of a hotel tower to find Jack Lord standing there, grim faced and stoic in his blue suit.

And that memory naturally brought Monk's atrocious improvised lyrics back into my head.

As we deplaned, we were greeted by airline hostesses who draped fragrant flower leis around our necks and welcomed us to the islands.

Much to my surprise, Monk accepted the lei and the kiss the hostess gave him on the cheek. It was a good thing he didn't ask me for a wipe, because I didn't bring any with me.

We had a one-hour layover in Honolulu before our forty-five-minute flight to Kauai. The airport was so nice, it wouldn't have bothered me to wait twice that long. The main terminal was an enormous open patio that wrapped around a Japanese garden and a koi pond filled with Jurassic carp that could probably chew off my arm. The balmy trade winds blew through the airport, giving the entire place the feel of a resort hotel.

We had to take the Wiki Wiki shuttle bus to the Inter-island Terminal for our connecting flight to Kauai. Luckily it was a short distance, because Monk couldn't stop repeating, "Wiki Wiki," and giggling during the drive.

As soon as we got there, I ditched Monk in the terminal on the excuse that I had to use the ladies' room. Which was the truth, but I also wanted to make a call in private.

I reached Dr. Kroger on my cell phone and told him what had happened.

"Amazing," Dr. Kroger said. He sounded astonished and not the least bit horrified. He obviously didn't see the situation from my point of view.

"That's one word for it," I said.

"I'm disappointed that he couldn't conquer his anxieties about being alone. On the other hand, this represents remarkable progress. Acting impulsively like this, going on a trip without forethought and obsessive planning, is a gigantic step for Adrian."

"He's not himself," I said.

"Everybody changes, Mrs. Teeger. Every day we're evolving into a new version of our previous selves. Don't shackle him to your preconceptions about who he should be."

I'd never heard such crap in my life.

"You don't understand, Dr. Kroger," I said. "Monk isn't evolved. He's on drugs."

"What drugs?"

"Whatever you gave him for his OCD."

"Dioxynl," Dr. Kroger said. "I prescribed that for him some time ago when his condition became totally debilitating for him. I'm surprised he took the medication again. He said he never would."

"Why did he say that?" I said. "Are there side effects?"

"Mild ones, but his were unique. The drug diminishes some aspects of his personality that mean more to him than relief from the limitations of his phobias and obsessions."

"You mean like losing all self-control and common sense?"

"The drug takes away his gift, the extraordinary

deductive skills from which he derives his identity,"
Dr. Kroger said. "In other words, Mrs. Teeger, when
he takes the drug, he's a lousy detective."

No wonder I'd never seen him take it before, no
matter how bad his OCD was.

"How long do the effects of this pill last?"

"About twelve hours," Dr. Kroger said. "Depending
on the dosage."

I glanced at my watch. Assuming he took the pills
shortly before the flight, there were about six more
hours of hell for me to endure, give or take an hour,
until the pill wore off and I'd begin experiencing the
hell I was more familiar with.

"What do I do when the drugs wear off and he's
back to being Monk?"

"What do you mean?"

"I mean this was supposed to be my vacation."

"That's between you and Adrian to work out," he
said. I could envision the amused smile on his face.
"Who knows? Maybe the two of you will have some
fun together."

I hung up. I couldn't help wondering if Dr. Kroger
put Monk up to this trip as a way of getting even
with me.

When I got to our gate, I couldn't find Monk,
though I have to admit I didn't look very hard. It's
not like I wanted Monk to intrude on my vacation—
not that I could even call it that anymore.

A heavyset Polynesian gate agent in a Hawaiian
Airlines aloha shirt and blue slacks announced that
our flight was ready for boarding.

Monk came rushing over just as passengers began
filing into the plane. He was wearing a bright yellow
aloha shirt decorated with hula dancers and was

eating chocolate-covered macadamia nuts right out of the box. The shirt and jacket he had worn on the plane were stuffed into his large shopping bag.

It may have been the first time I'd ever seen his naked arms. Usually he wore long-sleeved dress shirts buttoned at the cuffs.

I don't know what was more shocking to me: that he'd put his clothes into a bag without folding them or that he'd bought a brightly colored shirt with a pattern that didn't match at the seams.

I settled on the shirt and said so. "I can't believe you bought that shirt."

"Isn't it nice?"

"Yes, it's very nice," I said. "But it's not really you."

"We're in Hawaii. I'm feeling the aloha spirit. Aren't you?"

"Not yet."

"You need to loosen up," Monk said. "Stop being so uptight."

"*You're* calling *me* too uptight?"

"That's what the Monk is saying."

I narrowed my eyes at him accusingly. "Did Dr. Kroger put you up to this? Did he suggest that you follow me to Hawaii?"

"No," Monk said. "I wanted to get away from the rat race."

"You don't commute, you don't work in an office, you don't punch a time clock, and you hardly deal with people at all," I said. "What would you know about the rat race?"

"I live on the track. I saw two rats run across my fence last night," Monk said. "Or at least I think I did."

"It was probably a squirrel."

"Commonly known as an enormous rat." Monk smiled at the gate agent and tipped the open end of the candy box in his direction. "Would you like some?"

"Sure." The agent smiled, reached his hand inside the box, and took one of the nuts. "*Mahalo*, bro."

"Aloha." Monk popped another nut into his mouth and headed jauntily down the gangway into the plane.

I had an awful feeling that it was going to be a very, very long week. And I didn't even know about the murders then.

4

Mr. Monk Arrives

As we flew over Kauai on our approach to Lihue Airport, I was surprised by how rural the island seemed compared to Oahu. I'd expected it to be much more developed, with a Waikiki-like shoreline crammed with hotel towers. But it wasn't. The beaches looked virtually pristine, and the hotels were low-lying and spaced well apart, all against a backdrop of lush green mountains covered with rain forests and streaked with waterfalls.

The first thing that struck me as Monk and I walked through the tiny airport were all the smiling faces. Outside of Disneyland, I don't think I've ever seen so many people smiling.

But nobody was paying them to pretend it was the happiest place on earth. These were definitely real smiles—the smiles of people who'd experienced, or were about to experience, paradise. I know, because I had one of those smiles, and so did Monk. In fact, he had the biggest smile I'd ever seen before on his face. For a moment I was almost glad he'd come along. That moment passed quickly when I remembered that eventually his medication would wear off.

The air was warm and moist, and a nice breeze blew through the wide-open baggage-claim area. I was stunned to see Monk pulling only two suitcases, the same number that I'd brought, off the baggage carousel.

Once, when his apartment building was tented for termites, he had to stay at my house for a few days. He brought two suitcases with him that time, too. But he also hired movers to bring over his furniture and his refrigerator. For a trip to Mexico, I heard he'd brought his own food and water for a week.

"Didn't you pack a little light?" I said.

"I'm visiting Hawaii," Monk said. "I'm not moving here."

All I could figure was that he must have taken one of his magic pills last night so he'd have the nerve to make the plane reservations and the peace of mind to pack light; otherwise he never would have made the flight.

We took our suitcases to the curb, and right away I saw Candace and her fiancé waiting for us, standing in front of a Mustang convertible.

Candace was wearing a halter top, a short floral wrap tied around her waist, and a big sun hat. She looked like she'd just run out of the ocean to meet us. Like everybody else we'd seen, she was flashing a radiant smile. As long as I'd known her, she had been a little chubby and painfully self-conscious about her weight. She wasn't any thinner, so seeing her casually revealing so much skin made me realize just

how happy and self-confident she'd become. The
love of a good man can do that to a woman. I know
that from personal experience.

Brian Galloway, her twentysomething fiancé, was
wearing a loose-fitting Red Dirt tank top over a pair
of cargo shorts. There was a ragged straw hat on his
head and a pair of Ray-Bans that kept sliding down
his big, sunburned nose. That was the first feature
they'd fix if he ever went on *Extreme Makeover.* He had
a couple days' growth of stubble on his face, probably
less out of laziness than premeditation. It looked
good on him, and Candace probably told him so. He
had an average physique that seemed to be only a
couple beers and a bag of Cheetos away from flab-
bing out, which I guess made him a perfect match
for my best friend.

Candace shrieked and we ran toward each other
like little girls and embraced. Although we talked
every week, and e-mailed each other almost every
day, it had been at least a year since I'd seen her
face-to-face. She worked in advertising down in L.A.
and didn't get up to S.F. very often.

She asked about the flight and Julie and then, of
course, about the man standing right behind me.

"I thought you were coming alone," she whispered, looking over my shoulder at Monk.

"So did I," I whispered back.

"Did you meet him on the plane?"

"You could say that," I said, then spoke up. "This
is my boss, Adrian Monk."

"Your boss?" Brian said, making little quotation
marks in the air with his fingers. "Does he always
come with you on vacations?"

"It's a working vacation," I said. At least it was now.

"I bet," Brian said with a wink, and shook Monk's hand. "Brian Galloway."

Monk then turned and offered his hand to Candace. They also shook hands. It was astonishing. I'd never seen him shake anybody's hand without asking for a disinfectant wipe immediately afterward.

"It's nice to meet you," Monk said to her.

"*You're* Adrian Monk?" she replied, bewildered.

"The one and only. But you can call me Chad."

"I have heard so much about you," she said, glancing at me. "So very, very much."

"I'm a legend," he said without a hint of modesty.

I wanted to change the subject quickly, so I turned to Candace. "Aren't you going to introduce me to your fiancé? Or were you going to wait until after the wedding?"

"Oh, God, what's come over me?" she said. "Brian, this is Natalie."

"You're one lucky man." I offered him my hand and he pulled me into a hug instead, pressing me close and giving me a kiss on the cheek. His arms were strong, his body was warm, and he smelled of Coppertone and Brut. It felt nice to be enveloped in muscle and masculinity, and I was a little sad when the hug ended.

"I'm so happy you could come," Brian said. "I don't think Candy would've married me if you weren't here to be her maid of honor."

"She's waited a long time for this day," I said.

"I wasn't waiting for the *day*," Candy said. "I was waiting for the *man*. And I finally found him."

Candy gave his butt a playful squeeze.

"Congratulations to you both," Monk said. "I know you weren't expecting me, so I want to assure you I have no intention of crashing your wedding."

"Nonsense," Brian said. "You're invited, and we'll be hurt if you're not there. Isn't that true, sweets?"

"Absolutely, huggums," Candy said. "There's nothing sadder than going to a wedding alone. Trust me, I know."

Brian loaded the suitcases into the trunk and we piled into the Mustang, Monk and I taking the backseat for the drive to Poipu Beach with Sweets and Huggums. Candace and Brian weren't even married yet, and they already had pet names for each other. They were going to be a tough couple to hang out with.

The two-lane highway took us first through Lihue, which looked like a small Midwestern town that hadn't changed since the 1970s. The town struck me as being totally out of place amidst the tropical setting. I don't know what I was expecting. Maybe grass huts or something.

Just outside of town, though, any similarity with rural Middle America disappeared. The verdant splendor of the fields, set against the jagged mountains, was breathtaking. I'd never seen so many shades of green before.

"I love the way it smells here." Monk took a deep breath and let it out slowly. "It's a heady mix of Air Wick 'Blue Orchid,' 1998; Renuzit 'After the Rain,' 2001; and Glade 'Tropical Mist,' 1999; with an ever-so-slight hint of Lysol 'Summer Breeze,' 2003."

"You certainly know your air fresheners," Brian said.

"I have an extensive collection," Monk said.

Candace gave me a look over her shoulder, and I just smiled as if to say *That's Monk.*

"Are you in the air-freshener business?" Brian asked.

"I'm a detective," Monk said.

"You mean like a private eye?"

"Monk, PI, that's me. I even have a theme song. Want to hear it?"

Hell, no, I thought, and quickly spoke up. "You ought to tell Mr. Monk what you do for a living, Brian. I think it's a fascinating occupation."

"I'm a sales rep for a company that makes special-order furniture for hotel rooms, corporate offices, hospitals, restaurant chains, even jails."

"You think *that's* fascinating?" Monk asked me.

"Haven't you always wondered who makes that stuff?" I said. "Besides, he gets to travel all over the world."

"Thank God for cell phones or I'd never be able to find him," Candace said. "He spent the entire summer furnishing a resort in Australia."

"She was complaining about how hot it was in L.A.," Brian said, glancing at us in the rearview mirror. "You should try spending July down under. It's blistering."

"It's amazing to me to hear all the places that Brian has been and all the things he's done," Candace said. "He's experienced more in twenty-eight years than most people do in a lifetime—certainly more than I have ever done."

"Like what?" Monk asked.

"I've worked on a cattle ranch in Texas, volunteered with the Peace Corps in Somalia, interned with archeologists in Egypt, and spent a summer on a fishing trawler off the coast of Maine," he said. "That's how I got this scar on my leg. It was nearly chewed off by a marlin."

Candace looked admiringly at her fiancé and then shifted her gaze to me. "Isn't he wonderful?"

I nodded and smiled, though I had to wonder why a guy who'd led such an exciting life had settled for a career in the furniture business.

The Grand Kiahuna Poipu was a sprawling ocean-front resort that took its design cues from the sugar-cane plantation that had once occupied the property. The resort amenities included the hotel, six luxurious beachside villas that rented for $5,000 to $10,000 a day, hundreds of time-share condominiums, a championship golf course, a world-class spa, and a convention center.

The resort also offered state-of-the-art film and video production facilities, which made the Grand Kiahuna Poipu, with its palm-lined lagoon and its golden beach, the perfect setting for countless get-rich-quick infomercials, and psychic Dylan Swift's daily TV show, *Whispers from the Other Side*.

And yet, the resort was spread out over so much land, and the property so densely landscaped with monkeypod trees, palms, and thousands of different kinds of flowers, that it still managed to seem relaxed, intimate, and naturally tropical. I didn't get a sense as we drove in that I was entering a Vegas-style "vacation destination," though that was certainly what it was.

The massive main lobby was open on three sides

and overlooked the ocean; ceiling fans with blades shaped like palm fronds pushed around the humid air. The reception area was furnished with rattan chairs, decorated with maritime art, and trimmed everywhere with lustrous koa, a hardwood native to the islands.

I headed for the registration desk before Candace stopped me.

"No, no, let Brian take care of it for you," she said. "It's on us, remember?"

"Thank you," I said. "You have no idea how much I need this."

"There are some advantages to coming from an enormously wealthy family," she said. "You ought to know."

We both came from rich families, but I refused to take any money from my parents—not that they've offered. Candace took as much as her parents were willing to give, and then some.

"I try not to think about it," I said. "Especially when I'm paying my bills with my meager salary."

"Speaking of your job." Candace tipped her head toward Monk, who was checking in. "That's *really* Adrian Monk?"

"Yes and no," I said.

"He's nothing at all like you described. No human being could be like that. I always knew you had to be exaggerating those stories."

"I wasn't; you'll see," I said. "And I want to apologize in advance."

"I know what's really going on here. It's like when we were teenagers. When you had a crush on a boy, you'd tell everybody how gross he was and how you couldn't stand him, and two weeks later you'd be parked on Skyline Drive, necking with him in the backseat of your parents' station wagon."

"That's not what's happening, trust me," I said. "The only relationship between us is that of crazy employer and sane employee."

"Then why did you invite him to come with you?"

"I didn't. He followed me. He didn't want to be alone."

"You mean he couldn't survive without you."

"Yes," I said. "Exactly."

"How romantic," she said.

"No, I didn't mean it that way," I said, struggling to make myself clear. "He's obsessive-compulsive. He can't handle the challenges of everyday life without me."

"I'm sure that's true," she said with a grin.

I groaned with frustration, which seemed only to amuse her even more. I could see I wasn't going to win this. No matter what I said it would come out wrong, and she was having way too much fun at my expense.

"Just because it's the night before your wedding," I said, "don't think that will stop me from strangling you."

She laughed and gave me a hug. She's always been big on hugs. "It's so great that you're here, that *we're* here together, and that I'm finally getting married."

"I wouldn't have missed it for anything," I said.

That was when Monk came over, followed by a valet who had our suitcases on one trolley.

"Good news," Monk said. "We're in adjoining rooms."

Candace winked at me.

*   *   *

I double-checked with the front desk and made sure our rooms were even-numbered and on an even-numbered floor easily accessible by stairs so Monk wouldn't have to use the elevator. Monk didn't care about those details in his drugged-up state, but I knew he would a few hours later.

We were on the fourth floor, rooms 462 and 464. The rooms were tastefully decorated with rattan furniture, floral bedspreads, and fans much like the ones in the lobby. Each room had its own lanai, which is a fancy Hawaiian word for sundeck.

Monk and I both went out onto our individual lanais at about the same moment to admire our views. Our rooms faced the beach and the Grand Kiahuna Poipu's amazing pool, a slow-moving river that weaved through a misty rain forest filled with hidden rocky grottos and ending in a waterslide that spilled into a beachfront freshwater lagoon. It was packed with kids and teenagers.

Amidst the dense tropical foliage that surrounded the pool area were several "hidden" Jacuzzis. In one I could see two lovers snuggling in the burbling water, their BlackBerries and iPods within easy reach. In another two overweight, sunburned couples stood boiling like lobsters, each one holding a tropical drink stuffed with pineapple wedges and tiny umbrellas.

There were hundreds of chaise longues around the pool and on the sand, each topped with luxuriously thick cushions and shaded by umbrellas that resembled thatched roofs. There must have been a state law that made James Patterson and Nora Roberts required reading because everybody seemed to be engrossed in a book by one of those two authors.

Hammocks were strung between the dozens of lazy palms that lined the beach—they were all occupied, mostly by couples curled up close to one another. I made up my mind to snag a hammock for myself this week, even if it meant getting up at dawn to do it.

The private cabanas erected on the sand were attended by hostesses in skirts and bikini tops, serving drinks and food and offering thick white towels and plush bathrobes to the sun-shy tourists ensconced inside.

The beach was a sandy crescent that curved in front of the Kiahuna Poipu's half dozen exclusive four-thousand-square-foot bungalows, each with private palm-shaded lap pools and hot tubs. The properties were lushly landscaped, giving the rich and famous plenty of natural shade and privacy, even from above. Still, I've seen a few grainy *Enquirer* photos, taken with long lenses from boats on the water, of topless movie stars sunning themselves beside those private lap pools.

I glanced at Monk, who seemed more content and relaxed than I'd ever seen him before.

"It's paradise," I said.

Monk nodded. "What took us so long to get here?"

I knew it was a rhetorical question, but I answered it anyway. "Money and opportunity is my excuse. What's yours?"

"Fear," he replied without hesitation. "And guilt."

I understood the fear, but not the guilt. He saw the look on my face and answered the question evident in my expression.

"Trudy and I always talked about coming here but never seemed to find the time," Monk said. "After she was killed, I couldn't bring myself to come. For a long time I couldn't even bring myself to step outside."

"So what changed your mind today?"

"Fear and powerful pharmaceuticals," Monk said. "And you."

I knew what he meant, and I was touched. He wasn't saying he loved me or anything of that magnitude. What he was saying was that he *needed* me, and that he'd miss me if I were gone. But what meant the most to me was the acknowledgment that he felt safe with me, comfortable enough that he could take some emotional risks as long as I was there for him to lean on.

He was saying I was his friend.

I glanced at my watch. "I've got the rehearsal dinner in an hour. What are you going to do?"

"Explore the grounds a bit; then I think I'll go swimming."

I smiled at him. "*You* want to go swimming?"

Monk said, "The pool looks like fun."

"Do you even own a bathing suit?"

"I'll buy one," Monk said.

This is one amazing drug, I thought. If Monk took it once or twice a month, he could accomplish a lot of little things that are usually major undertakings for him. Like buying new socks. Getting his hair cut. And grocery shopping.

I wondered if there was more to Monk's decision not to take the drug than the loss of his detecting skills.

"I'd like to have a look around, too," I said. "Give me a minute to change and I'll go with you."

"Okay."

I went back into my room and, as I changed, I realized that I'd just blown my first opportunity to be alone. Monk was ready to go off on his own, and I'd invited myself along with him. I did it without thinking, and not out of worry or a sense of responsibility.

I did it because we're friends. Even though he could be more irritating than any person on earth, I enjoyed being with him. I guess when you get right down to it, that was how I was able to put up with all his eccentricities.

That, and he was paying me.

5

Mr. Monk and the Medium

It took Monk less than five minutes to buy a bathing suit from the Ralph Lauren store in the resort's shopping arcade right off the lobby. He just picked a simple pair of blue swim trunks off a sale table, checked the size, paid for it, and that was it. No biggie for anybody else, yet an amazing accomplishment for Monk.

We wandered out into a large, palm-lined garden on the other side of the hotel from the pool. The garden faced the beach and was filled with people sitting on white lawn chairs. At first I thought it was another wedding, but then I saw the TV cameras and recognized the man in front of the audience. It was Dylan Swift, the famous medium, taping an episode of his syndicated daily TV show.

I knew who he was, of course. I would have even if he didn't divide his time between Hawaii and San Francisco, where he started his shtick a few years ago on a local television station.

Everybody knew Dylan Swift. His books, with his

smiling face on the cover, were in every bookstore, grocery store, and 7-Eleven in the country. No matter where you went, Swift was watching you with his intense preternatural gaze, daring you not to look into his eyes and buy his book. It was kind of creepy.

Swift's popularity was helped in no small measure by the fact that he was incredibly good-looking. Today he wore a casual Tommy Bahama aloha shirt and tan slacks. His silk shirt was open just enough to show off his hairless chest and his brawny pectoral muscles. But his most prominent feature was his matinee-idol cleft chin, reminiscent of both Kirk Douglas and Dudley Do-Right. The question of whether his chin was natural or man-made was debated more often, and with more intensity, by his critics than whether or not he was a genuine psychic.

"Who is he?" Monk asked.

I'd long since stopped being shocked by Monk's total ignorance of American popular culture.

"Dylan Swift," I said. "He talks to dead people and relays their messages to their loved ones."

"That can't be done," Monk said.

"Tell that to the millions of people who watch his show and buy his books."

Swift moved through the crowd as if pulled along by some invisible force. The garden was like a giant Ouija board, and he was the game piece in the center.

"I'm getting something . . . . It's a name. It begins with the letter 'G' . . . yes, I clearly see a 'G,' " Swift said. He closed his eyes, cocked his head, and listened to something. " 'G' could be someone sitting here or it could be the name of someone close to one of you who passed on."

A man jerked his arm into the air and waved it

around, bobbing excitedly in his seat in front of Swift as if he'd just won a prize. He was in his sixties, a tubby little man in a bright aloha shirt and pleated shorts that he buckled practically at his chest. He wore sandals and white tube socks that nearly went up to his knobby, pale knees.

"My name is Gary," the man said, his double chin wobbling. "Could it be a message for me?"

"Yes, it is for you," Swift said. "Someone from the other side is whispering to me. A woman who was very close to you."

"My sister?"

"I'm sensing her name began with an *M* or an *E*, or perhaps contained both letters."

"Margaret," Gary said. "You're talking to Margaret?"

"Yes, that's right," Swift said. "She died recently."

"About three years ago," Gary said.

"Margaret looked out for her little brother," Swift said.

"I was her older brother," Gary said.

"Yes, but she was still very protective of you, wasn't she? As if you were her little brother. In fact, she saved your life once, didn't she?"

Gary nodded enthusiastically and squeezed his wife's hand. She was shaped just like him and dressed almost identically.

"When we were kids, we were fishing on the lake and I fell out of the boat," Gary said. "I got tangled up in the anchor line and almost drowned."

"Yes, and you would have, but she was there for you then and wants you to know she's still looking out for you now," Swift said.

I turned to go, but Monk was transfixed. I guess

curiosity was one aspect of his personality no drug could deaden.

"She's tried very hard to touch you from her realm," Swift said. "Margaret says you know when. She says it was in that moment of your darkest despair. When you got the news you hoped you'd never hear."

"You mean when I got the cancer diagnosis?"

Swift nodded. "That voice you heard in the back of your mind, the one that said, 'This isn't my time to die; I will fight,' that was her whispering to you. She wanted you to know you were going to be all right. And you are, aren't you?"

"I'm in complete remission." Gary began to sob. "Yes, I heard her. Tell her I heard. Tell her she gave me the strength to fight."

Swift put his hand on Gary's shoulder and gave him a reassuring squeeze. "Margaret knows that. And she wants you to know she loves you now and for eternity from the other side."

I applauded along with the rest of the audience. Swift lifted his head up and met Monk's gaze for a moment. Monk didn't look away. I'd seen that expression on Monk's face before; it was one he usually reserved for men he was intent on proving were killers. It was an unspoken challenge: *You can't fool me.*

The psychic was gravitating toward Monk. The last thing I wanted was Monk, in his drugged-out state, confronting Dylan Swift on national television.

"Maybe we should go, Mr. Monk," I said, taking him by the arm and leading him away.

"The man is a fraud," Monk said.

"Nobody has been able to prove it yet," I said.

"I could," Monk said.

"You're on vacation, remember?" I said. "You're here to have a good time."

"I'd enjoy it," Monk said, but he tagged along with me anyway.

I looked over my shoulder and saw Swift watching us go, a bemused expression on his face.

I would have liked to see Monk swimming.

I would have liked to have some pictures of it, too, as evidence to show Stottlemeyer and Disher that it really happened. I couldn't imagine Monk getting into a pool crowded with half-naked, sweaty, lotion-slathered adults and squealing kids with runny noses and full bladders.

But I missed that historic event. Instead I went to my best friend's rehearsal dinner. As much as I love Candace, I would have preferred to be in the pool with Monk.

None of her relatives nor any of Brian's were among the guests, just two dozen of their mutual friends from L.A. Her parents were on safari and couldn't be bothered to adjust their plans for something as insignificant as their daughter's wedding. Brian was an orphan whose parents died in a car accident, so he had neither parents nor relatives to invite.

There wasn't much to rehearse, either. The wedding was going to be quick and casual, out on the luau garden tomorrow morning. All I really had to do was stand beside Candace at the altar and remember to give her Brian's ring.

The dinner was a Hawaiian buffet served in an open-air restaurant on the lagoon, the terrace lit by torches. I'd tell you all about the food and the conversation but I was slammed by jet lag and too many of those tropical drinks, and headed to bed by ten. I called Julie to let her know I arrived safely, asked my Mom not to spoil my daughter beyond rehabilitation, and went to sleep.

I was awakened at seven the next morning by whimpering. No, it was more like mewling, and it was coming from Monk's room.

I dragged myself out of bed, pulled on a bathrobe, and shuffled over to the door between our rooms. I pressed my ear against the door.

"Mr. Monk?" I said. "Is that you?"

"I'm not sure," he said. "I've been asking myself the same question since dawn."

I tried the knob. The door was unlocked.

I walked in to find Monk standing in the corner, his back to the wall. He was wearing his usual suit, with his starched white shirt buttoned up to his neck. The bed was made, though the bedspread had been removed, folded, and placed out on the lanai. The aloha shirt and the bathing suit he'd worn yesterday were folded and placed in the garbage can.

"What happened?" I asked.

"I woke up in bed," Monk said. "Beneath that bedspread."

He tipped his head toward the bedspread as if it were a wild animal.

"Do you know how many people have sat on that bedspread?" Monk said. "Toilet seats in public restrooms are more sanitary, and I *slept under it.*"

Monk shivered from head to toe, then shook his head. He held out his hand toward me.

"Wipe," he said.

"I don't have any, I'm sorry. I haven't had a chance to pick some up yet."

"I didn't pack any either," he said. "Can you believe it? Was I insane?"

"Actually, you were more or less normal," I said. "Compared to other people, that is."

"It's like Dr. Jekyll and Mr. Hyde," Monk said. "Or Bruce Banner and the Hulk."

"You have no memory of what you did yesterday?"

"Worse," he said. "I remember it *all*."

He cringed and I cringed for him.

"You have to put it all out of your mind or you'll be paralyzed," I said. "I suggest you take another pill and grab the next flight home."

"I'm staying," Monk said.

"Why?"

"Because I'll go crazy at home by myself," Monk said. "I'm not very good alone. Besides, I need to unwind."

"Isn't that what you did yesterday?"

He recoiled from the thought, doing that full-body shiver of his.

"I'm sorry, Mr. Monk. That was a low blow."

Monk acknowledged my apology with a slight nod. "If you really want me to go, I will."

I almost said yes, but then realized that if I did, I'd feel even guiltier than I had leaving him behind in San Francisco.

"If you're going to stay, we need to have an understanding. You have to be on your best behavior."

"You won't even know I'm here. Except that I'm going to be with you all the time. More or less. Mostly more."

"Exactly, so this week doesn't count as my vacation. This is work. I still have all my vacation days coming to me."

"You don't have any vacation days."

"We'll have that fight another time," I said. "I'm here to relax."

"Me, too. You should start packing."

"Packing? For what?"

"Our move to new rooms," Monk said. "I can't stay in this one."

"Why not?"

His gaze drifted over to the desk. I saw three envelopes and four pieces of hotel stationery. I stifled a smile. In a strange way, it was a relief to have the Monk I knew back again.

"I see," I said.

I walked over to the desk, tore one of the pieces of stationery in half, and dropped the pieces into the trash can.

"Problem solved," I said.

I called housekeeping to come empty Monk's garbage and take his bedspread away before he set fire to it. Then I called the concierge to see if there was any place on the island that carried Sierra Springs bottled water, the only water Monk drank, and Wet Ones disinfectant wipes, the only wipes Monk trusted.

God was on my side. The hotel had a plentiful stock of Sierra Springs water and the gift shop sold Wet Ones. Crisis averted. I asked them to charge a case of each to Mr. Monk's account and bring them up to his room right away.

I also asked them to bring up a bowl of Chex cereal for him (he loves those little squares) and an order of macadamia pancakes, fresh pineapple, and hot coffee for me.

I showered, put on a sundress, and met Monk on his lanai for breakfast. He was still wearing his shirt, jacket, slacks, and loafers, despite the humidity and the heat.

"Aren't you uncomfortable in all that?" I asked.

He gave me a look. "No."

"Okay, but you're going to be overdressed for the wedding," I said. "It's Hawaii-casual."

"I can be Hawaii-casual." He went into his room, took off his coat, hung it up in the closet, and came back out on the lanai. "Voilà."

I was suffocating just looking at him.

"How about opening up your collar and rolling up your sleeves?"

"Maybe I should do a whole striptease while I'm at it," Monk said. And then he was stricken by a new thought. "Wait. Is this a *nudist* wedding?"

"No, of course not."

He sighed with relief and wagged a finger at me. "You had me going there for a minute."

"We're here to have fun, aren't we?"

"Not that kind of fun," he said.

6

Mr. Monk Speaks Up

The wedding ceremony took place in the hotel's secluded luau garden, which was ringed by a sunburst of blossoming tropical flowers—white orchids, crimson bougainvillea, yellow allamandas, blazing red anthuriums, cups of gold, and birds-of-paradise. Those flowers were complemented by stunning bouquets prepared for the wedding and placed throughout the garden. Even the guests themselves were flowery. All the guests, with the exception of Monk, wore fresh plumeria leis and floral aloha wear.

A Hawaiian band sang "*Ke Kali Nei Au*," which was to the islands what Peter, Paul, and Mary's "The Wedding Song" is on the mainland. But the music was hardly necessary. The singsong chirp of island birds and the natural rhythm of the waves was music enough.

Candace and Brian faced the Hawaiian minister in front of the grass-skirted stage where, at night, the hula dancers performed during the luau.

Candace wore a white wedding *holoku*, a long,

formfitting *mu'umu'u*, and a *haku* lei of white den-
drobium orchids, baby's breath, and roses on her
head. She was aglow with happiness. It brought tears
to my eyes.

Brian stood at her side in a white aloha shirt with
a light floral pattern, white linen pants, and a *maile*
lei of green leaves draped around his neck.

The minister, a heavyset Hawaiian in his thirties,
also wearing an aloha shirt, performed the Hawaiian
wedding blessing, which involved a lot of stuff in
Hawaiian and the exchanging of elaborate leis. Out
of the corner of my eye, I could see Monk fidgeting.
I prayed that he wasn't about to jump up and inter-
rupt the wedding to reorganize some flower arrangement that didn't meet his criteria.

The minister started to say something in English,
catching my attention again.

"If anyone here knows of any reason this couple
shouldn't be joined in holy matrimony, speak up
now or forever hold your peace."

I heard Monk clear his throat. I turned around and
looked at him. Everybody did.

He raised his hand.

"Yes?" the minister said.

Monk looked around. "Are you calling on me?"

"Yes, you," the minister said. "Is there something
you'd like to say?"

Monk stood up and tipped his head toward Brian,
whose face was tight with rage.

"He's not twenty-eight years old," Monk said.

"Yes, I am," Brian said.

"You have a smallpox vaccination scar on your
shoulder. They stopped giving those shots in the
United States in 1972."

"I got mine later, before I went to Somalia with the Peace Corps," Brian said. "Can we go on with the wedding now?"

Candace glared at me. I flushed with embarrassment. This was all my fault, and I felt terrible about it.

"That's another thing," Monk began.

If looks could kill, Monk would have been executed by a firing squad. Every single person in that garden was glaring at him.

"The marines engaged in relief efforts in Somalia in 1992," Monk said, "but the Peace Corps hasn't been there since 1970."

"Not *officially*," Brian said. "This was a covert operation."

Candace looked at Brian skeptically. "The Peace Corps runs covert missions?"

"Peace is a dangerous business, honey. Look, what does any of this have to do with why we're here today? We're getting married, aren't we? We love each other and we want to spend the rest of our lives together. That's what's important."

Candace smiled and nodded, taking his hands in hers. "Yes, of course." She turned to the minister. "Let's go on."

"Marlins don't have teeth," Monk said.

The minister looked up, clearly irritated. So was everybody else. "Excuse me?"

"Brian said he was bitten on the leg by a marlin while crewing on a fishing trawler. But marlins have no teeth and are fished only for sport, not commercially."

"It could have been a tuna, I don't know. It was a big fish and it had teeth. Does it matter what kind it was?" Brian said. "What is your problem? You got a thing for Candace or something?"

"I have a thing against pathological liars," Monk said. "You said you spent the summer in Australia and that it was sweltering in July. But the seasons are reversed south of the Equator. July is actually the dead of winter down under."

"It's hot in Australia all year round," Brian said.

"I don't think you were there at all," Monk said. "I think you were lying to cover the fact that you were actually with your wife."

Candace stared at Brian. "Your *wife*?"

"I'm not married," Brian said, then turned to Monk. "I'm trying to get married, but you keep interrupting."

"You've been very careful not to develop a tan line from your wedding band, but you have a slight callus where your ring finger meets your palm," Monk said. "It takes years to build up a callus from the slight friction of a ring against the skin. So, I'd say you've been married for at least five years now."

Candace grabbed Brian's left hand and ran her fingers over his palm. Her face reddened. "Oh, my God. He's right. You *are* married."

There were gasps from the shocked guests. There was probably a gasp from me in there, too. I'd seen Monk do these amazing deductions before, but never in a situation like this, never outside the setting of an investigation.

Candace staggered back from Brian. "Who are you?"

Brian shifted his weight nervously. He was caught, and he knew it.

"The man who loves you," Brian said. "A love so powerful that I wouldn't let a marriage to another woman prevent me from having you in my life."

"Is there a single thing you've told me about yourself that isn't a lie?"

"I'm in the furniture business," he said.

Candace slapped him across the face, the smack as loud as a gunshot.

"I never want to see you again," Candace said, her voice quavering. She yanked the lei off her head, threw it at Brian's face, and marched away. I started to go after her, but she dismissed me with a wave of her hand.

I turned back to Brian. "How could you?"

"How could I not? She's incredible," Brian said, crying now. "I love her."

"What about your wife?" I asked.

"I love her, too," he said. "I'm cursed with a tremendous capacity for love."

"You were going to divide your time between the two of them," Monk said, "and blame your absences on business trips."

"They never had to know about each other," Brian said. "I would have made Candace very happy."

"Where does your wife live?" Monk asked.

"In Summit, New Jersey," Brian said. "With the kids."

There was a path lined with palm trees that meandered through the resort property and along the beach. I found Monk standing on the path in front of the hotel, watching the tourists splashing around in the waves.

He stood there in his long-sleeved white shirt buttoned at the cuffs, his gray slacks, and brown loafers while everybody around him was in bathing suits or T-shirts and shorts or colorful aloha wear. There was something melancholy and Chaplinesque about him, so apart from the world around him.

Beyond him, I saw the azure sea and the frothing surf and all the people in the water, having fun body-surfing, swimming, and just getting knocked around by the waves. It looked so inviting, especially after spending an hour with my heartbroken friend. I wanted to run right past Monk into the waves and forget all my troubles.

But I didn't. Like most people, I'm a lot more care-free in my fantasies than I am in my life. I wondered, for a moment, if maybe Monk was the same way. Did he ever have the impulse to roll up his sleeves? To take off his loafers and walk barefoot in the hot sand?

Monk looked back at me and then shook his head. "Unbelievable, isn't it? How can people do that?"

I nodded in agreement. We hadn't seen each other since I left the aborted wedding to comfort Candace, so we hadn't had a chance to talk about it. "I don't understand how a person can claim to love someone and then deceive them so completely."

"Oh, I understand that." Monk started to stroll along the path following the beach going toward the private bungalows. "What makes no sense to me is swimming in the ocean."

"It's hot out, we're at the beach, and the water is warm and inviting," I said. "It's what people do in Hawaii."

"Don't they know that thousands of creatures live, eat, and empty themselves in there?"

"Empty themselves?"

"Fish don't have indoor plumbing," Monk said. "They swim around in their own excrement. And when we flush our toilets or wash something down the drain, where do you think it goes? Out there."

When he put it like that, even I had second thoughts about taking a swim. Two women in bikinis walked toward us. Monk lowered his gaze to his feet until they passed.

"How's your friend?" Monk asked his feet.

"Gone," I said. "She packed her bags and went straight to the airport."

"Why did she do that?"

"She's hurt, angry, and humiliated, Mr. Monk. She feels like a complete fool. You could have spared her the embarrassment if you'd told me that Brian was a fraud *before* the ceremony."

Monk raised his head again and was startled to see three women in bathing suits coming toward us. Instead of lowering his gaze, he looked over their heads.

"I didn't realize it until I was sitting there," Monk said, eyes on the sky.

"But he told you all that stuff yesterday."

"I heard what he said but I didn't recognize the significance in my altered state. That's why you should just say no to drugs," Monk said, glancing at me after the women walked by. "Are you mad at me?"

I was and I wasn't.

"I wish you could have found a way to expose Brian without humiliating Candace in front of all her friends. But you saved her from making a terrible mistake, and for that I'm grateful. Maybe someday she will be, too."

We approached a fork in the path. Two couples were walking toward us. The women were in bikini bottoms and wet T-shirts, the men in Speedos. Before we could pass one another, Monk yanked me onto the other path as if saving me from being run over by a truck.

"Does this mean we're going back to San Francisco today?" he asked eagerly.

"The tickets and reservations are nonrefundable, so Candace said I might as well stay and enjoy myself. *You're* welcome to go home if you like."

Monk stopped and cocked his head, looking at something. I'm not sure he even heard what I'd said.

I followed his gaze. We'd stopped in front of the private bungalows, which were shaded by lazy palms and shielded from prying eyes by a wall of greenery and flowers. The path we were on cut between two of the homes and ended in a tiny cul-de-sac, where I could see a black van marked *Medical Examiner* and two police cars.

Oh, hell, I thought.

"I wonder what's going on," Monk said.

"It's none of our business."

"Someone is dead."

"People die all the time. It doesn't mean it's murder."

"But it *could* be." Monk jumped up, trying to see over the hedge of bougainvillea, hibiscus, and heliconia into the backyard of one of the bungalows.

"Even if it is, so what?" I said. "*We're* on vacation."

"You told Candace when we arrived that this was a working vacation." Monk crossed in front of me to the opposite hedge.

"I lied," I said.

"And you still don't understand how people can deceive the ones they love?" Monk jumped up a couple of times. "This is the house."

He squatted down and separated the hedge to see into the yard. I crouched behind him and looked over his shoulder.

On the other side of the hedge was the hot tub, which doubled as a fountain, water spilling over the edge and splashing down some large lava rocks into the black-bottomed, pebbled lap pool.

The dead woman was floating faceup in the hot tub. Her eyes were wide-open and her skin was unnaturally white. Her lips were stretched in a taut rictus of a grin, her artificially red hair fanned out in the water like an Afro. She looked like an obscene parody of a circus clown.

She must have been in her late sixties and wore a one-piece bathing suit, the kind with an industrial-strength bra to hold up an enormous, sagging bosom and a skirt to hide the butt. My grandmother had a suit like that. The instant a woman puts one of those things on she's transformed into one of the elephant ballerinas from *Fantasia*. There should be a warning label sewn into those suits.

Two Hawaiian morgue assistants in short-sleeved white uniforms lifted the corpse out of the hot tub and laid it on a body bag on the patio.

A crime scene photographer took pictures of the dead woman and a bloodstained coconut on the patio, not far from the palm tree that shaded the hot tub.

A few yards away there was a chaise longue with a white blanket laid out on top of the thick cushion. I could see the spine of a John Grisham hardcover, a glass of water, and a big, floppy sun hat on the coffee table beside the chaise.

A uniformed police officer observed everything from the shade of a patio umbrella, sweat dampening his short-sleeved shirt.

" 'Ey! No make li'dat, bruddah." Someone spoke sharply behind us.

We looked up to see a big Hawaiian guy in his thirties standing in the path, hands on his hips right above the gun and the badge clipped to his belt. He was in shorts, flip-flops, and an aloha shirt that depicted a vintage seaplane landing on a tropical isle. There were laugh lines around his eyes and his chubby cheeks made me think he found more joy in life than sorrow. But he wasn't looking very happy at that moment. He was looking downright mean.

"Are you the detective in charge of this investigation?" Monk asked, rising to his feet.

"Ass right, brah. LT Ben Kealoha, Kauai police. Why boddah you?"

"I have no idea what you just said. I'm an American from America. I'm Adrian Monk and this is my assistant, Natalie Teeger."

"Fo' what you mek ass doing look-see in da *puka*?"

Monk turned to me. "I think we're going to need a translator."

I understood the detective. He was speaking in thick pidgin, which is not so different from California surfer-speak. I'm not a surfer, but I grew up in Monterey and dated quite a few of them. They spoke pidgin because their Hawaiian surfing idols did.

"This is Lt. Ben Kealoha. He wants to know what we're doing peeking through the bushes." I turned to Kealoha and gave him my friendliest smile. "Mr. Monk is a detective consultant to the San Francisco police. He was just indulging in a little professional curiosity. Would you mind telling us what happened?"

"Ka den. Da *makule* haole in da pool. Da coconut dun drop and wen brok da noggin of da *momona wahine*. She wen sink in da pool li' that," he said. "Dass why hard. Bummah."

I'd never heard pidgin spoken so fast before, and it didn't help me any that he was mixing in some Hawaiian words, but I still got the gist of it. I turned to Monk.

"He says it's an accident. The old woman was sitting in the hot tub, a coconut from the palm tree dropped on her head, knocked her out, and she drowned." I turned back to Kealoha. "Yikes. Talk about bad luck. I won't be sitting under any palm trees on this trip. We'll be on our way now, if that's okay with you. *Mahalo.*"

I started to go, but Monk didn't move. He just shook his head. "That's not what happened."

All the joy I felt about spending a week in Hawaii evaporated in that instant—because I knew what Monk was going to say next and what it meant for me. I silently mouthed the words as he spoke them.

"This woman was murdered," Monk said.

"Show me how you figga that, yeah?" Kealoha said, motioning us to follow him.

Monk went along eagerly, a smile on his face. He couldn't have been happier to stumble onto a corpse on the first day of his Hawaiian vacation. I looked at it differently. I saw it as evidence that I was cursed.

7

Mr. Monk and the Coconut

Kealoha opened the gate and led us into the side yard, his flip-flops slapping against his heels. We passed twin air conditioners and a row of trash cans that reeked of spoiled food. We walked around a palm tree, stepped over some fallen coconuts, and came into the backyard behind the chaise longue.

I got my first good look at the kind of accommodations $5000 a night will get you. The bungalow's spacious living room and gourmet kitchen were entirely open to the patio, thanks to interlocking panels of sliding glass that disappeared into pocket walls. High-end rattan furniture was arranged throughout the interior of the house and the patio, making it all one continuous open space.

Monk glanced back the way we'd come in, leaned over to one side and then the other, then went over to the chaise longue. He glanced at the hardcover book on the table, the sun hat, and then went over to the body.

He squatted beside the woman, sniffed her, and

examined the flesh-colored hearing aids in each of her ears.

Monk extended his hands, framing the scene like a director, zeroing in on the coconut before his attention was distracted by three decorative lava rocks in the planting area, which he carefully rearranged according to their size, from biggest to smallest.

Kealoha watched Monk with amusement. So did the two coroners and the uniformed officer.

"He for real?" Kealoha asked me.

I nodded. "It's his process."

Satisfied with his rocks, Monk turned to Kealoha.

"She's been dead two hours, judging by her skin and lividity, though it's hard to tell since she's been in the hot water and blazing sun. What's her name?"

"Helen Gruber," Kealoha said.

"How long have she and her husband been staying here?"

I almost asked Monk how he knew she was married, but then I spotted the diamond wedding ring on her finger. I don't know how I missed it before. The diamond was the size of a marble.

Kealoha shrugged. "Mebbe a week."

"A week?" Monk rolled his head, closed one eye, and held his hand out over the hot tub, palm up. "Where is her husband?"

Kealoha shrugged. "We're lookin'."

Monk frowned, stood up, and came over to us.

"She was hit on the head with a coconut and drowned," Monk said.

"Das what I say," Kealoha said.

"But it wasn't an accident," Monk said. "This entire scene was staged for your benefit. She wasn't even in the hot tub when she was killed."

Monk tipped his head toward the palm tree in the side yard. "The coconut came from *that* tree, not the one over by the hot tub. You can see the indentation in the dirt where the coconut was lying before the killer picked it up. There's also a soft spot on the coconut where it was resting against the moist ground."

Kealoha squatted beside the tree, examined the place where Monk said the coconut had been, then waved over the crime scene photographer.

"Aikane, make some snaps of dis. Tanks, eh?"

"The killer came in through the same gate we did, picked up the coconut, and sneaked up behind her inside the house," Monk said.

"In da house?" Kealoha said, standing up. "How you figga?"

"She's not wearing any suntan lotion. The book on the chaise longue is a large-print edition, so she obviously needs reading glasses. So where are they? The killer put out all these props and he did it in a hurry. Who found her?"

"Da maids," Kealoha said.

"When?"

"An hour or so."

Monk squinted up at the sun, looked at the hot tub again, then went into the house. We followed him. The bungalow had an open floor plan, the kitchen open to the living room, which was open to the patio. Only the bedrooms had doors. The high-pitched ceiling had exposed beams, the fans mounted on them spinning hard in a futile effort to circulate the cool, conditioned air around the house before it escaped outside.

Monk took a napkin off the marble counter in the

kitchen and opened the refrigerator. It was empty. He opened several of the cupboards, which were full of dishes, pots, and pans that looked as if they'd never been used. He leaned into the sink and peered into the drain.

"She was killed here," Monk said.

"How you know dat?"

"The victim has a slight horizontal bruise right below her collarbone," Monk said. "Based on her height, that's exactly where she would have hit the counter when she fell forward."

"You could be mistaken," Kealoha said, dumbfounded. So dumbfounded, in fact, that he was speaking perfect English.

Monk shook his head. "No, I couldn't."

Kealoha looked at me.

I nodded. "If Mr. Monk says it's murder, it is. Ask Capt. Leland Stottlemeyer on the SFPD; he'll tell you the same thing."

"I know this may seem like a strange accident to you, but that's the nature of island life. These kinds of things happen here all the time," Kealoha said. "Murders don't."

"They do now," Monk said.

Kealoha sighed, took a notepad out of his back pocket, and scribbled something on a page. He motioned to the uniformed officer.

"Kimo, call in some more officers. This is a crime scene; I want it secured until SID can get here, eh? Find Dr. Aki; tell him we got a body that needs cuttin'."

"He's fishing today, brah," the officer said.

"Ka den, call the coast guard, tell 'em to bring him

in, yeah?" Kealoha tore the page out of his pad and
gave it to the officer. "Here's my contact over there."

The officer went outside to make his calls. Monk
folded the napkin he was using and put it in his
pocket.

"You've slipped out of character," Monk said.

"You mean da pidgin stuff?" Kealoha said. "The
haole like their Hawaiians to be Hawaiian, so I do
my part. It's good for tourism and blows off people
I no wanna to talk to anyways."

I looked at Monk. "Why don't you tell Lieutenant
Kealoha who killed Mrs. Gruber and let's go. It's
noon and I'd really like to get to the beach today,
take a swim, and try one of those tropical drinks
stuffed with fruit and tiny umbrellas."

"I don't know who killed her yet."

"*Yet?*" Kealoha said.

"But I will," Monk said. "I'm on the case."

I was afraid of that, though he was only confirming
what I knew was true the moment he peeked through
the hedge. Monk wouldn't rest until the murder was
solved, which meant, by extension, that neither
would I.

Some vacation, huh?

"Let's grab a plate and talk story. I'll tell you
everything I know about the dead lady," Kealoha
said.

"A plate?" Monk asked.

"Lunch," Kealoha said, striding out of the house.

We piled into Kealoha's Crown Victoria, the standard transportation for cops everywhere, and he
drove us a couple of miles inland to Koloa and what

remained of the first sugar-plantation town in the islands. On the way he told us that Helen Gruber came from Cleveland, where her late first husband made his fortune in the paving business. She recently married Lance Vaughan, who'd been her personal trainer and was about thirty years younger than her.

Good for her, I thought. *If rich men can have trophy wives, why can't wealthy widows have their boy toys?*

Frontier-style wooden storefronts lined one side of Koloa Road; on the other were the ruins of the old sugar mill. The storefronts looked as if they hadn't changed much since the 1830s, except now they were selling eight-dollar scoops of ice cream and sixty-dollar T-shirts to tourists instead of taro and supplies to the fieldworkers.

We parked in front of an old cabin at the far end of the road, on the edge of a field of tall weeds and neglected sugarcane. There was a peeling sign out front that announced the place as Cokie's Grill. The restaurant had a sagging porch, screened windows, and a rusted corrugated-metal roof covered in green moss.

We got out, scattering a group of roosters that sought refuge under the porch and clucked at us. Monk stared at them as if they were alligators.

"What is this place?" Monk asked.

Kealoha stepped up onto the porch. "This was a camp house for the sugar-plantation workers. It's hardly changed, yeah?"

"It should be condemned," Monk said. "Why are we here?"

"Fo da boss grines," Kealoha said, opening the rickety screen door and ushering us in. "Best plate lunch on Kauai."

Monk turned to me, the color draining from his face. "Wipe."

I reached into my purse and handed him one as we went in.

The cramped little cabin still felt more like a home than a restaurant, though the smell of fried food and fish was everywhere. The white walls were peeling and yellowed with age and the hardwood floors creaked under our feet with each step.

There were just four tables inside, each covered with a red-checked tablecloth. The ladder-backed chairs were faded red, and smooth from years of use.

The only other customers were two impossibly old Hawaiian men in aloha shirts that hung on their bony frames, their skin dark and wrinkled, as if all the moisture had been wrung from their bodies. They sat at a table for three, playing cards and nursing Cokes.

The menu was a chalkboard mounted on the wall beside the open doorway into the kitchen, where an old woman in a *mu'umu'u* and an apron, her gray hair tied back into a bun, supervised three other similarly dressed, but younger, women at the grill. There were only three items on the menu: PLATE LUNCH $5. DRINK $1. SLICE PIE $2.

A zapper hung like a lantern in the far corner of the dining room, crackling every few seconds as another flying insect flew into the electric grid. Its wire grate was blackened with charred bugs and dismembered wings. Every time the zapper snapped, Monk winced with revulsion.

"Three plates, momma," Kealoha yelled, then led us to a table with three chairs.

I took a seat. "Is that your mom?"

Kealoha shook his head and sat down. "She's *ka-ma'aina*. She's been cooking so long, they say even the Menehune when eat da grines here."

"Who are they?" I asked.

"Hawaiian elves," Kealoha said. "They lived here for thousands of years, working only at night and building many great things, before they sailed away forever on their floating island. But some are still around, doing their mischievous magic and da kine in the night. They steal my car keys all the time."

Monk stood over us.

"Please sit down, Mr. Monk," Kealoha said.

"I can't," Monk said.

"Why not?" Kealoha asked.

"This table is wrong."

"What's wrong with it?"

I figured it out and stood up. "There are only three chairs."

"And there are three of us," Kealoha said. "We each have a place to sit."

"But three is an odd number," I said.

"So?" Kealoha said.

There was no point trying to explain it all to Kealoha, so I just got up and sat down at the next table, which had four chairs. After a moment so did Kealoha, a bewildered expression on his face. But Monk remained standing, staring at the table we'd left.

"We can't just leave it that way," he said.

Monk looked around. The other empty table had four chairs, too. If he took a chair from that table, it would also be uneven. He turned to the table where the two old men sat and motioned to their empty third chair.

"Do you mind?" He took hold of the chair with a

wipe in his hand, dragged it over to the table we had abandoned, and organized the seating so everything was evenly spaced.

Kealoha looked at me and whispered, "Is he okay in the head?"

I deftly avoided the question. "He's a brilliant detective."

Monk came over to our table and was about to sit down when he gasped and staggered back in horror.

"What is it?" I asked.

He pointed at his chair, his finger shaking. Kealoha rose from his seat and peered over the table. I looked down at the seat.

A tiny green lizard was on the chair.

Kealoha grinned. "That is our friend the gecko."

"He's not my friend," Monk said.

"They are good luck," Kealoha said. "They eat the mosquitoes and the cockroaches."

Monk shuddered. "There are cockroaches here?"

"Not when there are geckos," Kealoha said. "That's why we're glad our friends are everywhere."

I looked around, and so did Monk. I hadn't noticed them before, but the geckos were *everywhere*: on the ceiling, crawling on the walls, and huddled on the ground beneath the bug zapper. The gecko scampered off Monk's chair, but I knew there was no way he'd ever sit there, or anyplace else in this restaurant.

"Sweet mother of God," Monk croaked.

As if on cue, the old woman shuffled out of the kitchen with a tray containing three Styrofoam boxes and three Cokes without ice in plastic glasses. She passed around our drinks, then set the boxes down in front of us and opened them with a flourish. The entrées were in their individual divided sections, like frozen dinners. She set one of the boxes down in front of Monk's empty chair, gave him a cold look, and returned to the kitchen.

"*Mahalo nui loa*," Kealoha called to her appreciatively, and dug into his food with gusto.

I regarded my meal. There was some kind of meat covered in a thick brown gravy, a ball of white rice, a square of purpleish pasty stuff, and a mound of what looked like relish.

Monk peered at the entrées as if studying a specimen in formaldehyde. "Is that rooster?"

"No, it's pork 'n' gravy, a scoop of rice, and poi," Kealoha said, while taking a piece of meat and running it through the rice and relish before putting it in his mouth. Mixing foods like that was a definite no-no in Monk's book.

"It looks like rooster to me," Monk said.

"How would you know?" I said.

"The chef doesn't strike me as someone who would go far looking for the best cut of meat."

"Have you ever eaten rooster?"

"Hell, no," Monk said.

"It could be delicious," I said. I cut some of the meat, stabbed it with my fork, and ate a bite.

It was very tasty, whatever it was.

"What's poi?" I asked Kealoha, waving my fork over the pasty stuff.

"Fermented and mashed taro. You eat it like this." Kealoha dipped two fingers into the poi, scooped up some of the paste, and stuck it in his mouth with delight.

While Monk was still gaping at him in disgust, I slopped some poi up with my fingers and sucked them clean.

Monk stared at me. "Have you lost your mind?"

The poi tasted like Elmer's glue, but just to be cruel, I stuck my fingers into the poi for another helping and offered it to Monk.

"Want to try?" I asked, my fingers dripping poi.

"Have you been sneaking some of my drugs?"

"What kind of drugs do you have?" Kealoha asked casually.

"Mind-altering but strictly nonrecreational," Monk said. "There's nothing the least bit fun about them."

"Especially for whoever is around him when he's taking them," I said, eating the poi.

"I have a prescription," Monk said.

I pointed to the relish with my wet fingers. "What's this?"

"Gecko," Monk said with authority.

"Kimchi," Kealoha said. "Spicy pickled vegetables, garlic, and chilies."

Monk leaned down and whispered in my ear. "You have only his word for that."

"Dems 'ono grines," Kealoha said, "but don't smooch nobody after."

I scooped some up with my fingers and put it in my mouth. The kimchi was spicy and heavy on the garlic, but I liked it. My breath was going to be awful, but the odds of my getting close enough to anybody who'd notice were nil.

Kealoha grinned at me. "We eat dat wid a fork."

I shrugged. "You can't take me anywhere."

The zapper crackled and Monk jumped back, startled, colliding with the empty chairs at the table behind him.

"Okay, that's it, enough of this charade," Monk said, pointing his finger accusingly at Kealoha. "We didn't have anything to do with Helen Gruber's murder."

"Who said we did?" I asked.

Monk tipped his head toward Kealoha. "He thinks that's why I knew so much about the murder. He took us to this godforsaken hellhole to protect the crime scene and keep an eye on us while his officer called Captain Stottlemeyer."

I glanced at Kealoha, who was busy chewing. "Is that true?"

He shrugged indifferently. "I took you to lunch. I could have taken you to the station instead. But this is how we do things here, easygoing and friendly."

"Is that what you call trapping us in this reptile-infested insect pit?" Monk said. "This sort of police brutality would never be tolerated in America."

"Dis *is* America, bruddah."

Kealoha's cell phone rang. He flipped it open and answered the call, rising from his chair and stepping out of earshot. Even so, I noticed he stood between us and the door in case Monk wanted to make a mad dash for freedom.

"Why are you putting yourself through this?" I said to Monk as I continued eating.

"I didn't ask to come to this house of horror," Monk said, wincing as the zapper claimed another insect.

"You intruded on their homicide investigation."

"They wouldn't have known it was a murder if it weren't for me."

"You don't know that."

"I know they'll never solve it by themselves," Monk said.

"This is your vacation," I said. "You're here to relax, remember?"

"Solving murders is how I relax. It's when I don't have a murder to solve that I become tense."

"Then read a murder mystery," I said. "Have you ever tried that? Besides, the Kauai police haven't asked for your help."

"Look how they live. Do you really think they can handle a homicide investigation? You heard what he said. They rarely deal with murders here. They need me."

Kealoha stepped up to Monk. "Captain Stottlemeyer says you're a fraud, that Adrian Monk would never go to Hawaii."

"Let me talk to him," Monk said.

The detective held the phone out to him.

"Wait." Monk turned and reached his hand toward me, palm up. "Wipe."

I gave him a wipe. Monk reached for the phone with his wipe, but the cell slipped through his moist grip and fell on the floor.

"I need another wipe," Monk said, waving his hand at me. "Stat!"

"That wipe is still good," I said.

"No, it's not."

"You didn't touch the phone."

"The wipe made contact," he said.

"Yes, *it* did. *You* didn't."

"But now there's less wipe on the wipe," he said. "I need full wipe. Open your eyes, woman. *There are lizards on the walls.* This is a full-wipe situation."

Kealoha picked up the phone and held it to his ear. "Still there, Captain?" He listened for a moment, smiled at me, then nodded. "Yes, I will."

He snapped the phone shut and slipped it back into the pocket of his shorts. "The captain says you are definitely who you say you are, and he expressed his sympathies for Mrs. Teeger."

"Now that we've established who I am," Monk said, "Can we get out of here?"

"Better than that," Kealoha said. "We can talk to Helen Gruber's husband."

8

Mr. Monk and the Toblerones

Lance Vaughan sat on the edge of a chaise longue, elbows on his knees, his face in his hands, his shoulders heaving as he cried softly. His board shorts were wet, and his short-sleeved red surf shirt clung to his hard body like a second skin. He had curly brown hair that was made for a woman's fingers to comb, and tug, and twirl. I could see in an instant why Helen Gruber married this guy. I was tempted to propose myself. I felt a sudden, desperate need for a breath mint.

"Mr. Vaughan?" Kealoha said. "I'm Lt. Ben Kealoha of the Kauai police."

Lance looked up and I saw the tears running down his stubbled cheeks and the pain in those blue eyes. He wiped the tears away with the palms of his hands. It struck me as a very masculine gesture. I would have wiped tears away with my fingertips. I would have wiped his away if it weren't for my astonishing powers of self-control.

Kealoha gestured to us. "This is Adrian Monk, a

private detective who consults with the police department, and his associate, Natalie Teeger. We're deeply sorry for your loss."

"It's a cruel joke, isn't it?" Lance said.

"What you mean?" Kealoha said.

"How many times did Gilligan get conked with a coconut? Every damn week, and it always got a laugh," Lance said. "Helen was a strong, proud, beautiful woman. She deserved better."

"A better way to die?" Kealoha said.

"Yeah," Lance said. "Something with dignity. Something that would have given her a chance to fight back. It's like she got killed by a pie in the face."

"Is that barbed wire tattooed on your wrist?" Monk asked.

Lance ran his finger over the tattoo on his left arm. "I got it when I turned eighteen to go along with this garage band I was in. Helen thought it was sexy. I had to talk her out of celebrating our engagement by getting a matching tattoo of her own. Could you see a woman in her sixties with a tattoo like that? That's the kind of woman she was. She didn't care what anybody thought about anything. She grabbed what she wanted in life. She did things her way, without apology or regret, and I loved her for it."

"You live like that," Kealoha said, "you make a lot of enemies."

"You think she was killed by bad karma?"

Kealoha shook his head. "I think she was killed by a bad man."

It took a moment before the meaning sank in. Lance's hands curled into fists and he looked Kealoha in the eye. "You're saying she was *murdered*? Why would anyone want to kill my wife?"

"Das what we're going to find out," Kealoha said. "We need to ask you some questions."

"Why don't you have a tattoo on your right wrist?" Monk asked.

Kealoha regarded Monk with bewilderment. I'm sure Kealoha was trying to figure out what that question had to do with the investigation. Poor guy.

"I guess I never got around to it," Lance said.

"Don't you think it's time you did?"

"Where were you this morning, Mr. Vaughan?" Kealoha said.

Lance glared at the cop. "I know what's going on here. You look at me, you see a man much younger than Helen, and you immediately assume I married her for her money. That's it, isn't it?"

"It's happened before," Kealoha said unapologetically.

"I bet there are tattoo parlors all over Kauai," Monk said. "You could get it done today."

Kealoha gave Monk a hard look. Monk ignored it; he was too busy giving Lance a hard look of his own.

"Two years ago I was a personal trainer in Cleveland. Women threw themselves at me," Lance said. "I had my pick of twenty-two-year-old, surgically enhanced blond bimbos, but you know why I fell in love with Helen?"

"Because she was rich?" I said.

"Rich in character, Ms. Teeger. Rich in intelligence. Rich in her no-holds-barred appreciation of life. She was authentic. A real woman in every sense. She ignored her age, and so did I. She was the sexiest woman I've ever met."

"And probably the wealthiest, too," Kealoha said.

Monk took a pen out of his pocket. "Use this."

"For what?" Lance said.

"To draw barbed wire on your wrist until you can get into a tattoo parlor. You'll thank me later."

"Are you crazy?" Lance said.

"I'm not the one with mismatched wrists," Monk said.

"Where were you between the hours of eight and eleven A.M., Mr. Vaughan?" Kealoha interrupted.

"Snorkeling on the Na Pali Coast," Lance said. "I was on a Snorkel Rob cruise with two dozen other people. Snorkel Rob can tell you. I made the reservation two days ago."

"Why didn't your wife go with you?"

"She said if she wanted to look at goldfish, she would have gone to a pet store instead of flying all the way to Hawaii. But she didn't want to stand in the way of my having a good time," Lance said, choking up again. "If only I'd stayed, maybe I could have saved her."

"I could draw the barbed wire for you," Monk said. "I'm not much of an artist, but then again, neither was the guy who did your tattoo."

"Can you think of any reason why someone would want to kill your wife?" Kealoha said, as if Monk hadn't spoken at all.

He shook his head.

"Is anything missing?" Kealoha asked.

"A tattoo on his right wrist," Monk said. "Am I the only one who can see it?"

"Jewelry, money, important documents, something of value?" Kealoha elaborated.

"I don't know," Lance said. "I haven't looked."

"Would you mind taking a look-see now?" Kealoha waved over an officer. "Go through the house with Mr. Vaughan, okay?"

Lance got up and led the officer into the house.

Kealoha turned to Monk. "What do you think?"

"He's dangerously unbalanced," Monk said.

"You think he's violent?" Kealoha said.

"I think he's got a tattoo on one wrist and not on the other one," Monk said. "A man who is capable of that kind of insanity is capable of anything."

While Kealoha checked out Lance's alibi, I was determined get down to the beach and soak up some of the Hawaiian sunshine. I didn't care what Monk wanted to do with the rest of the day.

I headed straight back to my room with Monk in tow and already fidgeting with nervous energy. He was anxious to investigate something, *anything*, but he had nothing to go on until he heard back from Kealoha. I for one hoped that wouldn't happen for another couple of days.

I went into my room, slammed shut our adjoining door, and changed into my bikini, still simmering over the fact that Monk managed both to ruin my friend's wedding and stumble on a murder on his first full day in Hawaii.

The wedding part I could almost forgive him for, since he saved Candace from marrying a pathological liar and would-be bigamist, but I deeply resented the corpse.

Most people can go their whole lives without getting involved with a murder. Monk is lucky if he can go outside and get his morning paper off his stoop without tripping over a dead body. Murders happen around him with such astonishing frequency that it's long since gone beyond coincidental and borders on supernatural.

I guess on some level I knew the moment Monk showed up on the plane that it was inevitable that, one way or another, I'd get dragged into a homicide investigation in Hawaii. All I could hope for now was that Monk would find the killer quickly or that things would move slowly enough to leave plenty of time for me to lie in hammocks, take long walks on the beach, and float lazily in the pool.

I was slathering on suntan lotion, and continuing to bemoan my sad situation, when I heard Monk's voice on the other side of the door between our rooms. He was talking to someone.

I put on a bathrobe, out of temporary deference to Monk's timidity when it came to exposed female flesh, and opened the door to his room.

Monk stood at his refrigerator with one of the assistant managers from the front desk. The young man in the hotel's uniform floral shirt and khaki pants looked exasperated, but as if he were trying his best to be polite. His name tag identified him as Tetsuo Kapaka.

"I don't see the problem, sir," Tetsuo said, acknowledging me with a polite nod.

"There are two Toblerones in the refrigerator but one of everything else," Monk said.

"Yes," Tetsuo said.

"That's the problem," Monk said. "I'm sure other guests have complained about it."

"You're the first, sir," Tetsuo said.

"I ate the last one, just to get some peace, but while

I was out the maid replaced it," Monk said. "Can you believe that?"

"She was replenishing the minibar," Tetsuo said.

"Is that what you call it?"

"It's how the minibar system works."

"It's a corrupt system," Monk said. "Because now there are two Toblerones again."

"You could eat one."

"Aha!" Monk exclaimed. "That's exactly what you'd like me to do, keep eating those extra bars at six dollars apiece."

"You don't have to eat it, sir. You could ignore it."

"Yeah, right. That's like expecting me to sleep when there are towels in the bathroom that are rolled instead of folded."

Tetsuo's brow wrinkled with confusion. "Do the towels make noise?"

"Not that you or I would hear," I said. "Not even dogs can pick it up."

"I'll instruct the maids not to replenish your minibar for the duration of your stay," Tetsuo said to Monk.

"Admit it, this is just a clever scam by the management to force people into eating Toblerones at outrageously inflated prices."

"No, sir."

Monk lowered his voice. "Are you afraid of reprisals if you talk? Is that it? I'm a detective consulting with the Kauai PD. I can get you witness protection. We can rip this thing wide-open."

"If there's nothing else, Mr. Monk, I'll be going."

"How many Toblerones did Mrs. Gruber have in her SubZero refrigerator?"

"I don't know sir," Tetsuo said. "That wasn't among her complaints."

"What *was* she complaining about?" Monk said.

"Noise," Tetsuo said. "She said she couldn't get any peace with all the people screaming and yelling day and night all around her."

"There must have been a lot of parties going on if she could hear them," I said. "She wore hearing aids."

"That's the thing," Tetsuo said. "Those bungalows are very quiet and secluded. She could barely hear me while I was talking to her. If she was hearing voices, they were in her head."

"So what did you do?"

"I referred her to our manager, Martin Kamakele," Tetsuo said.

Monk narrowed his eyes. "Is he the mastermind behind the Toblerone plot?"

"I don't know, sir." Tetsuo turned to the door. "Have a nice stay, and don't hesitate to contact me if I can be of service."

Monk stared after Tetsuo as he left. "That's a man who lives in fear. There weren't any Toblerones in Helen Gruber's refrigerator. There wasn't any candy at all."

"Maybe she stumbled on the insidious Toblerone conspiracy and was killed to keep her quiet."

"You're joking, but those six-dollar bars add up," Monk said.

"You work on that," I said. "I'm going down to the beach."

"You can't."

"Why not?"

"We're in middle of a murder investigation."

"I'm going to the beach."

"I don't think you're going to have the time."

I opened my bathrobe and let it drop to my feet. Monk threw his arm up in front of his eyes and turned away like a vampire facing a crucifix. At least he didn't hiss.

"Mitch used to love this bikini. I haven't worn it in years. What do you think of it?"

"There's not enough of it," he said from behind his arm.

"Good," I said, and I left. As long as I was in a bikini, Monk wouldn't get near me.

9

Mr. Monk Gets a Message

I dove into the waves and tried not to think about Monk's description of the ocean, but I couldn't get it out of my head, no matter how warm and wonderful the water felt. All I could see in my mind was raw sewage and fish excrement.

That's what Monk does to a person. It's insidious.

I let myself drift in the waves back toward the shore. Weaving my way through all the people on towels and beach chairs, I strode up the hot sand and, to my delight, found an empty hammock between two palms.

Lying there, gently swaying in the humid breeze, letting the sun dry the water from my skin, was like being cuddled by Mother Nature herself. I felt warm, safe, and incredibly relaxed. I drifted into a sweet, languorous nap.

I was awakened by a slight chill. I opened my eyes to see a dark cloud blocking the sun. Within an instant I was soaked by a tremendous downpour of hard-driving rain. My instinct was to run for shelter, but it was a warm rain, and I was in my bikini, so I stayed right where I was, giggling like a child.

I wasn't the only one. The tourists in the ocean and the pool continued splashing around as if nothing had changed. Most of the people on the beach and on the chaise longues simply covered their heads with their towels, mostly to protect their magazines and books, Game Boys and laptops.

Even in the rain, Hawaii was paradise.

Almost as quickly as it began, the rain stopped and the cloud moved on. The sun shone even brighter, and so did everything else, the plants and flowers glistening with raindrops. The smell of the rain and all the fresh flowers filled the air and mingled with the salty spray of the sea.

Within a few minutes I was dry again, and thirsty. I needed something sweet and cold. I rolled out of my hammock, feeling all loose and lazy, and strolled slowly over to the poolside bar—a thatched-roof hut with several rattan bar stools in front.

I gave the bartender my room number and ordered a Lava Flow, a delicious concoction of frozen strawberries, coconut rum, piña colada mix, and bananas all whipped together and topped with a slice of pineapple and the requisite umbrella. I took my first sip and closed my eyes. I was so relaxed, I felt like I might dissolve into a puddle.

"Your husband misses you."

I opened my eyes to see Dylan Swift, the psychic, slide onto the stool beside me. He didn't bother introducing himself. I guess when your face is on a million books, and you've got your own TV show, you figure everybody knows you. Judging by the way everybody around the pool was staring at us, he was probably right.

"I'm single," I said, giving him the information his lame pickup line was designed to draw out of me. I'm not famous, but I didn't bother introducing myself, either. He could wait for my book, assuming I ever wrote one.

"You're a widow," Swift said, his gaze intense and piercing, like a surgical laser. It felt like my vision was improving just looking into his eyes. "And the bonds between you and your husband haven't been severed by death."

I was angry at the invasion of my privacy and pained by the truth of his observation, but I tried not to reveal either emotion.

"Am I supposed to be impressed?" I reached casually for my drink and nearly knocked it over.

"He's anxious to communicate with you, to ease your pain," Swift said. "But I sense it's not your mourning that he wishes to relieve. No, it's something else. Some unfinished business. You feel that he was wronged in some way."

"Mitch was killed two days before his twenty-seventh birthday," I said. "I'd say that was wrong."

I was surprised at how close to the surface my anger was and how easily I revealed it. I guess when it came to Mitch, my emotions were pretty raw.

Swift took the umbrella from my drink and twirled it between his fingers. "It was an accident that took him from you."

"He was shot out of the sky by enemy fire," I said. "It was hardly an accident."

"What I meant was that it wasn't his fault," Swift said. "He doesn't blame himself for what happened in Kosovo and neither should you."

"I don't," I said.

"But somebody does, and that troubles you," Swift said. "It fills you with rage and frustration. No matter what anyone in the military tells you, Mitch wants you to know he did everything a soldier should do. He wants you to be proud of him, to know that he was courageous, and not to doubt that he was the man you loved, right up until the end."

Against my will, tears were welling in my eyes, and that really pissed me off. The last thing I wanted to do was cry in front of this man. Or any man.

"I'm still not impressed," I said, taking another sip of my Lava Flow and trying to act as if we were discussing something like baseball or the weather instead of the death of my husband.

"I'm not trying to impress you or anybody else," Swift said. "I'm just relaying a message. You want to know what really happened to Mitch, don't you?"

"Can you tell me?" I asked, upset at how quickly I spoke and the desperation that revealed.

"I can't, but Mitch can," Swift said. "Unfortunately, the images, the symbols, they aren't so easy to read. Other voices and other sensations are crowding them out."

"I don't understand."

"My relationship with the spirit world is complicated. Imagine a thousand spirits in a room and just one cell phone for them to call out with. I am the cell phone. They are all fighting to be heard. But you know how unreliable cell phone reception is sometimes. It would be hard enough just hearing them clearly, but they don't speak to me in words so much as in feelings, images, tastes, smells, and sounds."

"Tell the others to wait their turn," I said. "Let Mitch talk."

"It doesn't work like that," Swift said. "And like a cell phone, I can't control who uses me. Sometimes, when I am near someone, a spirit who wants to reach that person will come through very forcefully. In other cases people come to me and ask to reach a specific loved one who has crossed over to the great beyond. That's more difficult."

"You have to make the cell phone ring on the other side and you hope the right spirit answers it."

Swift smiled enigmatically. I had a feeling he worked hard perfecting the enigmatic part. "Something like that."

"You haven't told me anything about my husband that you couldn't have found in a Google search or safely assumed based on the circumstances."

"You're a skeptic."

"I'm a realist," I said. I was lying. I wanted more than anything to believe he was talking to Mitch, and I hated myself for that yearning. "What do you want from me, Mr. Swift?"

"Call me Dylan, please."

"You haven't answered my question."

"I don't want anything from you, Natalie."

"So you *do* know who I am," I said accusingly.

"I know you were with Adrian Monk, and I need to see him," Swift said.

"Why?"

"To relay a message from the dead. Someone is desperate to communicate with him."

"Anyone in particular?" I asked.

"Helen Gruber," he said.

"That's pretty specific, considering the spirits rarely introduce themselves to you."

Swift smiled again, though there was nothing enigmatic about it this time. He was pleased.

"You've watched my show?"

"When I was stuck at home with the flu. I caught a few minutes here and there between my vomiting."

I was trying to be cutting, to dispel some of that smug confidence of his, but he seemed unperturbed.

"I've never felt such a strong connection to a spirit before. My bungalow is a few doors down from hers," Swift said. "It was as if her spirit contacted me on her way to the other side, moments after she was killed."

"How do you know she was killed?"

"I felt it. It was sudden. It . . ." He struggled for the right words. "It didn't come from inside, like a natural death. It came from behind. Someone came up behind her and struck her on the head; that's what I'm sensing."

He could have picked up most of the vague stuff he'd told me so far from the hotel staff or one of the police officers at the crime scene. It didn't take a psychic to presume a murder has taken place when you saw a morgue wagon and police cars parked on the street.

"There are things she wants me to share with Monk," Swift said.

He was putting me in an awkward predicament, forcing me to weigh my own selfish desires against my ethical duties as Monk's assistant.

It was bad enough that Monk had found a murder to solve, but he was so desperate to avoid enjoying

Hawaii that he was ready to launch an investigation into how his minibar was stocked.

Now here was Dylan Swift, a guy who supposedly talked to dead people, saying he had a collect call from the other side from the victim of the murder Monk was investigating.

If I brought Swift to him now, Monk would dedicate whatever time we weren't spending on the hoicide investigation to exposing the celebrity medium as a fraud. In fact, Monk was ready to do it when we stumbled on the filming of Swift's TV show the day before, an incident I hoped he was too drugged-up at the time to remember.

But that would change if Swift showed up claiming to speak for Helen Gruber. And I could kiss goodbye any hope of enjoying one moment of my vacation.

So I rationalized that part of my job as Adrian Monk's assistant was to be his gatekeeper and keep people from wasting his time. If Swift actually had something useful to contribute, I would bring him to Monk right away. But if he didn't, I'd spare Monk an unnecessary distraction and, in doing so, buy myself a little vacation time in paradise. No harm done.

I managed to convince myself I wasn't being selfish at all. I was being extraordinarily considerate and helpful.

"Share them with me," I said. "And I will pass them along to Mr. Monk."

He stared at me for a long moment, trying to come to a decision. That was fine with me; it gave me a chance to enjoy some more of my Lava Flow. Finally he sighed and began speaking.

"She doesn't know who killed her," Swift said.

"But she's flooded my mind with images and sensations. The smell of lilac. The light, sweet taste of *liliko'i* pie. I see Captain Ahab hiding in the shadows. I sense love taking flight. I feel barbed wire against flesh. I see a glimpse of a lumberjack standing by a pine tree holding a porcelain doll. You're not writing any of this down."

"I have a good memory," I said. "Did she give you anything more concrete than that?"

"She's not alone," he said.

"You mean she's not the first victim?"

"All I know is that there are other spirits who wanted to communicate with me about this. It didn't make a lot of sense to me then and it doesn't now. But I'm sure it will become clear as time goes on."

"The spirits said they'd call back?"

He rose from his stool and gave me a smile, this one full of amusement. Swift had quite a repertoire of smiles.

"Spirits this disturbed never stay quiet. They'll persist until their message is heard."

I was right not to take Swift to see Monk. Not only was none of his gibberish the least bit helpful, but he was obviously an attention-seeking fraud, trying to horn in on whatever publicity might arise from the murder investigation.

Swift started to walk away, then he stopped and looked over his shoulder at me.

"Mitch still likes that bikini on you," Swift said, nodding with approval. "I can see why."

I felt a shiver, as if Mitch himself had brushed his lips against the back of my neck.

10

Mr. Monk Rents a Car

I got a towel, wrapped it around my waist, and went to the lobby, Dylan Swift and his messages from beyond still very much on my mind.

I was on my way to the elevators when I saw Monk at one of the kiosks in the wide shopping arcade. The stand was made to look like a beach hut and was devoted to island jewelry. Monk was methodically sorting through the display of shark-tooth necklaces, to the obvious displeasure of the middle-aged Hawaiian proprietress behind the counter.

"Shopping, Mr. Monk?" I said as I approached.

Monk turned around, saw me in my bikini top, and looked right over my head. "I don't shop."

"Then what are you doing?"

"Having fun. That's what a vacation is for, isn't it?"

"It's okay if you look at me."

"I don't think so." He shifted his gaze back to the necklaces, which he was rearranging on a little carousel necklace tree. Each necklace had a single white shark tooth dangling from it.

"We're at the beach. All the women here are wearing swimsuits, tank tops, or halters," I said. "Look around and you'll see."

"I'd rather not."

"They're breasts, Mr. Monk, not wild animals."

"That's how they behave."

I sighed, giving up. "So if you're not shopping, what are you doing?"

"I'm arranging the teeth by type of shark and where they belong in the jaw."

"You call that fun?"

The proprietress groaned in misery.

Monk nodded enthusiastically, continuing to sort the necklaces. "It's a blast. There are about thirty-three kinds of sharks in Hawaii, and some have as many as thirteen rows of teeth. An average shark sheds eighteen hundred teeth a year, fifty thousand in a lifetime. There are all kinds of shark teeth on the necklaces here, hundreds of them, in no order whatsoever."

"So it's like a giant, enormously complex jigsaw puzzle."

"You can't do this at home. Only in Hawaii," Monk said. "I was lucky there wasn't a line when I got here."

"Or anybody since," the proprietress muttered.

"You can actually tell the difference between one shark tooth and another?" I asked.

Monk snorted derisively. "Of course. Who can't?"

"How long have you been here?"

"I've lost track of time in all the excitement."

"Three hours," the proprietress said. It was obvious by the stony expression on her unhappy face that she'd felt every single second of those hours pass by.

"I haven't had this much fun since those summers when my brother and I would shell a large bag of roasted peanuts, mix everything up, and compete to see who could reassemble the most nuts. Then we'd eat them. Those were some wild, wild times."

Looking past Monk, I noticed Lance Vaughan at the front desk with his luggage. He appeared to be checking out.

"Mr. Monk, look."

He shook his head. "I thought we settled that."

"Not at *me*, at the front desk."

Monk glanced at the front desk, then turned back and smiled at the proprietress. "This has been great. Really rad."

"Rad?" I said.

Monk looked at me, forgetting for an instant that I was in a bikini top. He quickly averted his eyes.

"Yes. That's what they say now. You really ought to try to stay in step with popular culture or you'll be left behind." Monk turned to the proprietress again. "I'll be back tomorrow."

"We're closed tomorrow," she said.

"When will you be back?"

"When are you going home?"

"Tuesday," he said.

"Wednesday," she said.

"Why are you closed so long?"

"A family emergency," she said.

Monk sighed sadly. "Are there any other shark tooth attractions on the island?"

"There are lots of places that have shark teeth," she said. "Lots of places *outside the hotel*."

"Oh, good, because I'm just getting warmed up," Monk said. He glanced over my head, which was his way of looking at me without looking at me. "Maybe you and I could go a round together sometime."

"Organizing shark teeth."

"It's a vacation, isn't it?" Monk said. "Have some fun."

With that, he headed over to the front desk, where Tetsuo was waiting on Lance.

"Going somewhere, Mr. Vaughan?" Monk said.

Lance, startled, turned around. "I'm changing rooms. I couldn't stay in that bungalow after . . ." His voice got so choked up, he couldn't finish. He cleared his throat and tried again. "I'm sure you understand, Mr. Monk."

"When we asked you about your wife, you didn't mention anything about her hearing voices."

Lance's expression hardened. "Where did you learn about that?"

Tetsuo lowered his head guiltily but didn't escape Lance's notice. Lance glared at him a moment, then shifted his gaze back to Monk.

"I didn't see the point of saying anything," Lance said. "Helen was a strong woman—that's how I want her to be remembered, not as someone who was slipping into dementia."

"How long had she been slipping?"

"She's been forgetful and disoriented for a while now, but she didn't start hearing voices until we got here. To be honest, it scared me. I had to get out of the house, get my own head straight, you know?"

"Is that why you went on the snorkeling trip without her?"

"Sure, it was one of the reasons," Lance said. "But I also have to keep myself fit. I couldn't spend two weeks here sitting by the pool. I'm a very physical guy; I need to work my body. As much as she wanted to, she couldn't keep up with me. Few people can. She accepted that. It was the only concession she made to her age."

"You could have made concessions instead," I said.

"And let my body go to hell?" Lance shook his head. "She wouldn't have liked that any more than I would have. She wanted me to be in top shape."

I was sure she did, in the same way a guy liked his young trophy wife to be thin, blond, and stacked. I doubted Helen would have married a guy thirty years younger than her if he had two chins and a beer gut. She could have found guys like that her own age.

Tetsuo handed Lance a card key. "Your room is ready, sir, courtesy of the Grand Kiahuna Poipu."

"Thanks." Lance took the key and looked at Monk. "Is there anything else?"

Monk shook his head. Lance picked up his suitcases and ambled off toward the elevators.

"You think he's the guy?" I asked.

Monk looked in my general direction, but not at me, and shrugged. "Who else could it be?"

"But he has an alibi," I said.

"The clever ones always do."

We started to walk away ourselves when Tetsuo called out to Monk.

"Sir, you have a phone message." Tetsuo handed Monk a slip of paper.

Monk glanced at it. "Lieutenant Kealoha has some

information. He'd like me to give him a call or stop by the station."

It would have been easier to call Kealoha, but I wanted to get out of the hotel and see some more of the island.

"Let's go to him," I said. "We need to get a rental car anyway."

"There's a Paradise Car Rental outlet located at the parking lot entrance to the shopping arcade," Tetsuo offered politely.

I went back up to my room, quickly changed into shorts and a shirt, and met Monk in the lobby again five minutes later. We started at one end of the U-shaped arcade and headed toward the exit, and the car rental counter, at the other end.

We rounded the corner and saw Brian, Candace's would-be husband, standing with his luggage at the rental counter, right in front of the exit to the parking lot. He was talking to the rental agent, a young white guy with sun-bleached blond hair wearing an aloha shirt covered with Paradise Car Rental's orchid logo. When Brian saw us, his face turned red with fury.

"There they are," he said, wagging a finger at us. "They probably know who did it."

"Did what?" Monk asked as we approached.

"Trashed my car," Brian said, tipping his head toward the parking lot. "Someone at the wedding did this. I'm certain of it."

We stepped outside and looked at Brian's Mustang convertible, parked in a row with several other identical Mustangs. But his was easy to spot. It was the one with the shattered windshield and a big rip down the center of the soft-top. Monk walked over and surveyed the car.

"This was an act of pure malice," Brian said.

"What about what you did to Candace?" I said.

"See?" Brian said to the agent. "She's practically admitting her involvement in this. But the joke is on her and her coldhearted, vindictive friends. I'm completely covered by insurance."

"Was there any other damage to the car that you'd like to report?" the agent asked. His name tag identified him as Tom, from Hermosa Beach, California.

"No," Brian said, as Monk returned.

"There's a scratch on the back bumper, three dings on the driver's door, bird droppings on the trunk, and a amoeba-shaped stain of indeterminate origin on the passenger seat," Monk said. "And he returned it with an uneven odometer."

"An uneven odometer?" Tom asked, clearly perplexed.

"It's at two hundred and seven miles. He didn't even have the common human decency to go the extra mile." Monk sneered at Brian. "How can you look at yourself in the mirror?"

Tom handed Brian a document on a clipboard.

"All you have to do is sign here and the shuttle bus will take you to the airport." He motioned to a Paradise Car Rental van idling at the curb a few yards away.

"You didn't note the scratches, dings and stains," Monk said to the agent.

"It doesn't matter," Tom said.

"That's a permanent stain."

"The interiors get stained all the time," Tom from Hermosa Beach said. "The red dirt alone will ruin the interior, if all the rain and sea air don't ruin the exterior first. Don't even get me started on what people spill in the cars or what we find under the seats. You don't want to know."

Monk shook his head. "No, I don't."

"And people drive them with no care or respect. Cars don't last long here. Luckily, there's a great body shop in Kapaa. All the companies use it."

Brian signed the document and handed the clipboard back to the agent.

"I hope you enjoyed your stay," Tom said.

Brian glowered at Monk and me, picked up his suitcases, and marched off to the shuttle. The agent turned to us.

"So what can I do for you this evening?"

"We'd like to rent a car," I said.

"Take your pick."

"We want one that's fresh off the boat," Monk said. "A car driven by only one or two very clean, sanitary people."

Tom looked at the wrecked Mustang. "That was the newest car we had. The rest have been here a couple months. You might try Global Rental in Lihue."

I glanced at the shuttle, which hadn't left yet. There were plenty of rental-car places at the airport.

"Mind if we hitch a ride on the shuttle to the airport?" I asked.

"Be my guest," Tom said.

I started walking to the shuttle.

"Do you really want to ride in a bus with that pitiful excuse for a man?" Monk said, walking alongside me.

"I'm not the one who is going to be uncomfortable," I said. "He is."

"Because seeing you staring at him will silently remind him of how he wronged your friend?"

"Who said anything about being silent?" I said. "I'm going to remind him as loudly, and as color-fully, as I possibly can for the entire drive. If you've got sensitive ears, you might want to keep them covered."

Brian would have bolted from the shuttle the instant we got to the airport, but he was slowed down by his luggage, so I got a few more choice words in before he escaped. Monk was so embarrassed by my language, I think he was tempted to run out, too.

The major car-rental companies, along with a few smaller operations, were all grouped together in a cul-de-sac adjacent to the airport parking lot. The shuttle dropped us off in front of Paradise Car Rental, but they didn't have any "fresh off the boat" cars available, so we went across the street to Global.

The rental agents at Global were young, Hawaiian, and apparently under strict orders never to stop smil-ing. They probably spent their off-hours with sore cheeks and grim faces to avoid the pain. Like their counterparts at Paradise, the pattern of their aloha shirts was their logo, which was the Earth as a steer-ing wheel.

"We can't rent a car here," Monk said.

"Why not?"

"Look at this place," Monk said. "It's in com-plete disarray."

I looked at the lot. I saw a hundred different Ford models parked in neat rows in numbered spaces. Monk should have been thrilled. "I don't see the problem."

"You must have jet lag. The vehicles are parked out there willy-nilly."

"Willy-nilly?" I said. "They are in numbered parking spots."

"They should be arranged by make, model, color, and year of production," he said as if it were a matter of common sense. "This is anarchy. If this is a sign of how organized they are, imagine how they maintain their cars."

I pointed across the street. "Look at the other rental companies, Mr. Monk. Their cars are all parked willy-nilly, too."

"At least now I know where the term 'willy-nilly' came from," Monk said. "It's Hawaiian for 'chaos.' "

An agent named Kimiko came over to help us. I asked for a convertible. Monk didn't care what we got as long as the car was fresh off the assembly line. Kimiko led us to a Mustang with only thirty-eight miles on the odometer—she said it had never been rented.

While Monk was inspecting the car for imperfections and I was filling out the rental form, a couple in their twenties, both sunburned, drove in with a Mustang that had been clipped on the front passenger side, shattering the headlight and crumpling the hood.

The couple told Kimiko they were sideswiped by a hit-and-run driver and gave her a copy of the police report. First Brian, now them. I checked the boxes on the form for every insurance plan they offered. It was going on Monk's credit card anyway.

"What a nice couple," Monk said, peering into their dented car.

"What makes you say that?" I said. "You don't know anything about them.

"They brought the car back with an even odometer. One hundred and twelve miles."

"It's a coincidence," I said. "They didn't do it on purpose."

"You're too cynical," Monk said. "Have some faith in your fellow man."

11

Mr. Monk Goes to Dinner

The cramped squad room of the Lihue police station resembled every other government office I had seen before. Everything was in shades of gray—the cinder-block walls, the file cabinets, the four metal desks, even the linoleum floors, where years of foot traffic had worn trails around the squad room. The only color came from the aloha shirts on the two detectives and the cluster of multicolored pushpins stuck in a black-and-white map of Kauai on a bulletin board behind Kealoha's desk.

Kealoha rose to greet us. "Hey, tanks for coming down."

"No beeg ting, bruddah," I said with a grin.

"Dat's good," Kealoha said.

"Do you have some new leads in the investigation?" Monk asked.

"Just mo' dead ends," Kealoha said. "The medical examiner confirms that Helen Gruber was killed sometime between eight and eleven A.M., which rules out Lance as her killer."

"His alibi checks out?"

"Like he said, he was on a Snorkel Rob catamaran cruising the Na Pali Coast, whale watching and snorkeling." Kealoha picked up a videotape from his desk. "Snorkel Rob has a crew member professionally videotape each trip; then at the end of the trip, they sell the tapes to the guests for fifty bucks each. I borrowed one."

There was a TV/VCR combo on a rolling cart near Kealoha's desk. The detective put the tape into the VCR and hit play. It was cued up to a scene on the boat. Lance was among a dozen tourists on deck watching the whales. Kealoha hit the fast-forward button, stopping at a shot of Lance ogling a young brunette in a tight surf shirt and G-string bikini bottoms as she dove off the boat. A few minutes further into the video, we saw Lance underwater, swimming amidst a school of tropical fish. Kealoha froze the image.

"Bummah," he said. "I liked him for this."

"The video could have been made days ago," Monk said. "How do we know it was taken this morning?"

"I got a sworn statement from the guy who shot the video; plus I'm tracking down all the haoles on the boat to corroborate what he told me," Kealoha said. "I've already talked to one couple from this video. They arrived last night from the mainland. So the video had to be made today. Dems da facts, brah."

"Did the guests on the boat ever go ashore during the excursion?"

"There's a couple of isolated beaches along the coast and they stopped at one of them for lunch. But if you're thinking maybe Lance slipped away from the group, got to a car hidden somewhere, and drove back to Poipu to kill his wife, fo'gedda 'bout it. What makes Na Pali so spectacular is that it's a rugged coastline of jagged, four-thousand-foot cliffs that are inaccessible by car."

"What about a helicopter?" I asked. "Don't they do tours of the Na Pali Coast?"

"It'd be crazy to try landing on one of those beaches, and even if you did, you couldn't do that without being seen by everybody on the boat," Kealoha said. "He's got a great alibi."

"Almost too great," Monk said. "I never trust people with great alibis. Or people who drink soda directly from the can. Or people who pierce any part of their bodies."

"I have pierced ears," I said.

"So do I," Kealoha said. "Nipples, too."

Monk shivered and pretended he didn't hear us. "He could have hired someone to kill his wife."

"I've talked to the Cleveland PD," Kealoha said. "They are checking out Lance and his bank accounts, too. I wouldn't be surprised if the Cleveland cops try to wrangle a trip here to deliver their news personally."

"So I guess that means there's nothing for us to do but enjoy the island while we wait," I said, hoping the Cleveland cops took their sweet time. "Shall we go, Mr. Monk?"

Monk drifted over to the map. "What's this?"

"Don't bother with that," Kealoha said, dismissing it with a wave of his hand. "It's stuff we're never gonna solve."

I wished he hadn't said that. With those words

and that simple gesture Kealoha had carelessly given Monk something else to obsess about.

"Why not?" Monk said.

"They're residential burglaries in Poipu. Most of the houses hit are vacation homes and condos that are only occasionally occupied by the owners. They can be vacant for months at a time or rented out every week."

"So by the time the owners notice something is missing, it could be days, weeks, or months after the crime was actually committed."

"It's jus li'dat." Kealoha sighed.

"What about witnesses? Has anybody seen anything unusual?"

"That's another problem. Lots of the neighboring homes or condos are either vacant or rented by one tourist after another. How do you know when somebody's a stranger if you're one too? We've asked the gardeners, mailmen, pool guys—the regulars—to keep an eye open, but they're no better than the tourists at noticing da kine."

"There must be at least a few cases where you have a rough idea when the burglary occurred. Didn't any alarms ever go off? Didn't anybody ever report freshly broken windows or jimmied-open doors?"

"A handful."

"When and where did they occur?"

Kealoha opened a binder on his desk and passed it to Monk, who scanned the pages.

I thought it was awfully convenient that Kealoha had the information so readily available. I was beginning to suspect that this was all a setup, that Kealoha *wanted* Monk to ask about the burglaries all along.

"These burglaries all occurred in broad daylight on weekdays," Monk said. "Why would the burglar take that risk?"

"I don't know," Kealoha said.

"This is odd," Monk said, referring to something he was reading. "According to these reports, some of the burglaries even happened in gated neighborhoods and security buildings. How did the burglars get in and out carrying stolen goods without anyone noticing?"

"It's a mystery." Kealoha shrugged and winked at me conspiratorially.

But I wasn't part of the conspiracy. I was a victim. He was practically confessing to unloading his cases on Monk and, by extension, making sure I had no opportunity at all to enjoy Kauai.

Monk pointed to a listing on the page. "An alarm was triggered three weeks ago at two fifteen P.M. at a house on Hoonani Road. Can you show me where that is on the map?"

Kealoha touched a pushpin on a road that ran along the coast on the southern edge of the island, not far from our hotel. "Right here."

"And this one four days ago at five P.M. on Lawai Road?"

Kealoha tapped a pin a little farther east, near where Lawai Road reached a dead end at Spouting Horn, which I knew from guidebooks was a fountain of water created by waves blasting through a narrow hole in an outcropping of lava rocks. I wondered if I'd actually get an opportunity to see it, or any of the island's other natural wonders, while I was here.

"What about this burglary last week at noon?"

"Here, on the Milo Hae Loop." Kealoha pointed to some homes along the Grand Kiahuna Poipu golf course.

And so it went. As Monk called out addresses from the binder, Kealoha showed him the corresponding pushpins on the map.

Monk closed the binder and stared at the map. After a long moment, he turned to Kealoha.

"Are you free for a round of golf tomorrow at eleven at the Grand Kiahuna Poipu?"

"I appreciate the invite, but I'm kind of working on this homicide case," Kealoha said. "And even if I wasn't, it's a very popular course. You'd never get a reservation for tomorrow on such short notice."

"Not even for official police business?"

"Is it?"

"It is if you want to apprehend a burglar," Monk said.

I decided not to speak to Monk until after we'd finished our dinner at the Royal Hawaiian and he'd given the waiter his credit card to pay the check.

The Royal Hawaiian was in the original Kiahuna Poipu plantation house. The restaurant was surrounded by a lush tropical garden and a meandering path lit by torches that led all the way down to the beach.

Although we couldn't see the ocean, we could hear the crashing surf and smell the sea breeze that wafted through the garden, picking up the floral fragrances. The dining room was paneled in rich koa wood, which gave the restaurant a distinctly Hawaiian elegance and justified the steep prices of the entrées.

I started with a warm macadamia-nut-and-goat-cheese salad with a passion-fruit vinaigrette followed by lemongrass seared island opah with udon noodles and a Thai basil-lime butter sauce.

Monk had a mixed green salad (which he promptly sorted out on a separate plate), followed by a grilled salmon fillet with white rice. He also had a 7UP with a slice of lemon to, as he put it, let loose a little.

I was trying to punish him with my silence but he didn't seem to notice. In fact, I think he liked it. Damn him.

While we ate, I thought about what a frustrating, and eventful, day it had been, beginning with a disastrous wedding ceremony and the discovery of a murdered woman. I met a medium who claimed to be channeling not only the dead woman, but my husband, too, and Monk decided to investigate all the unsolved burglaries on the island.

And this was just our first full day.

"You know Lieutenant Kealoha is using you," I said finally as the waiter returned and presented Monk with his Visa card, the check, the credit card receipt, and a pen on a little silver tray.

"No, he's not." Monk took out his own pen and began carefully signing the receipt.

"He tricked you into solving those burglaries for him."

"I don't mind," Monk said.

"*I* do," I said. "It's bad enough that you inserted yourself into a homicide investigation, but now you're taking on his entire caseload."

"You call that a caseload?" Monk said. "I could solve a year's worth of his cases in a week."

"That's exactly what he's hoping for."

Monk dropped his pen in disgust, then used the

straight edge of his table knife to carefully fold the receipt in half and tear it down the middle. Then he repeated the process on the two halves before waving over the waiter.

"Can I help you?" the waiter asked.

"I need you to void this transaction and print out another receipt for me," Monk said, piling the four scraps of the receipt onto the little tray.

"Did I make a mistake totaling the bill?"

"No, your addition was fine. I screwed up. My signature was a mess."

The waiter, baffled, picked up the tray and walked away.

I usually tried not to eat out with Monk unless he was paying cash. When he uses a credit card, he has to make sure he signs his name *just right*. It once took him six attempts over a period of twenty minutes to sign a receipt.

"I've got an idea, Mr. Monk," I said. "Why don't you go to work for the Kauai police full-time while we're here. That way, Kealoha can hang out with you all day while I enjoy my vacation. I'll see you at the airport on Tuesday and you can tell me all about the cases you solved."

"I don't understand what's bothering you. We're going golfing tomorrow morning, aren't we? That's not work. That's fun."

"It's only so you can stake out those houses on the course," I said.

"That's part of it," Monk said. "But it's mostly so I could get in a few holes of golf. We couldn't get on the course otherwise."

"You're saying *you* manipulated *him*."

"Let's just say I can be cunning when I want to be," Monk said. "It's like a superpower. I'm afraid if I use it too much, it will consume me."

The waiter returned with the check, the credit card, and the receipt. Monk straightened up, stretched, and attempted to sign his name again. He leaned down, his face so close to the table that his nose was nearly touching the receipt.

"Have you ever played golf?" I asked.

"Of course," Monk said. "I'm really quite good. I'm a par player."

I was skeptical. It takes considerable skill, born of years of practice and steady play, to reach that level.

"How come I've never seen a set of clubs in your house?"

"I only need one club," Monk said. "My forte is windmills."

"Windmills?"

"You have to time the putt perfectly or your ball won't go through the hole in the mill house; it will get hit by the windmill blade and knocked aside. A lot of amateurs get bogged down there, and the strokes really add up. It's a sad thing to see."

"You're talking about miniature golf. It's not the same thing as golf."

"I know that," Monk said, concentrating on his signature. "Miniature golf takes precision. It's like the difference between brain surgery and hacking off someone's leg with an ax."

"You're saying miniature golf takes *more* skill?"

"Have you ever seen a windmill or a castle on a PGA-ranked course?" Monk said. "I think not."

He sat up with a frown, eyed the receipt from different angles, then tore it up again in the careful way he had before. The waiter, who was standing off to one side watching us, came over to the table.

"Is there another problem, sir?"

"I need a new receipt. I think the signature line was crooked. You should really check it out before you bring over the next receipt," Monk said. "Borrow a level from the kitchen."

"Why would we have a level in the kitchen?"

"How could you run a restaurant without one?"

"Of course, my mistake, sir." The waiter took the tray and walked away.

Monk gave me a look. "He must be new."

Since Monk was going to be a while signing his name, I excused myself and went to the ladies' room, which gave me a chance to walk through the restaurant and admire the paintings of island flowers and luau dancers.

On my way back to the table, I passed by the restaurant front desk, where a slim woman in a low-cut sundress was waiting while the hostess bagged a to-go order for her.

The woman had a dark, Mediterranean complexion, hazel-brown eyes, a lithe body, and black hair tied into a ponytail that fell between her shoulder blades. I'd seen her before. She was the woman on the catamaran whose butt Lance was admiring. She wore a surf shirt in the video, so I noticed something about her this time I didn't see before: She had a tattoo on the top of her left breast.

It was a heart with wings.

Love taking flight. Dylan Swift's words came back to haunt me and a sudden chill brought shivers to my skin. That image was one of the things Helen Gruber's spirit had supposedly shared with him.

It could have been coincidence that a woman on the boat with the murdered woman's husband just happened to have a tattoo that could be interpreted as "love taking flight."

It could have meant nothing.

Or it could mean everything. I had to know which was the case.

I hurried back to the table, where Monk was still working on his signature.

"You've been signing your name for thirty years. You should have the hang of it by now."

"These are not exactly the optimum conditions. It's a tiny receipt with a minuscule space allotted to sign my name. It's tricky balancing the proportion of the letters with space between them and getting everything to fit. If I rush it, I could end up jamming my last name against the edge of the paper. I've seen it happen before."

I glanced back at the woman. She handed her credit card to the hostess, who rang up her bill.

"You're not being graded on your penmanship, Mr. Monk. It's just a signature."

"It's more than that," Monk said. "It's verification of your identity. It's an extension of who you are."

The woman signed her credit card receipt. It took her about one second. Nobody could possibly spend as much time signing his name as Monk did. I suspected there was another motivation besides attaining the perfect proportion and balance between his letters.

"I'm on to you, Mr. Monk," I said, reaching into

my purse and getting some cash. "I don't think this has anything to do with getting your signature right. I think this is all about you being cheap."

"I don't understand what you mean," he said.

I grabbed the receipt from him, tore it into pieces, and slapped some money, enough to cover our meals and the tip, on the table.

"You hate to pay," I said, getting up from the table. "So you do this thing with the signature until I get so frustrated that I pick up the tab. It's like you said; you can be cunning when you want to be."

"I only use my cunning for the good of mankind," Monk said, picking up his credit card and rising from his seat. "Not for personal gain."

I didn't bother arguing, but I promised myself that the next time we went out to dinner, I would let him sit there all night signing his name and I still wouldn't pay.

The woman gathered up her bag and walked out of the restaurant just ahead of us. We followed a few yards behind her through the tropical garden to the parking lot. Luckily for me, her Jeep was parked only a couple of spots down from our Mustang.

The night sky was much darker than in San Francisco, but the stars twinkled brighter here. The air was pleasantly warm, like a bed in the morning, and the fragrance was sweet, like freshly laundered sheets. I must have been tired, because I was obviously thinking about bed a lot.

"It's a great night for a drive," I said, putting the soft-top down. I had no idea how far the woman was going to take us, and I needed an excuse if she journeyed far from our hotel.

"That sounds nice," Monk said amiably.

The woman pulled out of her spot and, using skills I learned from watching *Rockford Files* reruns, I let a couple of cars slip in between us and her as she headed down Poipu Road. It was dark, the road lit only by the moon and the headlights of passing cars.

She made a left on Kapili, which took us down to the water, where the rays of the crescent moon reflected off the waves. There was no beach there, just black, craggy lava rocks, the surf smashing up against them in a frothy spray, creating a mist we could feel on our skin as we drove along Hoonani Road, which hugged the shoreline. On the other side of the street were condo complexes and private homes facing the water.

"It's so beautiful here, isn't it? Even when all you can see are the silhouettes of the palm trees cast against the moon."

"Not to mention the Jeep the woman from the catamaran is driving."

"Huh?" I said. That was really the best I could do under the circumstances.

"We're following one of the tourists who was on the Snorkel Rob cruise this morning."

"We are?" I tried to sound surprised and not guilty. Now I knew how the bad guys felt when he revealed their crimes.

"She was at the counter of the restaurant when we left."

"Really? Your powers of observation are absolutely amazing. I never would have recognized her."

"So it's a coincidence that we're following her."

"Of course it is," I said. "We're just taking a drive along the water."

"Then why did you slow down to let two cars get between us and her?"

"Because I'm a very courteous driver."

"I watch *The Rockford Files*, too. We watch it together."

She pulled into a condominium complex and parked behind one of the waterfront units. The condominiums were called the Whaler's Hideaway, the name written in rusted metal-strip scrawl on the low lava-rock wall that ringed the complex. Another one of Dylan Swift's images came back to me.

Captain Ahab hiding in the shadows.

A whaler hiding? It was a stretch, but here she was at Whaler's Hideaway. The image fit, just like "love taking flight" matched her tattoo. I felt a shiver go through me, and the opening notes of *The Twilight Zone* theme song played in my head.

I drove around to the front of the building, where it faced the Pacific, and parked on the street so we could see the unit she entered as well as all the others in the complex. Everybody had their drapes wide-open to take in the view. We could see into every unit, including hers.

And we could see Lance Vaughan greet her at the door, giving her a kiss on the lips. She squeezed his butt and took their food to the table on their lanai.

Monk turned to me. "How did you know?"

"Would you believe I deduced it?"

"No."

"Why not?" I said.

"Because if there was something to deduce, I would have deduced it. Deducing is what I do."

I sighed with defeat. I really didn't want to tell him, but I had to now.

"I had some help."

"From who?"

"Helen Gruber."

Monk gave me a look. "She's dead."

"I know, but she left you a message this afternoon."

"How could she if she's dead?"

"She talked to Dylan Swift," I said. "From the great beyond."

12

Mr. Monk Shows How It's Done

On the way back to the hotel and up to our adjoining rooms, I told Monk all about my encounter with Dylan Swift at the poolside bar. I recounted everything Swift said about the murder and the images and sensations Helen shared with him from the great beyond—the smell of lilac, a lumberjack holding a porcelain doll, the taste of *liliko'i* pie, Captain Ahab hiding in shadow, barbed wire against flesh, love taking flight, and a pine tree.

I sat on the edge of my bed and he sat in one of the two rattan easy chairs. I expected him to explode with anger or something, but he didn't. He just sat there calmly looking at me.

"I haven't checked but I bet there are two Toblerones in my minibar."

"Mr. Monk, did you hear a word I said?"

He nodded.

"And?"

"I wonder how many Toblerones are in your minibar." Monk got up and went to my minibar.

"I know I should have brought Swift straight to you but I was skeptical about this whole talking-to-the-dead thing."

"Because it's impossible. He's a fraud. Nobody can talk to the dead," Monk said, tugging at the minibar door. "You did the right thing keeping him away from me."

"I did?"

"He would have distracted me from the investigation, which needs my full attention," Monk said. "Where is the minibar key?"

"I gave it back to the front desk," I said. "I didn't want to be tempted by the stuff in there."

"I need a wipe and a hairpin," he said.

I opened my purse, found a Wet Ones and a hairpin, and gave them both to Monk. He used the wipe to clean the hairpin of all my deadly germs.

"You say Swift is a fraud, but two of the images that Swift saw connect Lance Vaughan to the woman on that boat," I said. "We wouldn't have known there was a relationship between Lance and her if it wasn't for Swift."

"So now you believe him?" Monk worked the hairpin into the minibar lock. "You think he talks to ghosts?"

"I don't know. But if those two images gave us a lead in the case, maybe the other stuff he told me will, too."

"You *want* to believe him," Monk said.

"No, I don't."

"Yes, you do. That's why you'd rather believe he can communicate with spirits than consider the most obvious explanation for his accuracy."

"Which is?"

"Swift must have seen Lance and that woman together before. When he learned that Helen was murdered, Swift figured there was a way to use that information to make it seem as if he were communicating with the dead and bolster his reputation as a medium."

The minibar lock clicked. Monk smiled, pleased with himself, and opened the little refrigerator. "Look at that, two Toblerone bars but one of everything else."

"Maybe Toblerone bars are simply more popular than everything else."

"You're so gullible," Monk said, closing the minibar. "But even so, to get you to believe in something as outrageous as talking to ghosts, Swift still would have had to win your sympathy first."

"He didn't win anything from me," I said.

"He softened you up somehow. He had to make you want to believe him," Monk said. "And I can only think of one way he could do that. He gave you a message from Mitch."

"I'm not that easy." I felt my eyes tearing up, my emotions betraying me. "You are the only person I've ever told about what happened to Mitch."

"You don't know what happened to Mitch," Monk said. "You only know the navy's version."

"They told me he was shot down over Kosovo, that he survived the crash but panicked on the ground, getting himself killed and endangering the lives of his crew."

"That doesn't mean it's true," Monk said as he sat down beside me on the edge of the bed. "The only people who know what really happened are the two crew members who survived. They could be lying to cover *their* cowardice, not Mitch's."

"The point, Mr. Monk, is that Swift knew all about that. None of it was ever made public."

Monk shook his head. "He only knew what you told him."

The tears really started coming now, but I didn't care. I was too angry and hurt.

"You think all it takes is one drink by the pool and I'll tell the first attractive man who comes along my most painful secrets?"

"You didn't know you were doing it."

"I wasn't drunk. I know what I said."

"Dylan Swift works in much the same way I do," Monk said. "He looks at a person and makes deductions. And then he uses that information to get you to tell him what he doesn't already know."

"I didn't tell him," I insisted, sniffling.

"What he does is called cold reading. I saw him do it yesterday during his show. It's a bit of trickery in which he pumps a person for information while simultaneously making it seem like he's getting his facts from the beyond. It's much easier to pull off with a crowd than with one person. What he did with you takes real finesse."

"I don't understand," I said, beginning to get hold of myself.

"Let's start with how he works a crowd. Last night, he wandered into the audience, sensing the letter G. Immediately a guy jumped up, said his name was Gary, and asked if the message was for him. In that instant, he told Dylan Swift the most important thing of all—that he was eager to be fooled and would do everything he could to help dupe himself. So, naturally, Swift picked Gary for the reading."

Monk went on to explain that as soon as someone responded, Swift looked at the person's age, hairstyle, jewelry, clothes, and the friends or family with him and made some simple deductions. Then Swift started throwing out educated guesses in questions that were shrewdly framed as statements.

Monk told me that instead of agreeing or disagreeing with Swift's guesses, most people would try to help him. They would freely volunteer additional information, giving Swift material with which to make more reasonable assumptions, and if he was right, they would think the dead were whispering in his ear. But if he was wrong, he could claim there was static on the line and, nine times out of ten, people would give him some suggestions to help him clarify the transmission.

"Swift told Gary that a woman he was very close to was reaching out to him. It was Gary who suggested it might be his sister," Monk said. "Swift said he 'sensed' that her name began with an 'M' or an 'E,' but to increase his odds of success, he refined the guess by saying the letters might just be in the name somewhere. It was Gary who volunteered that Swift must be talking about his sister Margaret."

I remembered it now. I could see how Swift got Gary to feed him the information he needed to appear as if he were channeling a spirit. But I didn't see how he did it with me.

"That's not what happened with me, Mr. Monk. The first thing he said to me was that my husband missed me. He already knew stuff . . . ."

"I'm sure he did," Monk said. "But think about

what you gave him. A standard ploy a medium uses is to say your dead loved one has some unresolved issues to deal with, that he was cheated or wronged. Did he say that?"

I nodded and sniffled.

"And what did you say?"

I remembered exactly what I said.

"Mitch was killed two days before his twenty-seventh birthday. I'd say that was wrong."

"It was an accident that took him from you," Swift said.

"He was shot out of the sky by enemy fire. It was hardly an accident."

I might as well have typed up Mitch's biography and handed it to Swift.

"Oh, my God, I'm such a fool." I started to cry again.

"No, you're not." Monk took my hand. "You just miss your husband very much."

I did and I always would; I knew that. What I didn't know was how close to the surface those feelings were and how easily I could be manipulated by them. I was ashamed of myself.

"Tissue," he said.

I sniffled, reached into my purse, and handed him a tissue.

"It's for you," he said.

I blew my nose and, in deference to Monk and his kindness, I took a Ziploc bag from my purse, put the Kleenex in the bag, and tossed the bag into the trash can.

It was obvious that Dylan Swift was a fraud. And yet something he said still gave me goose bumps.

"Everything you're saying makes sense, Mr. Monk, except for one thing. You remember that bikini I was wearing?"

Monk flushed with embarrassment and looked at his feet, as if I were wearing it at that moment.

"Vaguely," he said.

"I've had it for years. I bought it in Puerto Vallarta, where Mitch and I went for a weekend of romance, sun, and tequila, much to my parents' horror."

"I don't need to know this," Monk said.

"I lost my top making out in the water with Mitch. He had to get an emergency bikini from a beachside vendor while I stayed in the water. That was the one he picked out for me. After that, every time he saw me in that bikini, he'd remember how I lost the last one. He loved to see me in it."

"I don't want to know this," Monk said.

"Swift said that Mitch still loved my bikini. There's no way he could have known whether Mitch had ever seen me in it. For all Swift knew, I bought it last week."

"You still want to believe in him."

"I want to understand how I was fooled."

"These con men are very smart. They study up on fashion, songs, hairstyles, everything that is or was in vogue. He must have known the bathing suit was an older style, cut, or pattern and made a lucky guess."

"But what if he'd been wrong?"

"He'd have said, 'What Mitch is saying is that he still thinks you're beautiful and will always love you.'"

I felt my eyes tearing up again and it pissed me off. Was I that weak? That vulnerable?

"You'd better go, Mr. Monk, or I may cry all night."

"That's okay," Monk said. "I don't mind as long as you've got plenty of tissue."

We sat there without talking; the only sounds were my sniffles. I was aware, though, of the sting of the tears on my cheeks and the warmth of Monk's hand in mine.

"But I do wonder about those Toblerone bars," Monk said.

"You'd better go check."

"Maybe I should." Monk got up and paused at the open door to his room. "If I find two, would you like one of them?"

He wouldn't be able to sleep with two pieces of the same candy in a minibar filled with one piece of everything else. Even so, it was a nice gesture.

"Sure," I said. "I'd like that."

I ate the extra Toblerone and called home to talk with Julie and my mom. I left out everything about my day except the time I spent at the beach. Julie informed me I was boring. It sounded like Mom had already bought Julie enough clothes to last her until high school, so my daughter was in no hurry for me to get back.

I fell asleep within seconds of resting my head on the plump pillow. I was exhausted. I was jet-lagged. I was emotionally depleted. It was a deep, rejuvenating, dreamless sleep that ended at eight A.M. with the crowing from a chorus of roosters.

It was the last sound I expected to hear on a tropical island. Parrots, maybe. Or macaws. Not roosters. But I awoke totally refreshed.

I didn't knock on Monk's door to see if he was up. Instead, I slipped into a T-shirt and sweats and went down to the beach for a walk.

The sand had been smoothed by the surf during

the night and was damp from the morning drizzle. The air was moist, warm, and heavy.

There were a half dozen others walking on the sand, but it still felt as if I had the beach to myself. I walked past the Grand Kiahuna Poipu bungalows, but couldn't see over the hedges, even walking on my tippy-toes.

Farther up the beach, just above the surf line, an enormous seal and her pup were lying on the sand. A worker from the hotel was roping off a wide area around them with yellow caution tape. I stopped at the edge of the tape and looked at the seals.

The mother had a scarred brown coat; her pup's was jet-black. They both had faces that reminded me of golden retriever puppies. The mother looked back at me with her marble eyes.

"Those are monks," the hotel worker said. He was Polynesian, with a deeply tanned, deeply lined face.

"Monks?"

"Named for their solitary existence," the worker said. "They are an endangered species."

I nodded toward the mother. "What are those scars?"

The worker smiled slyly, showing all his crooked teeth. "From all her good lovin'. The male seals like it rough."

I gave the monk seals, and the hotel worker, a wide berth and continued on my walk.

The beach ended at a rocky point of lava rocks that stretched out into the bay. A well-worn footpath wound around the base of the point and ended at the sidewalk on Hoonani Road, right in front of the Whaler's Hideaway. As I walked past the condos,

I glanced up at the woman's unit, but the drapes were closed.

I crossed the street and went into the Whaler's Hideaway parking lot, following it around to the management office. There were doughnuts on the counter and a middle-aged woman behind it. She had a beehive hairdo and a willingness to talk.

I learned she was semiretired and worked part-time to subsidize her island lifestyle, which she couldn't manage to do with the money she'd saved as a schoolteacher. I learned her children and grandchildren never visited her when she lived in Flagstaff, but now that she had moved here, they wanted to see her all the time. And I learned the names of the "lovely couple" in condo A-3.

Roxanne Shaw and her boyfriend Curtis Potter. Both from Cleveland.

13

Mr. Monk Goes Golfing

When I emerged from the elevator on our floor, I saw three maids' carts in front of the open door to Monk's room. I went inside and found the maids folding bath towels on the bed, with Monk watching over them.

"No, no, Kawaiala, you fold it from left to right, and then from bottom to top. Try it again." Monk moved to the next maid as she was folding. "Wait, Meilani, make sure the corners touch. If you get that first crucial fold wrong, abort the procedure and go again."

"What are you doing, Mr. Monk?"

"Showing them how to properly fold a towel instead of rolling it." One of the maids' towels caught his eye. "Very good, Lana. You're getting the hang of it. Let's do it once more. Practice makes perfect."

"I found out about the woman we saw last night," I said. "Her name is—"

"Roxanne Shaw," Monk interrupted.

"How did you know?"

"I saw her signature on the credit card receipt on the counter as we left the restaurant. She has a very nice, even signature, by the way."

"Well, her name is not the big news. I found out that she's from—"

"Cleveland," Monk interrupted. "Just like Lance and Helen."

"How did you know that?" I said, trying to hide the disappointment in my voice.

"While we were following her, I noticed she'd covered the driver's seat with a beach towel to keep herself from getting burned on the hot upholstery. There was a big drawing of Chief Wahoo facing us the whole time."

"Who is Chief Wahoo?"

"The logo of the Cleveland Indians baseball team." Monk pulled me aside, out of earshot of the maids. "I learned some things this morning, too. Meilani cleaned Helen and Lance's bungalow. She says that Helen Gruber loved the pies on the island. She was always bringing pies back to the bungalow. But there was no pie in the refrigerator the morning she was killed."

"One of the sensations Swift said he was getting from the beyond was the taste of *liliko'i* pie."

"It was a safe guess," Monk said. "It's the most popular pie on the island, and the odds are good that tourists are going to try it while they're here. But where was her pie?"

"Maybe she ate the last slice at dinner," I said. "Or with breakfast yesterday morning."

"But there were no dirty dishes in the sink, and the maids hadn't come yet."

"What difference does it make?"

"I don't know," Monk said.

Kawaiala approached Monk with a folded towel. "How is this?"

Monk smiled. "Perfect. I think you've all got it now. Go forth and share your knowledge."

The maids shuffled out of the room and closed the door behind them, leaving the towels neatly stacked on Monk's bed.

"You taught the maids how to fold."

Monk sighed. "It feels so good to give something back to society."

I glanced at my watch. "We've got a golf game in three hours. You can rent clubs and shoes, but you're going to need to get yourself the right clothes."

"I'm not renting shoes. That's like asking me to wear another man's dirty underwear," Monk said. "What wrong with what I'm wearing?"

"You can't go on the course like that. You'll just draw attention to yourself. And they won't let you on the course with those shoes."

"Fine," Monk said. "Let's go shopping."

They sold golf clothes and accessories at the same men's store where Monk bought his bathing suit. I wish I could say it went as smoothly this time. I won't make you suffer by describing in painful detail what the next two hours of living hell were like for me. But to give you an idea of what I had to endure, Monk selected his golf shoes by counting the plastic cleats until he found an affordable pair with an even number of them. We went through a lot of shoes. And when the shopping was finally done, it took him fifteen minutes just to sign his credit card receipt.

Want my job? I didn't think so. How about taking

Monk along on your next vacation? I bet your whole body is tensing up just at the thought of it. Now you know how I was feeling.

Monk ended up buying khaki slacks and a short-sleeved, red polo-style shirt. He looked great and I told him so. It seemed to embarrass him, so I didn't press it. I hoped a little positive reinforcement might convince him to loosen up fashion-wise. Sometimes I want to reach out and unbutton his collar, because just seeing it makes me feel like I'm being strangled.

We drove the two or three miles to the Grand Kiahuna Poipu golf course. And once we got there, I was glad I came along. It was beautiful. The course was immaculately maintained and vividly green, set against the crisp, blue sky, the misty mountain peaks, and a dramatic view of Poipu Bay, the waves crashing against the serrated edge of the black cliffs and the rocks below. I don't know how anybody could concentrate on golf when there was so much to see.

We rented two sets of clubs and a golf cart and met Kealoha at the first tee. He was dressed, as usual, in an oversize, untucked aloha shirt and shorts and had his own set of clubs in a bag that looked as if it had been dragged across several continents.

"This is what I call police work." Kealoha grinned.

There were four tee boxes set at different distances from the hole. The black box was for championship players, the red box was for women, the white for the average golfer, and the gold was what they called the resort box, for occasional golfers looking for an easier, more relaxed game.

We all lined up to tee off from the white box and put on our gloves. Monk put one on each hand.

"Do you play a lot of golf, Lieutenant?" I asked Kealoha.

"Surfing and golfing are about all there is to do here," Kealoha said. "But it's a pricey hobby. I share this set of clubs with four other bruddahs."

"You'd never notice," I said.

"What about you?" Kealoha asked. "You play?"

"When I was growing up. My father belongs to a lot of country clubs," I said. "I haven't played in years, but when I did, I was pretty okay at it."

"Pretty okay." Kealoha nodded. "What's your handicap?"

"Eighteen."

"What about you?" Kealoha said to Monk.

"It's my game," Monk said, wiping down his club with an antiseptic wipe. "I don't have a handicap."

"You're only supposed to wear one glove," Kealoha said. "You're right-handed, so it would be on your left hand."

"Nobody wears just one glove," Monk said. "Except maybe Michael Jackson, and he's very strange."

The first hole was a par four. About 380 yards away, the putting green was ringed with sand bunkers. Luxury homes lined one edge of the dogleg-shaped fairway, and on the other was a grove of trees and a man-made lake.

We each teed off, me first, followed by Monk and Kealoha. Our balls ended up at roughly the same place, where the fairway curved toward the green.

We climbed into the golf cart, Kealoha at the wheel, Monk up front, me in the back, and we tooled down the fairway.

"I heard from the Cleveland PD this morning,"

Kealoha said. "Lance stands to inherit millions this time."

"*This* time?" Monk said.

"Helen Gruber isn't the first old biddy Lance has married and outlived," Kealoha said. "She's the third. There was Elizabeth Dahl, age seventy-six, in Philadelphia, and Beatrice Woodman, age sixty-eight, in Seattle."

A lumberjack holding a porcelain doll.

Woodman and Dahl.

Once again, two more images from Swift were on the money. Could those other spirits Swift said were trying to communicate with him about Lance have been Elizabeth Dahl and Beatrice Woodman?

I tried to give Monk a look, but he wouldn't look back at me, so I nudged him. He still ignored me. He knew what I was thinking and didn't want to deal with it. Either Swift did a lot of very quick digging into Lance's past or he was getting good information from the beyond.

I knew what Monk's explanation would be.

But what could it hurt to go back to Swift and ask what else the spirits were telling him? Even if Swift were a fraud, he could save us some time repeating research he'd already done.

But I didn't want to say any of this to Monk, at least not in front of Kealoha.

"Were Dahl and Woodman murdered?" Monk said.

"Cleveland cops tell me they died of natural causes." Kealoha brought the cart to a stop not far from where our golf balls lay on the grass. "Lance sure knows how to pick 'em, though Helen was his youngest and healthiest wife yet. She was also the richest."

"Maybe he got tired of waiting for nature to take its course," I said.

"You said you're talking to the other guests on the Na Pali catamaran trip," Monk said. "Have you spoken to Roxanne Shaw yet?"

Kealoha shook his head. "Nope, which one is she?"

"The one with the G-string," I said.

"Oh, yeah," Kealoha said. "I remember her from the video."

"I bet you do," I said.

Kealoha stopped the cart a few yards from our golf balls and we got out.

"I was looking forward to talking with her," Kealoha said. "Snorkel Rob says she only bought one ticket. Meaning she's traveling alone. There's nothing lonelier than being by yourself in paradise. I was thinking maybe she'd like some companionship from a lovable Hawaiian while she's on the island."

"I don't think so," Monk said, his back to us as he looked at the homes along the fairway. "We saw her with Lance last night. And she's from Cleveland."

Kealoha whistled, impressed. "You one sly mongoose, Mr. Monk. I'll check her out and we can talk to her together. But her alibi is as good as his."

I followed Monk's gaze. I could see some gardeners at one home, a pool man at another.

"Did the Cleveland PD check Lance's bank accounts?" I asked.

Kealoha nodded. "If Lance paid someone to kill his wife, the money didn't come from his account or his wife's. I'll ask the Cleveland PD to look at Roxanne's piggybank, but I gotta wonder if maybe we're looking in the wrong direction."

"Lance is the only one with a motive to kill his wife," Monk said.

"But how could he have done it without hiring someone else? He wasn't on the island at the time of her murder, and neither was Roxanne. Their alibis are confirmed by videotape and the other haoles on the boat."

"I know," Monk said.

"Maybe it was a thief who did it," Kealoha said.

"One who didn't steal anything?"

"It could happen." Kealoha carefully selected a three iron from his bag. "Maybe he freaked after clobbering her."

I wasn't worried about Lance's perfect alibi. After all, in Monk's last case, the suspect was having open-heart surgery at the time of the murder. And Monk *still* proved she did it. So I had faith, even if Kealoha didn't, that Monk would find the fatal flaw or the trickery in this alibi, too.

"You don't want to use that club," Monk said.

"Why not?"

"It's a three," Monk said. "Use a four or a six iron."

"But a three is better for this shot," Kealoha said.

"Three is never better," Monk said. "Trust me on this."

Kealoha gave me a look, put the three iron back, and took out a four. He went over to his ball and made his shot. The ball flew low and landed well short of the green. He scowled at Monk.

"I'm gonna start looking into the thief theory for the murder," Kealoha said.

"It's a waste of time," Monk said.

I also used a four iron and didn't do much better than Kealoha. Monk used a four and ended up landing in the sand bunker.

"Tough one." Kealoha suppressed a smile and climbed into the golf cart.

I couldn't resist rubbing it in myself. "Run into many sand traps around those windmills, Mr. Monk?"

We got back in the cart and drove up to the green. Monk was quiet, his gaze on the homes. Someone was installing a satellite dish on the roof of one of the houses. Monk checked his watch.

At the green, we each approached our golf balls and assessed the shots we had to make. Monk walked around the perimeter of the bunker. His ball sat in the center of the smoothly raked sand.

Monk stood there at the edge of the bunker, staring at the ball as if it were atop quicksand. I knew what he was thinking: How could he get to his ball without disturbing the raked sand? He was starting to sweat.

Kealoha, meanwhile, made his play. It took him one swing with an iron and three putts to get his ball into the hole for a score of two over par.

"Pretty okay," he said. "For me."

I glanced back at Monk, who wasn't paying any attention to either of us. He stepped gingerly across the bunker to his ball, a sand wedge in his hand.

Kealoha and I both stopped to watch him now.

Monk looked at the hole, then looked at his ball and swung. The ball shot up out of the bunker in a spray of sand and landed on the green, rolled, and stopped about one putt short of the flag.

"Excellent shot, Mr. Monk," I said, genuinely impressed.

But Monk was scowling. He backed out of the bunker, placing his feet in his old footprints, and marched up to the green.

"What were they thinking?" Monk said.

"Who?" I asked.

"Whoever designed this course. Didn't they realize what would happen if they put sand so close to the putting green?"

"Yeah. They created a hazard."

"I think they did it intentionally. They should be ashamed." Monk squatted at the edge of the green, faced the bunker, and started blowing sand off the carpet of grass.

"What are you doing?"

"Can't you see there's sand all over the grass?"

"It's okay," I said.

"It's not okay," Monk said. "Grass and sand do not coexist."

I looked back at Kealoha, who was staring at Monk in disbelief. "What are we gonna do?"

"I'm going to play on," I said, taking an iron out of my bag. I managed to finish the hole at three over par, and was quite happy with myself.

I turned to gloat, but nobody was paying attention to me. Kealoha was watching Monk, who'd blown and wiped as much sand off the green as he could and was now attempting to rake the bunker.

"It's your turn, Mr. Monk," I said.

"I'm busy."

We watched as he tried to rake the sand without actually stepping in it, but he couldn't, not without creating vertical lines, and that was a problem, since the trap had been raked horizontally before.

After several minutes, Monk set the rake aside, walked into the trap, and began wiping out all the rake marks by dragging the side of his shoe across the sand.

"What are you doing?" I said.

"Erasing and starting over."

I could see a foursome waiting to tee off, and judging by their body language—the way they were standing there, hands on their hips, pacing back and forth—they weren't happy.

"You're holding up the next set of players," I said.

"Go on without me," Monk said. "I'll catch up."

"What about the foursome?" Kealoha asked.

"They can play around me," Monk said. "Besides, they'll appreciate the care I've taken to restore the bunker."

"You don't have to rake it," I said. "You just smoothed it out with your shoes."

"It's not the same," Monk said. "It doesn't match the other bunkers."

He picked up the rake and began to work, careful to make his lines straight and even.

Kealoha just shook his head.

The foursome behind us started to play, hitting their balls down the first leg of the fairway. Soon there would be golf balls whizzing over our heads like bullets.

Monk finished and regarded his work. "That's better."

He took out a putter and squatted beside his ball, eyeing the lay of the green.

But then something caught his attention, something beyond the hole. I followed his gaze. He was looking at the houses along the fairway. A mailman was delivering a box to one of the homes. Monk checked his watch, rose to his feet, and put the ball in the hole with one putt. Four strokes. Par for the hole.

He turned to us with a smile. "That was fun, though what this hole really needs is a castle. Or a moat."

Kealoha looked back at the fairway, where the other golfers were staring at us. "We'd better move on to the next tee."

"I have a better idea," Monk said. "Let's catch a burglar instead."

14

Mr. Monk and the Towels

Kealoha drove the electric cart along a narrow asphalt road that crossed the golf course and branched off into a cul-de-sac in the neighborhood of fairway homes. At Monk's direction, Kealoha parked behind the U.S. Mail truck idling at the curb and we all got out.

The houses didn't seem any more extravagant than your average tract home on the mainland, but these were probably worth well into seven figures by virtue of where they were. There were no fences between the homes, only plants—and in some cases, low, decorative lava-rock walls that also served to mark boundaries. The landscaping of the homes was as manicured and lush as the golf course they faced.

The mailman was dropping off some boxes from Amazon on the front porch of a home and returning to his truck when we approached him. He was a muscular Polynesian man wearing an untucked, short-sleeved, blue U.S. Postal Service uniform shirt, dark blue shorts, and a safari hat. His eyes were hidden behind reflective, wraparound sunglasses.

"Can I help you?" the mailman asked.

Kealoha turned to Monk. "I don't know, can he?"

"Are you the regular mailman on this route?" Monk asked.

"Yeah," the mailman said.

"How long have you been doing it?"

"A couple of years."

Monk turned to Kealoha. "He's the guy. Well, one of them, anyway."

"What guy?"

"He's responsible for at least half a dozen of your unsolved burglaries, maybe more."

The mailman started for his truck again. "I don't know who you people are, but I've got mail to deliver and a schedule to keep."

"And that was your undoing," Monk said.

The mailman edged past Monk, but Kealoha stepped in front of him and lifted his shirt, revealing his round belly, his badge, and his gun.

"Hold up, brah. Police." Kealoha turned to Monk. "You think he's the burglar?"

"I haven't done nothing," the mailman said.

"Whoever committed the burglaries knew when the homes were occupied or empty, could get into security buildings and gated communities with ease, and was able to steal large items like computers and stereos in broad daylight without being seen."

"How does that point to him?" Kealoha asked.

"People file vacation holds or forwarding addresses for their mail when they go out of town, and that lets him know when the houses are going to be empty. He has the code or the keys for security buildings and gates so he can deliver mail and his presence isn't suspicious. And he carts out his stolen goods in Priority Mail boxes, so it looks like he's simply picking up or delivering parcels."

"Dat's a good theory," Kealoha said. "I'm gonna need a lot more than that to arrest this guy."

"Arrest me? For what? I haven't stolen anything," the mailman said. "See? My hands are empty."

"All the burglaries that you could pin down to a specific day or time took place on weekdays in broad daylight," Monk said. "Never at night, never on Sunday."

"The same schedule a mailman keeps," I said.

"They also all occurred at specific times of day in the same neighborhoods," Monk said. "The break-ins in this neighborhood, for instance, always happened around noon. The ones farther west happened at the end of the day."

"At the end of the mailman's daily route," Kealoha said, glancing at the suspect, who wisely stayed silent.

"I wanted to go golfing this morning to see who came through the neighborhood at noon," Monk said. "When I saw the mail truck, it all made sense."

"There's just one problem," Kealoha said. "We don't have any proof."

"Yeah," the mailman said with a sneer.

"Impound the truck and get a search warrant," Monk said. "I guarantee you'll find burglar's tools, some empty boxes, maybe even some stolen goods in the back."

"I suppose it's worth a shot." Kealoha looked at the mailman. "What do you think, bruddah?"

The mailman answered by barreling past Kealoha

into the driver's seat of his idling truck and speeding off, tires screeching.

Monk dashed to the golf cart, got behind the wheel, and floored it. As the tiny cart zipped past me, I jumped onto the back and grabbed hold.

"What are you doing?" I yelled as Monk steered us between two of the homes and across their backyards.

"Cutting him off," Monk said. "The road weaves around to the other side of the block."

"But we're in a golf cart. He'll mow us down."

"Hand me a pitching wedge," Monk said as we bounced along the grass.

I grabbed the club and was about to hand it to Monk when we burst through a hedge of bougainvilleas. I let go of the club and grabbed an armrest to avoid toppling out of the cart.

We were nearing the street. The mail truck was coming our way. If we didn't stop, within moments our two paths would cross.

"Hurry," Monk said.

I yanked another club from the bag and passed it up to Monk, who wedged it against the power pedal and his seat.

And then he casually jumped out of the moving cart onto the soft lawn.

I was stunned. It took me a second before it sank in that I was in the cart alone. I leaped off just as the cart shot into the street, directly into the path of the speeding truck.

The mailman swerved too hard to avoid the golf cart and the truck tipped over, sliding on its side across the asphalt in a shower of sparks before slamming into a palm tree.

The driverless golf cart scooted along between two more houses and out onto the golf course beyond.

Monk and I scrambled to our feet, ran to the postal truck, and pulled the dazed mailman from his seat. He had a few cuts and bruises, but he'd survive. We laid him down on the grass and then took stock of each other. My knees were scraped and Monk had some grass stains on his new pants, but otherwise we were both fine.

"Thanks a lot," I said to Monk.

"What did I do?"

"You jumped out of the cart!"

"Of course I did," Monk said. "I didn't want to get killed."

"What about me? You could have told me you were going to jump."

"You saw me, didn't you?"

"That's not the point," I said. "Before the driver jumps out of a moving vehicle he has an obligation to notify his passengers first."

"I beg to differ."

"It's common courtesy!"

That was when Kealoha came running up, drenched in sweat and totally out of breath.

"Why did you do that?" Kealoha managed to spit out between gasps.

"He was getting away," Monk said.

"We're on an island," Kealoha said, still huffing. "He was driving a mail truck. Where was he gonna go?"

"Oops," Monk said.

At that moment I happened to glance at the golf course, just in time see our cart as it splashed into the lake and abruptly sank, taking our clubs down with it.

I was glad the rentals were on Monk's credit card and not mine.

Although burglary tools and stolen goods were found in the mail truck, I was hoping the destruction of two vehicles, the loss of three bags of clubs, and the outrage of the golf course officials would dissuade Kealoha from passing along any more of his unsolved cases to Monk.

Not that Monk cared about the damage he'd caused. Playing a single hole of golf and chasing a bad guy left him in an ebullient mood and eager to do more sleuthing.

I was ready to do nothing more strenuous than lie in a hammock. I'd had enough excitement for one day.

Fortunately, there wasn't any detecting to do until Kealoha could get back to us with more background on Lance Vaughn and Roxanne Shaw. I figured I had some time, since Kealoha was going to have his hands full dealing with the events of the morning.

So we had a late lunch at Poipu Beach Park. We grabbed some tuna fish sandwiches at Brenneke's Deli. Monk had them cut off the crusts and he loaned them his tape measure so they could cut the sandwich exactly in half. We took our lunch across the street to one of the scattered picnic tables on the grass leading to the sand.

The beach beyond the park was packed with families and their kids, who were Boogie boarding and frolicking in the water. There was a fat monk seal basking in the sand, his slumber captured for posterity by two dozen camera-toting tourists.

"You know what that is?" I said.

"A monk seal."

"I understand they're the only seals that clean their fish before they eat them."

"Been working on that one long?"

"Since this morning," I admitted.

After we finished our lunch, we drove back to the hotel and parked in the self-parking lot beside another Mustang convertible. Monk got out and examined the other car.

"This is Brian's rental car," he said.

"Half the cars in this parking lot are Mustang convertibles. How can you tell?"

"A little innovation we call the license plate."

"You memorized the plate?"

"And the vehicle identification number," Monk said. "Besides, I recognize the three dings and the scratch."

"Good for you."

"They replaced the windshield and the soft-top." Monk peered in the driver's-side window. "The seat isn't stained anymore."

"So they cleaned it. That should make you happy." I headed for the lobby.

"But it was a permanent stain," Monk called after me.

"Apparently not." I kept going.

He caught up with me. "I think they replaced the seat."

"Okay."

"Why would they go to the expense of replacing

the seat to get rid of one stain but leave red-dirt-soiled carpets, the dings, and the scratch?"

"I don't know, Mr. Monk. More important, who cares?"

"It's just something to think about."

There were a million things I'd rather think about, but there was no point in telling Monk that. This was, after all, the same man who memorized the VIN of someone else's rental car.

We were walking across the lobby toward the elevators when we were intercepted by a short Hawaiian man in a silk aloha shirt, slacks, and nice leather shoes.

"Excuse me, Mr. Monk, may I have a word?" He offered Monk his hand. "I'm Martin Kamakele, manager of hotel operations."

They shook hands. I had a wipe ready before Monk could ask for it.

"You're in charge of how the minibars are stocked," Monk said, disinfecting his hands.

"Yes, that's one of my many responsibilities. I understand you instructed the cleaning personnel on the fourth floor to fold the bath towels instead of rolling them."

"There's no need to thank me."

"I appreciate that you have a personal preference for folded towels, and we very much want you to be comfortable during your stay," Kamakele said. "But we can't fold all the towels in the hotel."

"It's the only way to treat a towel."

"It's the most time-consuming way. Folding towels takes three times as long as rolling them, and our cleaning crew is on a very tight schedule. Following your instructions made them fall two hours behind in their duties."

"Do their duties include stocking everybody's minibar with one extraneous Toblerone?"

"We will gladly fold your towels, but I'm afraid we'll continue to roll the others."

"But I'll know they're rolled," Monk said. "How do you expect me to sleep in a building filled with rolled towels?"

Kamakele looked to me for a little help, but he wasn't going to get any. This was between him and Monk.

"I don't know what to tell you, sir," Kamakele said.

"Tell me you'll fold the towels," Monk said.

"I'm sorry."

Now Monk and Kamakele were both looking at me for help. I sighed and addressed the manager.

"This towel situation is going to make it very hard for Mr. Monk to concentrate. I don't know if you're aware of this, but he's working closely with the Kauai Police Department on the investigation of Helen Gruber's homicide. He's a very famous detective."

"I'm familiar with Mr. Monk's reputation," Kamakele said. "Before I came here, I was head of operations at the Belmont Hotel in San Francisco."

"Then you know how quickly he works when he's thinking clearly. He could solve this murder before word reaches the mainland that it even happened. But if he's distracted . . . well, this investigation could plod on for weeks and the inevitable negative publicity would have time to spread. Who knows what impact that might have on your occupancy rate?"

"I see." Kamakele chewed on his lip for a moment. "I think we can work something out. How would you like to stay in the bungalow formerly occupied by the late Mrs. Gruber? It's fully detached; you won't be in a building with rolled towels. Your towels will all be folded."

"But it's a closed crime scene," Monk said.

"Not any longer. The police officially released it this morning."

"We can't afford five thousand dollars a night," I said. "Or anything close to that."

"Guests who can afford those rates won't stay at the scene of a homicide," Kamakele said. "Until we can completely renovate the bungalow and offer it as entirely new, I'm afraid it's going to stay empty. You can have it for what you're paying now."

I looked at Monk, commanding him with my gaze to agree to the offer. He did.

"Excellent," Kamakele said. "I'll have your things moved over immediately."

"Did you ever meet Mrs. Gruber?" Monk asked.

Kamakele nodded. "She was referred to me by the front desk. Mrs. Gruber was driving them crazy. She said she was hearing voices. I'm sure she was, but they were all in her head. It's so sad when that happens."

"Did you offer to move her?"

"Yes, but all of our bungalows were occupied. I offered her one of our suites in here instead, but she refused. She said if the noise was loud out there, it must be even worse in the building."

"What about her husband?" Monk asked. "Did you ever talk with him?"

"We exchanged pleasantries when I welcomed him

and his wife to our hotel, escorted them to their bungalow, and presented them with a complimentary bottle of our finest champagne. Beyond that, no, we never spoke. But they seemed very much in love."

"You mentioned you worked in San Francisco," I said. "Did you know Dylan Swift back then?"

"He conducted his Great Beyond seminars at the Belmont. When I came to Kauai to oversee the remodeling of the hotel for the new owners and I learned they were adding a production facility, I was instrumental in convincing Dylan to produce half of his TV shows here."

"Why?" Monk asked with obvious disapproval.

"To add some cachet to our production facilities, which are primarily utilized by infomercial programs, and to advertise our resort," Kamakele said. "Not only do we benefit from the publicity, but nearly thirty percent of our guests stay here specifically to be in the audience for his program or to attend one of his seminars. And he gets an amazing backdrop for his show. He shoots the other half of his shows in San Francisco. In fact, he's going back there on Monday."

"Do you believe he can talk to the dead?" I asked.

"My father died five years ago, but thanks to Dylan, I still talk to him every week."

15

Mr. Monk and the Medium Meet Again

I don't understand people who are reluctant to sleep in a room where someone has died or buy a house where a murder has occurred. Homes have histories—within their walls lives are created, spent, and lost. That's . . . well, life.

What gets me is that the same people who won't set foot in a house where someone has died don't think twice about living on a cliff in a landslide zone. Or in woods prone to wildfires. Or in a high-rise apartment constructed on a fault line. Or in a housing tract spread out on a floodplain. Or in a neighborhood adjacent to a toxic landfill.

They'll ignore those risks for the view, the solitude, the cachet, a shorter commute, or a good deal.

Not me. I had no qualms about enjoying the decadent luxuries of the $5,000-a-night private, oceanfront bungalow where Helen Gruber met her fate.

To Monk's credit, neither did he.

Of course, if you want to get technical about it, her body was in the Jacuzzi. I'd have no problem going in the hot tub, either, but I'd sit where I could keep my eye on the palm tree. Yes, I know Helen Gruber wasn't actually hit by a falling coconut—she was clobbered with one in the kitchen by her killer (who I was still betting was her husband, despite his airtight alibi). Even so, there was no harm in playing it safe.

Monk claimed one of the guest rooms for himself, so I took the master bedroom, which had its own private marbled bath and another hot tub. I changed into my bikini and was on my way for a quick dip in our private lap pool, detecting be damned, when there was a knock at the door.

I was hoping it was room service—maybe we qualified for the "Welcome to Kauai" bottle of champagne despite the fact that we weren't paying the going rate for the bungalow.

I opened the door to find Dylan Swift standing there. He wasn't grinning this time.

"Hello, Natalie. Is Mr. Monk available?"

So much for these being private *bungalows*, I thought. "How did you know we were here?"

"I'm in the bungalow next door and I saw you move in. I really need to speak with Mr. Monk. The spirits won't give me any peace until I relay their messages."

"I relayed them."

"There are more. Day and night, all I'm getting are images and sensations from Helen. She's very adamant about getting her messages through to this world."

"You're wasting your time. He's not going to believe you anyway, and I sure as hell don't. I know how you got all that information about Mitch out of me, and I'm telling you now, it won't happen again. I'm not falling for it."

That was when Monk, back in his usual attire, emerged from his room. "Is this the guy who talks to dead people?"

"He's the one," I said.

Swift treated that as his grand introduction, and he strode in as if stepping onto a stage in front of an audience. He offered his hand to Monk.

"Dylan Swift. It's pleasure to meet you."

Monk didn't shake his hand. "I don't particularly like shaking hands, especially with crooks and con men."

"Which am I?"

"Both," Monk said.

"I'm not surprised that you doubt my gift, Mr. Monk. In fact, I welcome your skepticism."

"You do?"

"You're a detective; you work with facts. You have an analytical mind. Whether you believe what I tell you or not doesn't matter to me. You'll only consider information you believe is useful, and that's all I ask."

"What you say is true," Monk said. "I often arrive at the truth by considering the lies first."

Monk glanced at me, noticed I was in my bikini, and abruptly looked away. I went back to the bedroom to grab my bathrobe but I could still hear them talking.

"Did anything I told Natalie yesterday prove to be useful?" Swift asked.

"No," Monk said.

"Maybe I'll do better this time."

Swift walked past Monk into the backyard. He seemed drawn to the hot tub. I put on my bathrobe and followed them out.

"In my experience, I've found that it helps me make a connection when people bring me personal items that belong to the deceased."

"I'm sure it does," Monk said. "It's much easier to make educated guesses that way. Cuts down on the amount of effort you have to put into extracting information and making it look like revelations."

"Rarely do I get the opportunity to stand at the very spot where the deceased passed on," Swift said, ignoring Monk's comments. "It's like standing at the doorway to the other side."

He closed his eyes, held his hands out, and began to shake. After a moment he opened his eyes, cocked his head, and did an about-face, returning to the house.

"Are you sure she died in the hot tub?" Swift said to Monk.

"I didn't say where she died."

"I'm sensing it was inside the house."

"Why don't you just ask Helen where it was?"

"It doesn't work that way," Swift said.

"Of course not," Monk said. "That kind of clarity and specificity wouldn't leave you much wiggle room for bad guesses."

"You are applying corporeal laws to the spiritual world. That's like asking fish to breathe air instead of water. Our expectations and our physics simply don't apply there. Everything about their world is different from ours, including how they communicate. They don't need words to convey ideas."

"How convenient for you," I said.

"Actually, it's very inconvenient and frustrating for me, Natalie, as well as the spirits. It's not like reading a letter or trying to translate Chinese into English. It's much more complex than that. Imagine standing on a freeway and trying to hear what people are saying in the passing cars. That's what this is like. So they try to use images, sensations, and emotions to convey what they wish to express, but even that is inadequate to the task."

"Sounds to me like a lot of excuses designed to allow you to be vague and inaccurate," Monk said. "And avoid being accused of fraud."

Swift went to the edge of the kitchen and waved his hands in front of him, as if clearing cobwebs or smoke. "She died here. I sense a chill, a tight space."

"She's in a drawer at the morgue," I said. "It doesn't get much colder or tighter than that."

"I see a flower, a rose, the thorns dripping blood, but I don't know what these images mean."

"If you're waiting for me or Natalie to offer suggestions, think again," Monk said. "We aren't rubes. We know how this is done."

"You suspect her husband of the murder, don't you?" Swift said.

"The husband is always the number one suspect when his spouse is killed," Monk said. "That's hardly a revelation."

"Helen suspects him, too. I'm sensing her distrust, feeling her anger. There were arguments, violent ones, about his fidelity. But she found peace here these last few days. She loved Hawaii. She loved the people and she loved the food. Helen was a sensualist, particularly when it came to food. Every day she brought home fresh pineapple and pie."

"You could have seen that from your front door," Monk said. "You don't need a view into the other side."

Swift sighed wearily. "Mr. Monk, I accept that you don't believe me, but it's not necessary to counter everything I say. Take what I give you or not; it's your choice."

"I'm choosing not to. I think you're a fraud who exploits a person's vulnerability for personal gain. It's criminal."

"Whose vulnerability am I exploiting now?"

"Hers," Monk said, looking at me. I was surprised.

Swift turned to me. "Are you vulnerable, Natalie?"

I was about to say no, but then I realized that wasn't true. "I am when it comes to my husband."

"You shouldn't be," Swift said.

I wanted to slap him. "You have no right to tell me how I should feel. You don't know anything about me or him."

"I know that Mitch ran, but not because he was afraid. It was to draw the Serb patrol away from his injured crew. He made himself a target to save them. I can feel his sense of duty, the responsibility he felt to his men."

I started to tremble, goose bumps rising on my skin. Swift's words rang true. Mitch always put duty before me, Julie, or himself. His first instinct wouldn't have been to save himself; it would have been to save his men.

But how could Swift have known that? How could he have known *any* of it? Nothing I'd ever said to Swift could have given him all that information. It was as if he'd been there on the ground in Kosovo himself. Or maybe—

No, I couldn't believe it. Rationally, I knew it

couldn't be true. But emotionally and physically, I felt as if Mitch were with us, reaching out to me. I could sense his presence.

My expression must have betrayed everything I was feeling, because Monk looked at me, and then his face flushed with anger. I'd never seen Monk angry like that before. But he didn't express it by yelling. Instead he turned to Swift and spoke in a very low, measured voice.

"Get out," Monk said. "Now."

"No, wait," I said, and looked Swift in the eye. "Why did the crew say he was a coward? He gave his life for them. Why didn't the crew tell the navy he was a hero?"

"They didn't understand. They just saw him run. That's how he's showing it to me. He didn't stop to explain himself before he acted; he just did it. I don't sense that he blames them for misinterpreting his actions. Neither should you. He wants you to let it go."

I sat down on the edge of the couch. My heart was racing. My eyes filled with tears.

Monk took Swift firmly by the arm, led him to the door, and opened it. "Don't come back."

"I haven't hurt her, Mr. Monk. I've given her peace. I can give you the same thing."

Monk pushed him out the door and slammed it shut. He walked into the kitchen, staring at his hands.

"Wipe," he said.

I sniffled, got up, and went to get my purse in my room. I took out two wipes and handed them to Monk, who scrubbed his hands as if they were covered in muck. He looked like he was trying to wash off more than germs. He was trying to wipe away the whole experience.

"What if you're wrong?" I said. "What if he really can talk to the dead?"

"He can't," Monk said. "He told you what you wanted to hear. That's what he does."

"But what happened to Mitch in Kosovo was a secret; it was never made public. The file is sealed and classified. Swift couldn't have found out the details so quickly. It's just not possible."

"And talking to dead people is?"

"Fine. It's not possible. So tell me, Mr. Monk, how could Swift have known what happened to Mitch?"

"I don't know how yet," Monk said. "But I will."

16

Mr. Monk and the Peanuts

After the experience with Swift, I had to get away from Monk, the bungalow, everything. I needed to clear my head, so I went to the beach. I dove into the water, swam past the waves, and floated on my back on the surface, arms and legs outstretched.

I looked up into that endless blue sky and just drifted, away from the land, away from my troubles, away from myself.

Soon I wasn't thinking at all. I was part of the sea and the sky and nothing else. I don't know how long I stayed that way, but I became aware of another presence near me. I turned my head and saw a monk seal floating on his back beside me, regarding me curiously with his puppylike eyes.

I wasn't startled or scared. I felt completely relaxed and, apparently, so did he. We floated together for a few moments, looking at each other, and then he rolled over and slipped under the water, passing beneath me and out to sea.

I floated for a few more minutes, then swam back

to the beach, bodysurfing on a wave and letting it carry me to the shore. It was so much fun, I went back and rode the waves like a kid for a while before using the outdoor shower and returning to the bungalow sunburned but relaxed.

Monk wasn't there when I returned to the bungalow. I took another shower, slathered some lotion on my red skin, and dressed in a sleeveless blouse and shorts.

When I emerged from my room, it was raining hard outside. The sliding walls to the patio were still wide-open, letting the moist, warm air into the otherwise dry house. It was nice, though my clothes began to stick to my skin, making me itch.

Monk sat at the kitchen table, his back to me, with a big pile of peanut shells in front of him. I walked to his side and saw that he'd shelled almost the entire bag of peanuts. He must have walked up to the grocery store while I was at the beach. Knowing Monk, I figured that errand must have kept him, and the clerks at the grocery store, occupied for some time. I was tempted to visit the store just to see how he'd reorganized the fruits, vegetables, meats, and everything else.

"What are you up to?" I asked.

"I thought you might enjoy a friendly game of peanuts," Monk said.

I pulled out a chair and sat down. "You read my mind. What are the rules?"

"You've never played?"

"I've led a sheltered life."

"It's a deceptively simple game. Just match the peanuts to the shells they came in. The person who puts together the most nuts wins."

"How do you resist eating them?"

"It's that temptation that gives the game its edgy quality."

Monk shelled the last nut. "Would you like to shuffle the shells and nuts?"

"I trust you."

He pushed the two separate piles of shells and nuts into the center of the table.

"Ready. Set. Go."

His hands moved so fast that, at first, all I could do was watch him try different combinations of nut and shell. It was amazing how fast he sorted through them. After a moment I began. I picked up a nut and then I picked up a shell. They didn't fit. I picked up another shell. It didn't fit either.

I glanced over at him. He'd already rejoined several peanuts with their shells.

Monk smiled at me. "Isn't this fun?"

"It's almost too much excitement."

How did he do it? I wondered if it was more a matter of memory than matching the shapes. I ate my peanut and picked another one from the pile to try my luck with.

"There's a personal question I'd like to ask you," I said, "but if it's out of line, it's okay for you to tell me that. I won't mind."

"You can ask me anything you want." Monk busily married nuts to shells, happily occupied with his task.

"All I know about Trudy's death is that she was killed by a car bomb. I'd like to help you find out the rest. But I'm kind of lost."

"So am I."

I knew Trudy was a reporter and that she was

meeting someone in a parking garage when she was killed, but that was it.

"I'd like to know what you know," I said. "I want to be prepared so that if something new comes up, I can understand what it means and how it might lead to the person who planted the bomb."

"I know who did it," Monk said.

"You do?" I popped the nut in my mouth and picked out another one. Monk's pile of reshelled peanuts was getting higher by the second.

"Warwick Tennyson. I found him in New York. He built the bomb with a cell-phone detonator and put it in her car."

"Why did he do it?"

"For two thousand dollars in cash. That's all Trudy's life was worth to him. Tennyson didn't know who hired him; he'd met him only once, in that same parking garage. It was dark. He never saw his face. But he saw his hands. Whoever wanted Trudy dead had six fingers on his right hand."

"Six fingers?" I said. "He's got to be lying."

"I believe him," Monk said.

"There can't be that many people out there with six fingers on one hand."

"You'd be surprised," Monk said. "Most have them amputated so they don't look like freaks."

"This guy may enjoy being a freak."

"Or he's a jokester and the finger was a fake, something he wore that day for fun, knowing it would draw Tennyson's attention and be misleading."

"What happened to Warwick Tennyson?"

"He died of cancer," Monk said.

"In prison?"

Monk shook his head no. "A free man. He died

two days after I talked to him in the hospital. You could say he gave me a deathbed confession."

"At least her murderer is dead and his last days were spent in pain and misery."

"Tennyson built the bomb, but he didn't make the phone call that detonated it," Monk said. "Whoever hired him did. That's her killer."

"Is there anything Trudy could tell you that would help you find him?"

Monk stopped the reshelling and looked at me. "Spirits don't speak from beyond. Dylan Swift is a con man."

"But for the sake of argument, let's say that he could talk to Trudy," I said. "What guidance would you seek from her?"

"How to go on with my life without her."

"I mean, about who killed her."

Monk shrugged his shoulders and tilted his head from side to side. "She could tell me why she was in the parking garage, who she was there to meet, and what story she was working on."

"Could it hurt to ask Swift?"

"You tell me," Monk said. "Does it hurt?"

"It's feeling the loss again. It's an old pain," I said. "But I actually feel better now."

"Nothing has changed," Monk said.

"Maybe I have."

"All he did was tell you what you already wanted to believe is true."

"So what if he did?" I said. "That might be what I needed to hear. Just because the navy says Mitch was a coward doesn't mean it's true. I know the kind of man he was better than anybody. Swift described what really happened to Mitch in Kosovo."

"You don't know that."

"In my heart I do. I just needed someone else to say it, that's all. Whether Swift made it up or not, I believe it."

Monk joined two more peanuts with their shells, then realized there were no more peanuts left, but quite a few orphaned shells.

There wasn't a single reshelled peanut in front of me. While Monk was talking, I must have eaten the other peanuts without even realizing I was doing it.

"Oops," I said. "You win."

"You made the rookie mistake," Monk said. "You gave in to salty temptation."

"It's the story of my life," I said.

There was a knock at the door. We shared a look. Monk's entire body seemed to stiffen. He clearly thought it was Swift again.

"Who is it?" Monk called out.

"Your brah, the LT," Kealoha replied.

Monk sagged with relief, and I went to the door to let Kealoha in. The rain had stopped, but he was all wet anyway and didn't seem to care. He walked in, looking a little bewildered.

"When you get into a case, you really get into it," Kealoha said.

"It's not what you think," I said.

"You mean you haven't moved into the dead woman's bungalow?"

"We have, but not because of anything that has to do with the murder," I said. "It's because Mr. Monk can't sleep in the hotel if everybody else's towels are rolled and only his are folded. But the hotel couldn't rent out this bungalow because of the murder, and since it's freestanding, and all the towels are folded here, we moved."

Kealoha stared at me for a long moment. "You say that like it actually makes sense to you."

"It makes Monk sense," I said.

"It's common sense," Monk said. "But you two know that; you're just razzin' me."

"What's up, Lieutenant?" I asked.

"I got some BG on Roxanne Shaw," Kealoha said. "She works as a hairdresser at a beauty salon in Cleveland. On a hunch, I checked Helen Gruber's credit history. She went to the Rose every two weeks for the last couple of years."

"The *Rose*?" I gave Monk a look but he ignored me.

"Das the name of the beauty parlor where Roxanne works," Kealoha said.

A rose, with thorns dripping blood, was also one of the images communicated to Swift by Helen Gruber—or so he claimed. I was still skeptical, but getting less so each time one of Swift's messages proved to be true.

"So Lance and Roxanne were definitely involved before they came to Hawaii," Monk said.

"That don't make 'em murderers," Kealoha said.

"Lance marries rich women so he can get their money when they die," I said. "He was cheating on Helen with Roxanne. What if Helen found out?"

"What if she did?" Kealoha said.

"She'd divorce him and leave him with nothing. You don't get many motives better than that," I said, drawing on the depth of my inexperience at homicide investigation.

"He's got such a strong motive for murder that he'd almost have to be an idiot to have killed her," Kealoha said.

"Or have a perfect alibi," Monk said.

"Which he has," Kealoha said. "We're focusing now on the theory that she was killed by a would-be thief who didn't mean to murder her, just knock her out."

"You have any suspects?" I asked.

"Not yet. We'll round up all the known felons on the island and squeeze 'em. Maybe our postman knows some of the other burglars working Poipu and would like to cut a deal by rattin' 'em out."

"Why would a burglar risk robbing a bungalow he knows is occupied?" Monk said. "If he came in from the side yard, he would have seen her in the kitchen. He could have walked away."

"Maybe he figured the rewards were worth the risks."

Monk shook his head. "It doesn't feel right."

"It does to me, and it's my case. I appreciate all the help you given me, Mr. Monk. It's been a pleasure meeting you both." He shook my hand and then Monk's. "I'll let you know how it all turns out. Enjoy the rest of your vacation. Aloha."

"Aloha," I said.

Kealoha smiled at us both and walked out. Monk frowned and rolled his shoulders.

"A rose?" I said. "Swift did it again. He knew about the hair salon before Kealoha did."

"I'm not surprised. Swift has known about Roxanne Shaw longer than we have and has had more time to investigate her."

"Has it ever occurred to you that Dylan Swift might have some kind of spiritual connection?"

"No, it hasn't. The simplest and most obvious explanation is usually the correct one."

"Then Lance Vaughan and Roxanne Shaw had nothing to with Helen Gruber's murder."

"Why do you say that?"

"Because given their airtight alibis, it's the simplest and most obvious explanation. But you don't buy that, do you?"

Monk grimaced. "The rain has stopped. Let's take a walk."

I wasn't a psychic, or in contact with the spirit world, but I could predict with absolute certainty where our walk would take us.

17

Mr. Monk Takes a Walk

Here's what I've learned about Hawaiian sunsets. Just when you think you've seen the most beautiful one ever, a golden sun falling behind burnt-amber clouds, along comes one even more spectacular the next day, with brilliant streaks of purple chasing across a cobalt-blue sky.

It was dusk when Monk and I started our walk, and my third Hawaiian sunset was every bit as breathtaking as the previous two. The sky was pink. The sun and the yellow clouds seemed to float on the dark purple ocean swells like a school of dolphins leaping to catch the last few rays of light.

Tourists and locals lined up on the beach and along the Hoonani Road seawall in front of the Whaler's Hideaway to watch the sunset and capture it forever, if not in their memories, then in photos and videos, thus saving their brain cells for more ATM codes and Web site passwords.

We stood at the seawall watching the sunset, but I knew Monk was a lot more interested in the view of Roxanne Shaw's condo behind us. But her shutters were closed, frustrating his efforts to spy.

Just as the sun was about to drop below the horizon, a shirtless Hawaiian man holding a torch ran out from the Grand Kiahuna Poipu and onto the lava rocks that jutted out into the bay. Hidden speakers strategically placed on the hotel grounds played a song with lots of pounding drums and lyrics in native Hawaiian. I had no idea what the singers were saying, but I'm sure it was something reverential and spiritual and not "Baby One More Time."

The man with the torch moved so deftly across the sharp, slippery rocks, it was almost ethereal. He stopped at the tip of the promontory, lit a standing torch with his own, then dove into the sea to symbolize the belief that the spot is the jumping-off place for souls into the next world (I knew that much from reading the guidebook).

If that was true, perhaps there was more than marketing savvy behind Swift's decision to produce his program at the Grand Kiahuna Poipu. If he *did* talk to spirits, it couldn't hurt to have his studio adjacent to the big door to the great beyond.

It got dark very quickly. I would have liked to linger for a while longer, but Monk was impatient and started walking toward the Whaler's Hideaway condos without me.

I hurried and caught up with him.

"Why are you so antsy?" I said.

"Murder does that to me."

"Do you know how Lance did it?"

"No."

"But you know *something*, don't you?"

"I always know something; that's not the problem.

It's all the missing somethings between the some-things I know or I think I know and the somethings that aren't somethings yet but I'm pretty sure *will* be."

What frightened me was that I understood exactly what he was saying. I wasn't entirely sure what that meant about my own psychological and emotional health, but it couldn't be good.

We stopped outside Roxanne's door. There wasn't a doorbell, just a ceramic tile with a notice painted on it asking us to leave our shoes outside so we wouldn't stain the carpets with red dirt. *Mahalo.*

Monk knocked on the door. After a moment or two it was opened a crack by Roxanne Shaw. She was wearing a bikini top and denim shorts.

"Yes?" she asked.

"Good evening, Ms. Shaw. I'm Adrian Monk, and this is Natalie Teeger. We're working with the police on the investigation of Helen Gruber's murder."

"Who?" she said, trying her best to look confused.

"The wife of your lover, Lance Vaughan, aka Curtis Potter. We know he's here. Those are his sandals beside the mat."

She looked down at the flip-flops, and before she could muster a lie, Lance stepped from behind her, shirtless and wearing aloha-style board shorts.

My breath caught in my throat. I usually don't go for the muscled, six-pack-abs type of guys, but he was perfect. Muscled, but not *too* muscled. He was incredibly attractive as long as he didn't say a word, but he had to go and break the spell.

"It's not what it looks like," Lance said. "We met on the catamaran tour and then ran into each other on the beach this evening. She invited me up to dinner. I didn't want to be alone in my grief, that's all."

"Spare us the lies, Lance," I said. "We saw you both together last night. We know she's from Cleveland and that she was Helen's hairstylist at the Rose."

"They go back together much longer than that," Monk said. "Lance and Roxanne have been lovers since they were teenagers."

"How do you know that?" Roxanne said.

"God, Roxy, would you please *think* before you speak?" Lance groaned. "He was guessing."

"Actually, I wasn't. The story of your lives is written on the tattoos on your bodies. You have a barbed-wire tattoo on your left arm, but not your right, that you said you got when you were eighteen."

"Not that again," Lance said.

"Ms. Shaw has a barbed-wire tattoo around her right ankle," Monk said. "Those tattoos are a set that symbolizes your bond to each other."

I looked down at her ankle, noticing the tattoo for the first time. I resolved to be a lot more observant.

Another young couple, carrying groceries in both hands, came up the path behind us and headed to the condo directly next door. They were about the same age as Lance and Roxanne and were dressed in silk aloha shirts and shorts.

"Maybe you'd better come in," Roxanne said to us, opening the door wide and stepping aside to let us pass.

I slipped off my shoes, and walked in.

Monk started to follow, but Roxanne stopped him.

"You have to take off your shoes." She tipped her head toward the notice on the door.

"That's only a suggestion," Monk said.

"It's the rules. There's white carpet all over this apartment. If you stain it, we'll get charged for the cleaning and possible replacement."

"I can vouch for that," said the woman next door as she kicked off her sandals. "That's brand-new carpet in that unit, and the last tenants had to pay for it. They tracked red dirt all over the place."

"I don't have dirt on my shoes," Monk said.

The man set down the grocery bags and fumbled in his pockets for his house keys. "Yes, you do."

Monk lifted up one of his feet and saw the rust-colored dirt on his sole.

"So, I'll just wipe my feet." Monk began wiping his feet on the welcome mat. "I'm a great wiper."

"That's not good enough," Roxanne said.

"You're letting in all the mosquitoes. Take off your shoes and get inside already," Lance said. "What's the big deal?"

"You're a deeply troubled man," Monk said, dragging his feet across the mat. "You abide by an arbitrary and crackpot rule about shoes but you have no problem indulging in casual adultery."

The couple next door stared at Lance and Roxanne.

"You're into swapping?" the woman said.

"They are and they aren't," Monk said, continuing to wipe his shoes. "She picks out older women for him to sleep with. I don't know if she sleeps around or not, but I don't think so."

"Would you please come inside?" Roxanne whined, deeply embarrassed.

"You see that heart on her breast?" Monk asked, almost running in place. The neighbors leaned in close and stared at the tattoo. "The heart symbolizes

her love for Lance, the wings her willingness to let
him go and have affairs with other people."

"Cool," the man said.

"What about you two?" the woman asked, shifting
her gaze between me and Monk.

"Us?" I said. "We aren't involved."

"We're investigating them," Monk said, motioning
to Lance and Roxanne. He was getting a little breath-
less from his shoe wiping.

The woman nodded knowingly. "I totally get it.
We like to investigate, too."

Monk smiled and turned to me. "See, I'm not the
only one who does it on vacation."

"That's the best time." The man winked at me and
unlocked their door. "When you four are done, you're
welcome to come over for drinks. We're up late."

They went inside their condo and closed the door.

"What a nice couple," Monk said to me. "It might
be nice to talk shop with them later."

He may be a brilliant detective, but there are times
when Monk is completely clueless. I shoved him off
the welcome mat, picked it up, and set it down on
the carpet.

"Get in and stand on this," I said, pointing down
at the mat. It was an order, not a suggestion.

Monk seemed to sense that. He took a big step
from the door onto the mat, careful not to touch the
carpet. I slammed the door shut behind him.

"Okay, what the hell is going on here?" I asked.

"Here's what happened," Monk said, and started
wiping his shoes on the mat again. "Lance and Roxanne fell in love and were a couple until greed got
the better of them. Somehow they came into contact
with Elizabeth Dahl, a wealthy widow who fell for

Lance. They saw a chance to exploit that attraction for money."

"You can stop with the shoes," I said. "You're inside now. You've probably got no soles left anyway."

"Oh." He stopped cleaning his feet, rolled his head, adjusted his shoulders, and continued talking. "Roxanne agreed to let Lance marry Elizabeth Dahl, as long as he got a healthy allowance that she could share and they continued to see each other on the side."

"You make it sound so tawdry," Lance said.

"And it isn't?" I said incredulously. "I think the word was created specifically to describe the two of you."

"Lizzie knew exactly what the deal was."

"Easy for you to say now that she's dead," Monk said.

"It was Lizzie's idea," Roxanne said. "She came to us and made us an offer. If I would share Lance with her, she would share her money with us. Liz got what she wanted out of it. She got to share Lance's body and his love with me."

"And you got her money," I said.

"There was nothing cruel about it," Roxanne said. "It made her happy."

"It made us all happy," Lance said. "No harm, no foul."

"Until she died and the money left to you wasn't quite enough to set you up for life," Monk said. "So you went searching for someone else with whom you could repeat the lucrative arrangement."

Monk started to take a step toward them, but Roxanne wagged her finger at him as if he were a misbehaving child. He stepped back onto his little island.

"You moved to Seattle," Monk continued, "where

no one knew you and you could look for a wealthy new benefactress for Lance to marry. His job as a personal trainer and yours as a hairstylist gave you an opportunity to screen plenty of potential lovers for him. Like Beatrice Woodman, whom I'm certain we'll find was a client at the hair salon before she became Lance's personal-training client and, eventually, his wife."

"That's not how it was. We didn't set out to find someone. Someone found me," Lance said. "Beatrice was a bright, vivacious, but lonely woman who longed for companionship and passion in her life again. I knew I had enough love in my heart for her and Roxanne. Lizzie taught me that, and I knew that doing this would honor her memory and the special relationship we had."

"But as soon as Beatrice Woodman died, you moved to Cleveland and found another widow to seduce," Monk said. "You started the scheme all over again."

"So he's a professional, live-in boy toy and she's his pimp," I said. "How romantic."

"Roxanne is the love of my life," Lance said, slipping his arm possessively around her waist.

"And yet you marry other women for their money," I said, then glanced at Roxanne. "What could you possibly see in this jerk?"

"His compassion," Roxanne said. "His heart."

"Mega dittos, baby, right back at you," Lance said to her. "Roxy wants older women who are at the end of their lives to have one last chance to experience the joy and passion that she has with me every moment . . . and that they've never had. It's an act of unselfish kindness, and I love her for it."

"No, honey, it's you that's making the sacrifice," Roxanne said. "And I love *you* for it."

I thought I was going to puke. Roxanne kissed Lance on the cheek, then looked Monk in the eye.

"If you ask me," she said, "he's an angel."

"Of death," Monk said.

"I had nothing to do with their deaths," Lance said. "But I had everything to do with the happiness my wives experienced before they passed on."

"I doubt Helen Gruber would agree," Monk said.

"I didn't kill her," Lance said.

"You're the one with the best motive," Monk said.

"And Roxanne is the runner-up," I added.

"We were both on a catamaran on the Na Pali Coast when Helen was murdered," Lance said. "There's no way we could have killed her, and you know that."

He seemed awfully proud of the alibi, to me. "Did Helen know you brought your little love honey with you to Hawaii and that you were off playing together?"

"Of course," Lance said. "Helen knew all about Roxanne."

"We know you're lying," I said.

"Really?" Lance said. "How?"

I almost said, *Because Helen told us,* but I caught myself.

"Because your story is a bucket of crap," I said. "You go from city to city, seducing lonely old women and draining their bank accounts, and you think that makes you a humanitarian."

"Lieutenant Kealoha will want to talk with you both," Monk said. "So I wouldn't start looking for a new city and another rich old woman just yet."

"Nobody wants Helen's murderer brought to justice more than I do," Lance said. "We're here to help for as long as it takes."

By then, I had had more of those two than I could stand.

"I'll notify the Nobel committee." I opened the front door and walked out, lingering a moment on the path to wait for Monk.

He stepped off the mat onto the carpet, then lifted his foot.

"See?" Monk said. "No stain."

He turned and walked the remaining two steps to the door on the carpet before closing the door behind him.

"Can you believe those people?" I said to him as he joined me and we started walking back toward the hotel.

"I don't believe anything about them. Except the part about seducing old women and taking their money."

"They must have hired someone to kill Helen."

"I don't think so," Monk said.

"Then how did they do it? There's no doubt they were on the boat at the time of the killing."

Monk stopped and looked back toward the condo. "Maybe we should ask the other detectives."

"What other detectives?"

"The ones staying next door to Lance and Roxanne," Monk said. "They don't mind investigating on their vacation. They might be able to give us a new perspective on things."

"I'm sure they could. But they aren't detectives. They're swingers."

"I'm a pretty good dancer myself."

"They have sex with other couples, Mr. Monk. That's what they meant by investigating people. They enjoy an entirely different kind of detecting."

He grimaced as if he'd just eaten something very sour and marched on toward the hotel. "What does this island do to people?"

"It must be the balmy air."

Thinking about the swinging couple again reminded me of something significant that happened during that conversation outside Roxanne's door. It had slipped passed me in the midst of all my frustration with Monk and his dirty shoes.

I suppressed a smile. "What did you think of Roxanne's breasts?"

"I don't notice that kind of thing."

"You saw her heart-with-wings tattoo, so you must have had a good look at her hooters."

"I saw the tattoos but I blocked out everything else," Monk said. "I'm still blocking it out."

"I see. So what do you think—are her breasts real?"

"No."

"How do you know?"

"They have an unnatural shape, and she has tiny surgical scars near her armpits."

"So if you saw all that, what exactly are you blocking out?"

"As much as I can."

"What's left?

"I don't know," Monk said. "I'm blocking it out."

"I don't get it," I said. "You avert your gaze from any woman in a bikini, but you obviously gave Roxanne a thorough once-over."

"I was looking for clues," Monk said. "It's an entirely different kind of looking than other looking."

God help me, but I understood what he was saying. He saw the details, the pixels instead of the picture, while searching for anything that might not fit together the way it should.

It was what made him Monk. It was what made him such a brilliant detective.

His life was all about organization, symmetry, and order. And mystery is, by nature, disorder. He approached an unsolved murder the way he approached life: putting every piece of evidence, every fact, in its proper place, restoring order, and, with it, uncovering the solution to the crime.

"But that's how you always look at everything," I said. "So why avert your gaze at all?"

Monk shrugged. "It's who I am."

I couldn't argue with that. "You're a complicated man, and no one understands you but your woman."

Monk nodded. "I'm the cat who won't cop out when there's danger all about."

"Monk," I said. "Adrian Monk."

"Right on," he said.

18

Mr. Monk Goes Sightseeing

I went to sleep early that night, sinking deep into the plush comfort of my $5,000-a-night bed. I don't know if the bed was really any plusher than the one in the hotel room. I couldn't tell you if the mattress springs were made of gold or if the pillows were stuffed with the down of some rare Peruvian goose, but I figured they weren't just charging for the view and the square footage.

My dreams were all about Mitch, and they played out like a fast-forward scan through home videos of our life together. It's a dream I've had before, and I usually wake up from it in tears. But that morning I awoke at peace, perhaps because in some way I felt Mitch was also at peace.

I credit that to Dylan Swift. I didn't know whether or not he was really in contact with Mitch. But Swift helped me overcome the guilt and anger I'd been carrying around since the day a navy officer showed up at my door to give me the news that Mitch was dead. I wondered if Swift could do the same for

Monk, thereby accomplishing what years of therapy couldn't achieve.

I knew Monk would never stop trying to solve Trudy's murder, and nobody, least of all me, would expect him to. But maybe hearing from Trudy through Swift would relieve some of Monk's guilt and help him accept that it was okay to move on with his life, even to find love again with another woman.

Of course, that would mean Monk would have to set aside his doubts about Swift. Because the thing is, it didn't matter if Swift was a medium or not. Just the exercise of pretending that he was might help Monk finally deal with his complicated feelings of loss.

But I knew there was no way Monk could ever ignore his misgivings about Swift, not for a moment of wishful thinking or even, dare I say it, a genuine contact with the spirit world.

When I finally got out of bed, it was gray and rainy outside, but it was still pleasantly warm and the air smelled pure and fresh. I was energized, completely relaxed, and ready to take on the day.

Monk was standing on a chair in the living room, shifting his gaze between one of the ceiling fans and his watch.

"Good morning," I said.

"Not really."

I went to the kitchen. I'd set the timer on the coffeemaker the night before, so there was a fresh pot of Kona coffee waiting for me. The aroma was rich and enticing.

"You mean because you know Lance and Roxanne killed Helen Gruber but you can't prove it."

"That's not it," Monk said.

"Okay." I poured myself a cup of coffee and sat down at the table.

"How can you sit there calmly in the midst of this disaster?"

"Blissful ignorance," I said. The coffee was wonderful. I made a mental note to take a couple pounds of Kona beans home with me. Maybe a crate.

"You can't hear it? You can't see it?"

"What? The rain? The weather will probably get better, but even if it doesn't, it's still Hawaii, and it's beautiful even when the sun isn't shining."

"Not that," Monk said. "It's the ceiling fans."

I looked up at them. "They're working, aren't they?"

"At different speeds," Monk said. "I've been watching them all night."

"All night?" I said. "You haven't slept?"

"How could I? I could hear the difference in pitch."

"No way," I said. "That simply isn't possible."

"I really need a stopwatch to get the precise timing of each fan. You didn't bring a stopwatch, did you?"

"No, I didn't."

"Neither did I. Can you believe that? That's what happens when you pack in a hurry. You always forget something essential."

I got up and poured Monk a cup of coffee. "I'm sure the hotel can fix the fans. Why don't you sit down and have some coffee? It's from Kona beans grown right here on the islands. You'll love it."

"What if they can't fix them? Then they'd want us to move back into the hotel, which is teeming with rolled towels."

"Teeming?"

"It isn't pretty." Monk stepped off the chair and sat down across from me at the table.

"The fans weren't bothering you yesterday."

"They were working then." Monk took a sip of his coffee.

"You don't think that maybe you're projecting your frustration onto the fans?"

"What frustration?"

"At not being able to prove Lance and Roxanne killed Helen Gruber."

"I'll prove it," Monk said, his gaze drifting up to the fans. "Can't you hear that?"

"How?"

"Be quiet and listen real hard."

"I'm talking about the murder," I said. "How are you going to prove they did it? Even the police have given up on Lance and Roxanne."

"It will come to me. I'm thinking of nothing else." Monk stood up and pointed at the ceiling. "Look at that. The third fan is doing at least one revolution less per minute than the first fan. And the fifth fan . . . well, don't even get me started on that one."

I set my coffee cup aside.

"I'll tell you what we're going to do," I said. "We'll order breakfast from room service and then we'll go sightseeing. And while we're gone, the staff can fix the fans."

"These are precision instruments, Natalie. I doubt the staff is up to the task. They didn't even know how to fold towels. Maybe I should stay and supervise."

"You're coming with me, Mr. Monk," I said. "You need a change of scenery. It will do you good."

"I'm not a big fan of scenery."

"Do you want to solve this case or not? You need

to focus and you can't do it here, staring at the ceiling fans."

He sighed. "Can we look around for a stopwatch?"

"Sure," I said. "It's not like we can get along without one."

"Then I'm in."

The rain stopped while we were eating breakfast, but the skies remained clogged with clouds, blocking the sun but doing little to cool the heat. I could almost feel the moisture evaporating up off the asphalt as we walked out onto the parking lot.

I headed to where I thought I'd parked our Mustang but it wasn't there. There were so many identical cars in the vast lot, it wasn't going to be easy pick out ours. I looked at the key fob in my hand and saw a panic button that would set off the car alarm.

I aimed the fob out in front of me and hit the panic button. No alarms went off. I aimed it in a different direction and tried the same thing.

"What are you doing?" Monk asked.

"I'm trying to find our car," I said. "I forgot where I parked it."

"No, you didn't," Monk said. "It was parked here. Fifth row, eleven spaces in from the left, right beside the car Brian rented, which is this one. I remember the VIN number."

"Then where's our car?"

"It was stolen sometime last night." Monk crouched and examined the asphalt around the car parked in our spot, a Ford 500. "It's dry under this car, which means it was parked here before the rain. It started raining at two-eleven A.M."

"You can tell the exact time it started raining from examining the ground?"

Monk shook his head. "I was up."

"That's right. I forgot." I took out my cell phone and called Lieutenant Kealoha. He showed up about ten minutes later with an amused expression on his face.

"Crime seems to follow you two around," he said.

"Not me," I said, tipping my head toward Monk. "Him."

"Don't be too hard on yourselves; this kinda thing happens all the time. We'll get the car back."

"How can you be so sure?" Monk asked.

"Where are they gonna take it? We live on an island, brah. Just about everything we have, from cars to milk, has to be shipped in by boat or plane. Even the sugar now comes from somewheres else. Probably some kids took the car for a joyride."

"And if it wasn't kids?" I asked.

Kealoha shrugged. "It'll be stripped for parts, but we'll find what's left of it. Not a lotta places to ditch a car here."

"We'll need a police report to take back to the rental agency," I said. "And a ride there."

"I hope you took the insurance."

While I filled out a bunch of forms at Global Rental, Monk went across the street to EconoRides to pick out our next fresh-off-the-boat ride. Even though it wasn't our fault, I figured Global wouldn't be too eager to rent us another car after we had lost the brand-new one they rented us before. I was right.

Over at EconoRides, Monk managed to find us another Mustang convertible that came off the same boat as our previous car and had only four miles on it, about the distance from Nawiliwili Harbor to the rental lot.

I filled out another stack of forms and made sure to get every insurance plan offered. I neglected to mention that the last car we'd rented ended up getting stolen.

By the time we got on the road, the sun was peeking out through the clouds. I put the top down and steered us north toward Makana Peak, which was the mythical Bali Hai in *South Pacific*. I wanted to see those idyllic beaches set against that famous peak.

Monk was quiet, wrapped up in his own thoughts, so I turned on the radio to a station playing soft Hawaiian music that was heavy on ukulele.

The glimmering blue ocean was to our right. The lush mountain rain forests were to our left. The music of the islands carried on the wind. The air was rich with the sweet scents of a thousand tropical flowers. I was completely immersed in the Kauai experience. For all of two minutes before Monk spoke up.

"We have to get a stopwatch."

"We will," I said, trying in vain to regain that feeling of complete immersion. It was like trying to get back to sleep in a hurry to jump back into your dream after being rudely awakened. "Enjoy the fresh air. Look at all the beautiful scenery. Who knows when—or if—you'll ever get back here again."

"We should get it now."

"What's the hurry?"

"This way we can stop by the hotel and drop it off for the workmen; otherwise they might not get the timing of the fans exactly right."

"The hotel is in the opposite direction. We're not going back that way just to drop off a stopwatch. Try to relax. If the timing of the fans is still wrong, we'll have the repairmen come back."

"But what if they've already gone home for the day?"

"We'll turn the fans off," I said. "Then they'll all be moving at the same rate. A dead stop. Problem solved."

I saw a sign for the Wailua Falls and nearly passed the turnoff. I made a neck-snapping, hard left turn onto a narrow road riddled with potholes. The road snaked toward the mountains through fields choked with overgrown weeds.

We bumped along for twenty minutes until we saw cars parked in the red muck on either side of the road, which ended in a muddy cul-de-sac where a couple dozen tourists stood, their backs to us.

A Hawaiian man in a yellow rain slicker sold pineapple and coconut wedges from the back of a pickup truck. He cut the fruit with a small ax and served the halves to the tourists on newspapers. Roosters, clucking and crowing, scurried amidst the people.

I made a U-turn and found a parking spot on the road facing back toward the highway. We got out and joined the tourists who were pressed up against a chest-high Cyclone fence that overlooked the Wailua Falls and the verdant canyon below.

We had to stand on our tiptoes and peer over the hedge of weeds on the other side of the fence to see the twin falls, which spilled down eighty feet into a dark pond that fed a tiny river in a thick grove of trees. In the distance, the serrated ridges of the mountains were shrouded in haze. It made a pretty picture, one that I told Monk was used in the main titles of *Fantasy Island*.

"Minus the roosters, the weeds, and the potholes, I assume," he said.

"Yes."

"No wonder it was called Fantasy Island. The reality is pretty miserable."

"I think there's something very appealing about the undeveloped feel of this weedy lookout," I said. "If this sightseeing spot were anywhere else in the world, the parking lot would be paved, there would be signs telling us where to take the best photos, and there would be a gift shop selling hot dogs instead of that guy hacking pineapples with an ax."

"Exactly," Monk said. "Let's go there."

Adrian Monk was a study in contradictions. He could walk into a blood-splattered crime scene and examine a decaying corpse without hesitation, and yet he was totally unnerved by some wild roosters and a little mud.

We drove back to the highway and over the rickety bridge that spanned the picturesque Wailua River. To our left, the abandoned and decaying Coco Palms Hotel, its thatched-roof bungalows pummeled by Hurricane Iniki in '92, sat on the edge of a dense coconut grove overlooking the golden beach where the river met the sea. The resort was a tiki icon, harkening back to another era. Looking at the building, I could almost hear Elvis Presley singing "Blue Hawaii."

Actually, I *was* hearing it. On the radio. It was too perfect.

Once we crossed the bridge, the Kuhio Highway became the main drag of Wailua, a ramshackle town of Western-style storefronts and minimalls. My stomach was growling, so I parked in front of Namura Saimin, a place I'd read about in the guidebook.

"What are we doing here?" Monk asked.

"Having lunch. This is supposed to be the best saimin place in the Hawaiian islands," I said, getting out of the car before he could argue with me.

Monk eyed the place dubiously. "What's saimin?"

"It's like a soup. Noodles, boiled eggs, bok choy, green onion, pork, peas, wonton, and SPAM all in a dried-shrimp broth. It's a delicacy. They also make wonderful pies."

"I wonder if they have gecko on the menu."

"If not on the menu," I said with a smile, "certainly on the walls."

We opened the screen door and walked in. There were no tables, just a very low counter with tiny stools that must have been designed with the Menehune in mind.

The restaurant was crowded with locals slurping from enormous bowls of saimin. I saw two empty stools. I hurried over and sat down on one of them before someone else could walk in and snag them. I moved so fast that I scraped my knees again trying to fit them underneath the counter.

Monk stood beside me, behind the empty stool.

"Sit down, Mr. Monk."

"When hell freezes over." He did a full-body cringe. "And even then, probably not."

"Why?" I asked. "There's nothing on the stool, and the counter looks clean to me."

He motioned to the wall. I expected to see a gecko crawling up the faded wood, but instead it was a sign that read: PLEASE DON'T STICK GUM UNDER THE COUNTER.

"There's nothing to worry about. I didn't get any gum on my knees." I turned to the Hawaiian man next to me. "Did you get any gum on yours?"

The man shook his head and slurped up some noodles.

"See, it's clean." I turned back to see Monk staring at the Hawaiian woman sitting beside him. Each time she slurped up some soup, she spit some broth on the counter in front of Monk's stool.

She became aware of Monk staring disapprovingly at her. She looked over her shoulder at him and he mimed wiping his mouth. The woman, obviously offended, turned back to her soup and slurped even louder.

I could see this just wasn't going to work out.

"Okay, Mr. Monk. You win." I sighed and got up from the counter. "We'll find somewhere else to eat."

Just as we were about to walk out, I spotted the *liliko'i* pies on display by the cash register. If I couldn't eat there, at least I could take some of their famous dessert with me.

"Wait," I said as we reached the door. "I want to get a slice of pie."

"You can't get just a slice," Monk said.

"Yes, I can," I said, pointing to the menu on the wall. "They sell it by the slice."

"But if you buy a slice, the pie won't be whole," he said. "An entire pie will be wasted."

"No, it won't. They'll simply sell more slices from the same pie."

"Who would buy a piece from a pie that's already been eaten?"

"I'm not sticking my face in the pie. They cut the

slice out and I eat the slice. I never come into physical contact with the rest of the pie."

"The sanctity of the pie is still being violated."

I gave him a look. "The *sanctity of the pie*?"

"You have to respect it. You should buy the whole pie," Monk said. "It's the right thing to do."

"What am I going to do with an entire pie?"

"Take it back and put it in the refrigerator."

"The refrigerator in my room is way too small and crowded with—" I stopped myself. I'd forgotten we were staying in the bungalow now. "Good idea, Mr. Monk. I guess it hasn't sunk in yet that we've moved. We've got a whole refrigerator we can fill up."

I motioned to the waitress, a woman old enough to be my great-grandmother, and ordered a pie. She put it in a box. I was reaching into my purse for the money to pay her when I saw the look on Monk's face.

It was an expression of pure contentment, total self-confidence, and sweet victory.

I didn't know how it happened, but I knew for certain that it had. Our sightseeing for the day was over and my relaxing vacation was about to begin.

Monk had solved the case.

19

Mr. Monk and the Pie

We went straight to the Lihue police station to see Lieutenant Kealoha. Monk suggested that Kealoha re-interview the maids and that he send a forensics team back to the bungalow right away to examine an area they overlooked the first time.

Kealoha began to defend the forensics team, but it wasn't necessary. Nobody would have blamed them for their omission. It would have been like dusting the inside of the chimney for prints. There's no reason to do it unless you think the killer is Santa Claus.

We waited at the station with Kealoha while his men did as Monk suggested. I was starving, so Kealoha shared his SPAM musubi and li hing mui with me. Monk declined. The musubi was a chunk of SPAM on a square of rice, wrapped in dry seaweed. It wasn't bad. But the li hing mui, which was dried salted fruit, was hard to swallow. I wanted to be polite, so I choked it down with a smile and even took a second piece.

I wanted to return the favor by sharing my pie with Kealoha, but Monk wouldn't let me. He said he needed it for something.

So, bored and eager for something sweet to wash the taste of the li hing mui out of my mouth, I left the two of them and walked down the street to a shack that served Shave Ice in sixty different flavors, from guava to root beer.

The Shave Ice was like a Sno-Kone, only instead of using crushed ice, they gathered the fine powder created by shaving a block of ice with a knife. The ball of powder was placed on top of a scoop of macadamia-nut ice cream in a cup and doused with fruit syrup.

The chilly dessert flash-froze my brain and gave me a sugar jolt that was like being revived with defibrilator paddles. Shave Ice is refreshing and sweet but it should come with a surgeon general's warning.

When I got back to the police station, Kealoha was beaming. In the time I'd been gone, Monk had solved two burglaries and a missing-person case. And more important, the forensics team had reported back from the bungalow. When I asked what they'd found, Monk wouldn't tell me.

"It will ruin the surprise," he said.

Kealoha went off to find Lance Vaughan and Roxanne Shaw and bring them to our bungalow, where we would meet them all, and the truth behind Helen Gruber's murder would finally be revealed.

Monk was so wrapped up in the case, he didn't even notice the fans when we came in or remember that we hadn't bought a stopwatch. This proved to me that I was right about him projecting his frustrations. Either that or the fans were actually synchronized now, but I had a hard time believing that.

He wouldn't let me put the pie in the refrigerator, so I set it on the kitchen table. I knew he was setting the stage for his summation, which is the moment he lives for in any investigation. To be honest, I like it, too, even though I'm usually more of an onlooker than a participant.

We didn't have to wait long. Within a moment or two of our arrival, Kealoha strode in with Lance and Roxanne. They were trailed by two uniformed officers, which must have telegraphed to the couple what was coming.

Apparently they weren't the only ones who knew what the future held. Dylan Swift strode in behind them.

"Whoa, hold up, bruddah," Kealoha said. "Who are you?"

"I'm Dylan Swift," he said, as if he'd just been asked what that big, yellow, fiery-looking thing was up in the sky.

"Is that supposed to mean something to me?"

"I've been assisting Mr. Monk on this investigation," Swift said.

"No, he hasn't," Monk said.

"Yes, he has," I said, earning a glare from Monk.

I didn't care whether Swift was a con man or not; he'd helped me, and I thought he'd earned the opportunity to see Monk in action.

"I know you," Roxanne said to Swift. "You're that guy who talks to ghosts. I read your book, *A Spiritual Guide to Better Lovemaking: Sex Secrets from Beyond the Grave.*"

"He wrote that?" Lance glanced at Swift, then back at Roxanne. "Is that where you learned the—"

She nodded. "Uh-huh."

When Lance looked at Swift this time, it was with an expression close to reverence.

"I'm here as an advocate for the dead," Swift said. "To give them a voice in what happens here today."

"Them?" Kealoha said.

"The women who've loved Lance Vaughan and died in his embrace," Swift said.

"No one has died in my arms," Lance said.

"Not unless you're talking about what poets call 'the little death,'" Roxanne said. "I experience that in his arms once, and sometimes twice, a day."

Monk shifted his weight impatiently. "Are you all going to keep talking or would you like to know how Lance murdered his wife?"

"I didn't kill my wife; you know that," Lance said. "It's impossible. I was snorkeling on the Na Pali Coast when she was murdered."

"Actually, you weren't," Monk said.

"There are a dozen witnesses who saw me, and a videotape that proves I was there."

"You were out on the water Wednesday morning, there's no doubt about that, and you certainly made sure everybody saw you. The only problem is, that wasn't when Helen was killed. She was murdered the night before."

"But the medical examiner said she died two hours before her body was discovered," Kealoha said.

"He was fooled, and so was I, even though all the clues were right in front of me that very first day. But I didn't realize it until Natalie bought that *liliko'i* pie at lunch today." Monk motioned to the pie on the table.

"Here's what happened," he continued. "Lance hit Helen over the head with a coconut and drowned her in the hot tub Tuesday night. Then he emptied the Sub-Zero refrigerator of all the pies and pineapple she'd brought home, removed the shelves, and stuffed her inside to keep her fresh. In the morning he put her in the hot tub to thaw and confuse the medical examiner about the real time of death."

"I didn't do any of it," Lance said. "I couldn't kill my wife and stuff her in the refrigerator. It's obscene."

"The cold, cramped space. It was the refrigerator," Swift said, facing Monk. "*That's* what she was trying to tell us. You understood the message I gave you and solved the case."

"You told Monk about the refrigerator?" Kealoha said, then shifted his gaze to Monk. "I thought it was buying the *liliko'i* pie that gave you the solution."

"It was. I didn't listen to anything this fake told me."

"Maybe if you'd listened to me, you would have solved the murder days ago," Swift said. "But at least Helen's words stayed in the back of your mind and you finally realized their meaning today."

"What I realized was that the maids said that Helen loved *liliko'i* pie and pineapples and kept bringing them home."

"Helen told you that, too, in her way," Swift interrupted.

He was right. I remembered that.

Monk ignored him and continued where he left off. "But where were the pies? The refrigerator was empty the day of the murder, one of the shelves was in backward, and the trash cans outside smelled of rotting food. That's because Lance threw out the pies to make room for Helen's corpse."

I remembered the smell now, and Monk adjusting the refrigerator shelf. He was right. All the clues were there that morning. But it was true that Swift also told us everything we needed to know. So the solution was right in front of us, *twice*, but we still didn't see it.

"You're making this up as you go along," Lance said. "It's ridiculous, and there's no evidence to back it up. Because it never happened."

Monk turned to Kealoha. "You want to tell Lance what the crime scene technicians found in the refrigerator today?"

"We found Helen Gruber's hair, some specks of her blood, traces of chlorine, and her footprints against the inside wall."

That was why Monk wouldn't let me put the pie in the refrigerator. It was unsanitary.

Lance shook his head. "No, you planted it all. I didn't kill her."

Swift suddenly let out an agonized wail, startling us all, and dropped to his knees, his head hanging down.

Monk groaned and went into the kitchen.

I put my hand on Swift's shoulder. "Mr. Swift? Are you all right?"

When he lifted his head, tears were streaming down his cheeks.

"How could you, Lance?" he said in a disembodied, distinctly feminine voice. It gave me chills. "I loved you. I gave you everything you wanted."

Lance stared at him in disbelief. *"Helen?"*

Roxanne began to whimper. I had trouble breathing. It was as if I'd stepped into a horror movie. Kealoha and the officers were frozen in place. But Monk didn't seem to notice. He was puttering around in the kitchen as if nothing unusual were happening.

"What did I ever do to deserve such cruelty?" Swift said in that soft, otherworldly voice.

Lance fell to his knees in front of Swift and grabbed him by the shoulders. "Helen, if that's you, tell them the truth. Tell them I'm innocent."

"I thought we'd be together forever, but after what you've done, you'll never join me here. You're going straight to hell, Lance."

And with that, Swift promptly fainted.

"Helen!" Lance screamed, shaking Swift. "Tell them!"

The officers grabbed Lance, yanked him to his feet, and handcuffed him.

"Book him, Dan-O," Kealoha said. "Murder one."

"No!" Lance yelled as one of the officers dragged him outside while reading him his rights.

"I've always wanted to say that," Kealoha said with a grin.

The other officer led away Roxanne, who was crying softly and muttering, "This isn't right."

Monk stepped out of the kitchen with several plates, a knife, and a spatula. "Would anyone like some pie?"

"How can you think about pie right now?" I said. "Can't you see that Swift has fainted?"

"Yes, it was quite a performance. I'm waiting to see his head spin completely around."

Monk set down his things, went to his room, and came back out a moment later with a tape measure.

Kealoha called the paramedics on his cell phone. I

put a pillow under Swift's head, got a wet towel, and dabbed his brow.

Monk used the tape measure to determine the circumference of the plate so he could cut the pie into even slices.

"Did Swift really know about all of this?" Kealoha asked me.

I told him about all the images Swift had given us from Helen, how we'd later discovered their meaning in relation to the case, and how Monk had explained it all away as a con job. When I was finished, I could hear the siren from the ambulance as it raced toward the beach house.

"Your explanations for Swift's so-called visions all make sense, Mr. Monk," Kealoha said. "Except for one thing. How did he know that Helen was in the refrigerator?"

"He didn't," Monk said. "He was talking about the morgue. It was a lucky break for him that the refrigerator ended up being involved."

Swift's eyes fluttered and he began to regain consciousness.

"Awaking right on cue," Monk said, carefully cutting the pie. "What a shock."

Swift opened his eyes and seemed startled. He tried to sit up, but I gently eased his head back down onto the pillow.

"Relax," I said.

"What happened?"

"You started speaking to Lance as Helen and then you fainted," I said. "The paramedics will be here any minute now."

"I was channeling her?" Swift said.

"She had some sex tips to share for your next book," Monk said. "But no one was taking notes."

"I don't remember any of it. She must have completely possessed me."

"That's how it looked," Kealoha said.

"I've never channeled a spirit so powerfully before, but these circumstances are unusual," he said. "We're in the place where she died. We were with the man who killed her. And her spirit is very forceful. I'm sensing her even now."

"Is this where your head spins?" Monk slid a piece of pie onto a plate. "Or will you levitate? Because I'd like to see how you do that."

The ambulance screeched to a stop outside our open front door and, a moment later, two paramedics rushed in, wheeling a gurney.

Monk sat at the table and casually ate his pie as the paramedics examined Swift and then lifted him up onto the gurney. At this point, Kealoha joined Monk at the table and helped himself to a slice of pie.

As Swift was being wheeled out the door, he took a last look at Monk.

"Helen wants to thank you. They all do. They are at peace now."

If Monk heard him, he made no sign of it.

I walked alongside the gurney to the ambulance. Just as the paramedics were about to load Swift inside for the ride to the hospital, I took Swift's hand and gave it a squeeze.

"Thank you," I said.

"I didn't do anything," he said. "I'm just the messenger."

"It was a message I needed to hear."

"I have another one, but it isn't for you," Swift

said as the paramedics lifted his gurney into the ambulance. "Tell Monk that I'm getting a strange image. It's connected to him somehow. I don't know what it means. It's a hand with six fingers."

And with that, one of the paramedics climbed into the ambulance, his partner closed the doors, and they drove off.

20

Mr. Monk Does a Favor

With the investigation of Helen Gruber's murder behind us, there was nothing standing in the way of my enjoying everything the island had to offer. I changed into my bikini, grabbed a towel and my Kauai guidebook, and headed for the beach, leaving Monk and Kealoha with a quick good-bye as I raced out the door.

I went to the Grand Kiahuna Poipu activity hut to check out some snorkeling equipment and buy a Ziploc bag of fish food. While I was there, I made reservations for Monk and myself to attend the resort's Sunday-night luau.

The best place for snorkeling, or so the guidebook told me, was a secluded little cove just past the resort property and right in front of the ruins of a condo complex decimated by Hurricane Iniki.

The condo complex was laid out in a staple shape, the courtyard in the center choked with weeds as tall as trees, the dry pool filled with sand, rusted chaise longues, and enormous chunks of concrete. The ocean-facing units were entirely stripped away; only the iron skeleton remained.

The tiny beach in front of the ruins was empty, too cluttered with black boulders and concrete blocks to be much of a tanning spot. The water in the cove was shallow and calm and filled with lava rocks, creating lots of nooks and crannies for tropical fish to dart around in.

I put on my snorkel gear and walked backward into the sea until I was about chest-deep. The water was warm and perfectly clear. I could see scores of colorful fish. I dove and paddled out to sea.

After that, I lost all track of time. It was as if I were swimming in the aquarium in the waiting room of my daughter's dentist's office. I half expected to go around the next rock and see the enormous face of some kid with braces staring at me, his nose pressed against the glass.

All I had to do was throw out a few kernels of food, and out of nowhere I was swarmed by fish tickling my skin and poking against my mask.

I thought about nothing, my mind a complete blank as I floated along, dispensing food, admiring one brightly colored fish after another.

In some ways, it was like being in a sensory-deprivation tank. It was just me and the fish and the gentle current. I was in a deeply relaxing snorkel trance that wasn't broken until I tossed out some food and an eel shot out of the rocks and into my face like a jack-in-the-box.

I screamed and jerked upright, scrambling for footing, sucking in water, and scraping my left leg across the razor-sharp surface of a lava rock.

It was only as I stood there, coughing and bleeding, my mask askew, that I realized I was in only about three feet of water.

Still coughing, I staggered back toward the beach, sat down in the surf, and pulled off my flippers. As the water lapped against the two-inch-long cut below my knee, I experienced for the first time what it really means to have salt rubbed in a wound. It was like being scrubbed with a loofah made of glass shards.

While I was drying myself off, careful not to get blood on the towel, I noticed how tight and itchy my back was. I couldn't see it, but I knew I had a nasty sunburn. How many hours had I been out there, floating facedown, my back cooking in the sun? I wouldn't be wearing my bikini top again that trip. It was going to be T-shirts for me for the rest of the week.

But despite my discomfort, I couldn't remember the last time I felt better or more truly well rested. I gathered up my things and trudged back to the resort.

Monk was leading a trio of maids out the front door when I came in through the back patio.

"See you tomorrow. If you have any questions before then, don't hesitate to call," Monk said, waving at them as they left with their carts, vacuums, buckets, and mops. "Aloha."

When he turned around, I expected him to avert his gaze away from my shocking nakedness. But instead he hurried over to me, looking at my left leg.

"What happened to you?"

"I was snorkeling and scratched my leg on a rock. It's no biggie."

"Not if you enjoy infection, gangrene, and amputation."

"It's not that bad, Mr. Monk."

"I want you to sit down and put your leg up on a chair."

He took me by the arm and led me to the kitchen table. As I was sitting down, he noticed my back. He gasped. Based on his reaction, you'd think the flesh had been stripped away and he was looking at my exposed spine.

"I got a little sunburned," I said. "It happens to everybody here."

"Why didn't you just douse yourself with gasoline and light a match?" He pulled out a chair and I lifted my injured leg up onto it. "Don't move."

Monk hurried to his room and came back a moment later with a small gym bag, which he set on the tabletop. He dragged a chair beside me, took a pair of rubber surgical gloves from the bag, and put them on.

"What's in the bag?" I asked.

"Haven't you ever seen a shaving kit before?"

He pulled out iodine, antiseptic cream, cotton swabs, gauze bandages, tweezers, scissors, tape, and enough medical supplies to stock a small hospital.

"You brought all that just for shaving?"

"I might nick myself," Monk said.

"Or get shot in the chest and have to remove the bullet yourself."

He soaked a swab with iodine, picked it up with the tweezers, and then gently dabbed my wound. The iodine stung again, but not as bad as the salt water.

"I'm sorry," Monk said, glancing up at me. "But it has to be done."

"It's okay."

Monk held my leg with one hand and tended to my cut with the other. While he dressed the wound, I watched him. I was deeply moved by this simple gesture, by his tenderness. Gone was any awkwardness he felt about my nakedness. His concern for me trumped his own anxieties. Well, most of them anyway. He still wouldn't touch me without gloves.

"What have you been up to while I was snorkeling?" I asked him.

"Showing the maids how to vacuum, mop, and dust," Monk said. "We had a lot of fun."

"You've been doing that since I left?"

"I'm on vacation, so I'm cutting loose, being a little wild."

He finished bandaging my cut and, using the tweezers, put all the used swabs into a Ziploc bag, which he sealed and put into another bag.

"Turn around," he said.

"Why?"

"So I can put some cream on your back," Monk said.

"You'd do that?"

He went to the kitchen, got some paper towels, and wound them around his gloved right hand until it looked like he was wearing an oven mitt. "If my hair were on fire, would you put out the flames? Would you throw me a life preserver if I were drowning?"

"Of course."

"It's the same thing." Monk came back, squeezed

some lotion out of a tube onto my shoulders, and started to rub it in with the paper towel.

It felt as if he were using a blowtorch. I yelped in pain and jerked away from him.

"What's wrong?" he asked.

"You might as well be using sandpaper. My skin is very sensitive, especially when it's burned. If you're going to do this for me, you're going to have to use your hands."

"You mean you want me to touch your body?"

"You can keep your gloves on if that will make you more comfortable."

Monk went to the kitchen and got a trash bag. He unwound the paper towels, stuffed them into the trash bag, tied it shut, and came back to his seat. He squeezed some more cream onto my shoulders, took a deep breath, and began to massage it into my skin.

I could see his reflection off the glass tabletop and the disgusted scowl on his face. It wasn't touching me that he found repulsive (at least, I hope not). The gloves weren't preventing him from feeling the greasy consistency of the cream between his fingers. He didn't like it. But he was doing a good job. The cream cooled my skin and immediately soothed the sting. And his light, tentative massage didn't feel bad, either.

"That feels good," I said.

"I'm sorry," Monk said. "I'll stop."

"No, no, go on. I thought making me feel better was the idea."

"I'm providing medical attention."

"Right. That's exactly what it feels like, good medical attention."

"I'm glad," Monk said.

He rubbed the cream in some more.

"I'm planning on spending the day tomorrow sightseeing and buying some souvenirs. Maybe see Spouting Horn and Waimea Canyon or go in the other direction and see Hanalei," I said. "Since you're finished investigating, you ought to come with me."

"I'm not finished."

"You caught Helen's killers," I said.

"But I haven't caught Swift."

I turned around. "What are you talking about?"

Monk held his hands in front of him as if they were covered with manure. "I'm going to reveal him for the fraud that he is."

"Please, Mr. Monk, don't."

Grimacing, Monk took one lotion-covered glove off with his other gloved hand. "He's a con man. He takes advantage of grief and loss for his own personal gain."

"Maybe. But he helped me. He could help you, too."

"I don't need his kind of help." Monk put the glove in a bag and took a fresh glove out of his shaving kit. "He doesn't talk to dead people. He tricked you. That's what he does."

I considered whether or not to tell Monk what Swift said about Trudy, but I decided it would only strengthen Monk's resolve to ruin the man. So that left me with just one option.

"I'm asking you as a favor to me," I said. "Please just leave him alone."

Monk looked at me for a long time. "I'll do it for you, not for him."

I gave him a kiss on the forehead. "Thank you, Mr. Monk."

"Now would you do a favor for me?"

"Sure."

"Could you put this glove on my hand?" Monk said.

I took the fresh glove from him and pulled it over his left hand, which he then used to take off the dirty glove from his right hand. He disposed of the lotion-covered glove in another bag, then removed the new glove from his left hand and put it in a bag, too. It was a strangely fascinating process to watch. I could have taken his gloves off for him, but to be honest, it didn't occur to me and he didn't ask.

"Do you go through all of that when you shave?"

"Of course I do," Monk said. "Me and every man in America."

21

Mr. Monk Goes Sightseeing Again

We ordered dinner from room service. Our meals were delivered personally by Martin Kamakele, the manager of hotel operations. It wasn't because we were VIPs who deserved extra-special attention. It was because Kamakele was upset that Monk kept his maids for three hours, putting them way behind in their work on the other bungalows and forcing the hotel to pay them overtime.

Kamakele implored Monk not distract the maids from their work anymore.

Monk agreed on one condition: On Monday, Kamakele would gather the entire cleaning staff together and let Monk instruct them in the history, theory, and proper handling of the dust rag, the mop, the broom, and the vacuum. Kamakele reluctantly gave in.

"You'll thank me later," Monk said.

We ate our dinner out on the patio and watched the sunset. Afterward Monk insisted on playing another game of peanuts. Since I was playing on a full stomach, I managed not to eat my pieces this time. He still easily beat me. I put one peanut back in its shell, but that was only because I cheated. I marked a shell with my fingernail so I could find it later. I think Monk knew, but he must have let me get away with it out of pity.

I spent the rest of the night going over the guidebook and a map of the island, figuring out all the things we were going to do on Sunday and learning facts about interesting sights.

First thing the next morning, we got in the car and set off for Waimea Canyon, which Mark Twain called "the Grand Canyon of the Pacific" because, really, what other big canyon is there to compare it to? Can you think of one? I can't. I'm sure there are others, but they aren't widely known.

Waimea Canyon is 3,600 feet deep, ten miles long, and a mile wide. It was a sixty-mile drive along the coast and up a winding road into the mountains to get there, but I didn't mind, even though my tender back burned from the contact with the seat. The scenery was spectacular. We saw craggy peaks, lush meadows, golden beaches, and the red Waimea River. Legend says the river runs red with the blood of Komali'u, the daughter of a tribal chief who was killed atop a waterfall by a lover she had spurned.

I thought Monk would like that story, maybe argue that someone else killed her, or that she was murdered somewhere else and dropped in the river. But he wasn't paying attention. He was too freaked out. The higher we climbed into the mountains, the more anxious he became.

Monk couldn't get out of the car at the first Waimea Canyon lookout spot. He sat there hugging himself, his eyes squeezed tightly shut, as if he were actually standing on the precipice instead of safely buckled in his seat, a good ten yards away from the cliff's edge. He couldn't even see the gorge from where he was.

So I got out, walked to the railing, and took in the view by myself. Instead of being all dry and dusty like the Grand Canyon, it was covered with dense green growth, and I could see a waterfall across the expanse. I wish I could tell you more, but I got only about sixty seconds to absorb the sight before Monk started honking the horn in a panic.

That was my one and only glimpse of the canyon, outside of the photos in my guidebook. To keep Monk from hyperventilating, I turned the car around and drove back down to the flatlands of the town of Waimea. By the time we got there and parked in front of a row of shops, Monk was calm again, though a little weak-kneed when he got out of the car.

"I think I have altitude sickness," Monk said.

"You were only up there for a few minutes. Your apartment in San Francisco is higher above sea level than that."

"I know. That's why I try not to reach for anything on a high shelf at home."

We were standing in front of a gift shop. T-shirts hung in the window, and a postcard carousel propped open the front door.

"I'm going inside to look for something for Julie," I said. "Maybe you'd like to rearrange the postcards by geographical location, size, or paper stock."

"I want to get her something too."

We went inside. The tiny store was stuffed with all kinds of cheap T-shirts, bathing suits, shorts, hats, wraps, and beach towels. They also sold videos of island sights, CDs of Hawaiian music, jewelry, Kona coffee, taro chips, macadamia nuts and cookies, suntan lotion, throwaway sunglasses, and hula dolls.

I was looking for something unique that Julie wouldn't be able to find at home. I was wandering around the store, looking at this and that, when I stumbled on their selection of Red Dirt shirts. I was sorting through them, hunting for one in Julie's size, when Monk joined me again with a package in his hand.

"I found something for her," he said.

I looked at what he was holding. "You're getting her Q-tips?"

"Hawaiian Q-tips," he said.

"Those are the same ones she can get at home," I said.

"But I'm buying them here."

"You should get her something uniquely Hawaiian, like one of these Red Dirt shirts. They're made right here on Kauai."

I told Monk the story behind the shirts. The story was almost as unusual as the shirts themselves. Hurricane Iniki destroyed a guy's T-shirt factory, soaking his entire inventory in water and mud. But it wasn't the total disaster it first appeared to be. He discovered he liked the unique, dyed color the mud gave his clothes. So instead of throwing out his ruined stock, he made dirt-stained garments his new business.

"You're buying her a dirty shirt?" Monk asked incredulously.

"They're dyed. They aren't caked with mud. There's a difference."

"No, there isn't."

"People dye shirts with all kinds of things. They've got shirts here dyed with coffee, beer, hemp, chocolate, and wine. It's fun stuff."

"It's disgusting. What do they do here? Wear a shirt for a week and then sell it?"

"These aren't used shirts," I said. "They've never been worn."

Monk suddenly became intensely aware of all the dyed shirts around him. He drew himself in, careful not to brush any part of his body against one of the shirts, which wasn't easy in the cramped store.

"Why would you want to buy your daughter clothes soaked with beer, sweat, and vomit?"

"I didn't say anything about sweat and vomit. Do you see any clothes dyed with sweat and vomit?"

"They probably save those for special occasions," Monk said. "Like human sacrifices."

"Don't you think you're overreacting just a bit?"

"We're talking about people who buy dirty clothes and eat in restaurants crawling with lizards." Monk lowered his voice, careful not be heard by the Hawaiian proprietor. "Cannibalism is hardly out of the question."

I took two Red Dirt shirts off the display and held them up to Monk. "Which do you like best? The T-shirt or the tank top?"

"I think I'm going to be sick."

Monk backed away and headed for the door, weaving his way cautiously through the aisles as if a shirt might leap out and attack him.

My cell phone rang. I reached into my purse and answered it.

"Hey, Natalie," Captain Stottlemeyer said. "How's the vacation going?"

I glanced at Monk, who was standing outside, taking deep breaths.

"It's been great, Captain. We're staying one step ahead of the cannibals. Monk even managed to solve a murder."

"So I've heard," Stottlemeyer said.

"Lieutenant Kealoha called you?"

"No, I read about it in the *Chronicle*. And *USA Today*. And I heard it on the radio driving into work."

"But Mr. Monk hasn't talked to anybody about it."

"Dylan Swift has. When did Monk start working with psychics?"

I looked outside again. Monk had started reorganizing the postcard display. He wasn't going to like this news. I didn't like it much, either.

"He hasn't," I said.

"You wouldn't know that from listening to Swift. They talked to him in the ER, where he was recovering from being possessed by the spirits who helped Monk."

I felt betrayed, used, and pissed off. "What did Lieutenant Kealoha say?"

"He didn't talk to anybody, as far as I know, but a couple of his uniforms did, and they back up Swift's story. They said he spoke in tongues or something. You don't know about this?"

"We haven't read a newspaper or turned on a TV since we got here."

"But you were there, right? Is any of what Swift says true?"

"Yes and no," I said, then gave Stottlemeyer a short rundown on our encounters with Swift. "Monk thinks he's a publicity-hungry fraud."

"Monk is right."

"I was kind of hoping he wasn't this time."

"I know how you feel," the captain said. "It would do wonders for my self-esteem if he got things wrong once in a while."

"This wasn't about my self-esteem. It was more about wish fulfillment."

"They're one and the same for me."

I thanked the captain for the call, bought a Red Dirt shirt and a shark-tooth necklace for Julie, and went outside, where Monk was still occupied with the postcards.

"You bought one of those disgusting shirts, didn't you?" Monk said.

"I had them triple-bag it and tie it shut. I'll put the bag in the trunk and wipe my hands with a disinfectant wipe."

"Aren't you worried that if she wears that shirt to school someone might report you to Child Protective Services?"

"I'll take the risk."

"I'll testify as a character witness."

"Thanks, I appreciate that," I said.

I put the bag in the trunk, we got in the car, and I started driving us back toward Poipu.

"You know how I asked you to do me a favor and not go after Dylan Swift?"

Monk nodded.

"Forget it," I said. "Get him."

"What changed your mind?"

"He did." I told Monk about my conversation with Stottlemeyer and Swift's claims that he helped Monk solve Helen Gruber's murder.

"I'll go to the taping of his show today," Monk said, "and reveal him for the fraud that he is."

"It's Sunday, Mr. Monk. I don't think he tapes today."

"I'll go tomorrow."

"Martin Kamakele told us that Swift was going back to San Francisco on Monday."

"Then I'll catch him there," Monk said.

"You may not have to wait that long. I didn't tell you this before, but Swift said last night that he has a message for you."

"What is it?"

Before I could tell him, something flashed in my peripheral vision. I looked to my left and saw a truck, its gigantic bumper gleaming like fangs, running the red light into the intersection and speeding right at me.

I didn't even have a chance to scream.

When the truck clipped the front of our car, the steering-wheel air bag punched into my face like a boxer's glove, and everything began spinning. It was like being in a carnival Tilt-A-Whirl while being smothered with a pillow.

When I opened my eyes, my ears were ringing, my chest was sore where the seat belt yanked against my flesh, and my face stung as if I'd been slapped on both cheeks. But I was alive and all the departments of my body were reporting back that everything was okay.

Monk lifted his face from the dashboard air bag as if he'd been startled awake from a nap. He seemed dazed but unhurt.

We both looked at each other without saying a word, then looked out the cracked windshield.

The car had spun completely around and we were facing the way we had come. The front end was smashed and the truck that clipped us was gone. People were beginning to stream out of the shops and restaurants and into the street to see what had happened.

"I think I've had enough sightseeing for today," Monk said.

22

Mr. Monk and Mr. Swift

A handful of tourists and locals had gathered on the sidewalk, eating Shave Ice and watching two guys hitch our smashed Mustang up to the tow truck that would take it back to Lihue. There were so few cars on the road that Lieutenant Kealoha was doing double duty, interviewing us in the intersection and directing traffic.

"So you're sure you had the green light," he said.

"Positive," I said. "Besides, if we were the ones at fault, don't you think the truck driver would have stuck around?"

Kealoha shrugged. "Maybe he didn't have a license or was driving without insurance and didn't want no trouble. What else can you tell me?"

"It happened so fast. All I saw were those enormous bumpers, like you have on your patrol car, and next thing I knew, I was looking at my air bag."

Kealoha shifted his gaze to Monk, who was examining the broken glass and the tire skid marks on the street.

"What about you?"

"The pickup truck was brown with dirt caked on the license plate, but I saw the letter 'N' and the number seven. The bumper was dented and the left front headlight was broken, so it was in an accident before. The driver was white, in his mid-thirties, a hundred and ninety pounds, with bleached-blond hair like surfers have, a bushy goatee, and a silver stud in his left ear. There were dead bugs on the windshield, mostly butterflies, though I can't tell you what kind."

Kealoha stared at him. "That's all you saw?"

"I only caught a glimpse."

"We'll put out an APB, which on an island like this means calling a few of your bruddahs and asking them to keep their eyes open."

Monk crouched over one of the skid marks. "This is odd. He must have seen us in the intersection, but he didn't slow down."

"That's why he hit you," Kealoha said.

"You'd think he would have slammed on his brakes and tried to avoid the collision, even if only at the last second. But he didn't. He just plowed right through us and kept going."

"Maybe he was in a hurry," Kealoha said. "Or he was being chased."

"There weren't any other cars," I said. "We would have seen them."

Monk looked perplexed. "It doesn't make any sense."

Kealoha closed his notebook. "You certain you don't want me to take you to the hospital, make sure nothing's broke?"

We both shook our heads, but the mention of the hospital reminded me about Dylan Swift.

"What have you heard from Swift?"

"Nothing, but I've heard from the reporters he's been blabbing to," Kealoha said. "I told 'em all, 'No comment,' and I ordered those idiot officers of mine to keep their mouths shut. How about you?"

"No reporters have called us. All I can figure is that the hotel operator wasn't told that we'd moved into Helen Gruber's bungalow. And Swift certainly didn't tell them. He doesn't want us contradicting him."

"Lance wouldn't talk to them. He's hired some big-ticket criminal defense attorney out of L.A. who will be his mouthpiece," Kealoha said. "He'll be here this afternoon. Meantime, we let Roxanne walk. We've got a solid circumstantial case against Lance but nothing to hold her on. If she had something to do with the murder, Lance is keeping quiet about it."

"Where's Swift now?" Monk asked.

"Back in his bungalow, I suppose. They didn't keep him at Wilcox Memorial; there wasn't anything wrong with him that an exorcism couldn't cure."

"Or a jail sentence," Monk said.

Kealoha dropped us off in front of the Grand Kiahuna Poipu lobby. He lowered his window as we got out of his car.

"When are you heading back to Frisco?" he asked.

"Tuesday," I said. "Why?"

"I'm trying to decide whether to bring in some off-duty officers and rejigger the work schedule. Since you two arrived on Kauai, the crime rate has skyrocketed."

"Maybe you should lock us up."

"The thought has occurred to me." He grinned and drove off.

I turned and saw that Monk was already inside the lobby, reading a copy of the *Honolulu Advertiser*. There was a picture of Dylan Swift on the front page.

I joined Monk and read the article over his shoulder.

LIHUE—Did a murdered woman solve her own killing from beyond the grave? According to famed psychic Dylan Swift, that's exactly what happened.

Swift is an internationally known medium and best-selling author who claims to talk to the dead. He tapes many episodes of his nationally televised daily TV series at the Grand Kiahuna Poipu, where vacationing Cleveland resident Helen Gruber was found dead Wednesday in the hot tub of her bungalow, apparently the victim of an accident.

Shortly thereafter, Swift began receiving "messages" from Helen indicating that she'd been murdered. He immediately relayed the information to San Francisco detective Adrian Monk, another guest at the hotel, who was aiding local police in their investigation.

Sources at the Kauai Police Department confirm that, based on Swift's information, Monk and the homicide investigators were able to build a case against Helen Gruber's husband, Lance Vaughan, for murder.

But sources say it was Swift's channeling Helen herself, in a dramatic confrontation with her husband at the scene of the crime Saturday, that provided the final clues. Vaughan was promptly arrested and charged with first-degree murder.

Vaughan was allegedly involved in an affair with Roxanne Shaw, also of Cleveland, who was visiting the island as well. No charges were filed against Shaw, who was questioned and released. She declined comment.

Swift was taken to Wilcox Memorial Hospital's emergency room, where he was being treated for undisclosed trauma relating to his "channeling."

"Without Helen's voice to guide us," Swift told reporters, "her murder might never have been solved. I'm glad I was able to serve a small role in seeing that justice was served."

Monk didn't bother reading the rest of the story. He carefully folded the paper and set it down on a table. "What was Swift's message for me?"

"He saw a hand with six fingers."

Monk rolled his shoulders and narrowed his eyes. I knew that meant he was mulling the facts, trying to put things together, seeing how they fit . . . or how they didn't.

"Who else knows about that man?" I asked.

"Me, Captain Stottlemeyer, Lieutenant Disher, and you," Monk said. "And the man who killed my wife."

Monk marched through the lobby, through the pool area, and straight to the bungalow across from ours. He pounded on the door. Swift opened the door, holding an ice pack in one hand.

"This is a pleasant surprise," he said, and stepped back, ushering us in.

The floor plan of the bungalow was identical to

ours, but the furniture was considerably more upscale and masculine, all dark koa wood and leather. The decor was less tropically floral, leaning more heavily on maritime paintings of sailing ships braving rough seas.

"We came to see how you were feeling," Monk said.

"I burned myself making breakfast," he said, showing us the nasty blister on his hand under his ice pack, "but otherwise I'm fine. Spiritual possession causes some disorientation and headaches immediately afterward but usually doesn't have any lasting physical effects."

"I was thinking more about all the talking you've been doing to the press," Monk said. "I'm surprised you still have a voice."

"The more I can foster greater understanding among the general public about the afterlife, the better they will be able to cope with death and grieving."

It was such a line of crap, and it made me so angry that I couldn't contain myself. "You're trying to capitalize on Helen Gruber's murder to promote yourself, your books, your seminars, and your TV show. It's disgusting."

"I thought you knew me better than that, Natalie."

"So did I, until I read what you were saying in the newspaper."

"Someone at the hospital or one of those officers alerted the media, not me. I simply answered their questions as honestly as I could."

"Maybe you can answer a few of mine," Monk said.

"Of course."

"Natalie said you had a message for me."

Swift seemed to relax. He nodded and took a seat, beckoning us to sit on the couch opposite him, which we did.

"I was hoping that you would ask. After I first met you, I had a startling vision of a hand with six fingers. I thought it might symbolize something about Helen's murder. But I saw it again last night, after the case was solved, so I knew that it was about you. I'm feeling the letter *T* very strongly. Is there someone close to you whose name begins with *T*?"

"My wife, Trudy."

"Has she passed on?"

Monk nodded. "She was murdered. A car bomb."

I wondered why Monk was playing along, giving Swift information to work with. Was it to draw Swift out or was Monk unable to resist his own curiosity, his need to hear from Trudy one more time, even if the message was false?

"I sense tremendous frustration, so much uncertainty. There are questions Trudy needs answered. Until then, she can't truly be at peace."

"I can't either. It's always been like that with us," Monk said. "We've always felt the same way. It was as if we were one person instead of two."

"That is love, Mr. Monk, the greatest force in the universe. It binds us together even in death."

I was startled by the honesty of Monk's admission, that he would reveal so much to a man he didn't trust. Monk wasn't simply playing along; he was opening himself up completely. Was that the price of exposing Swift or was Monk hoping for some greater truth to emerge?

"She needs to know what happened," Swift said. "She needs to know why she died."

"I don't know," Monk said sadly. "I was hoping she could tell me."

"There are things she wishes to tell you, things you might be able to use to free you both from the questions that haunt you."

"Tell me," Monk said.

"There were other deaths. Women. Many of them. But not in San Francisco. I sense so much terror, so much pain. I see a hunchback carrying a statue of Christ on his shoulder."

"Corcovado," I said.

Monk and Swift looked at me. "It means 'hunchback.' It's a mountain in Rio de Janeiro with an enormous statue of Christ the Redeemer atop it. You can see the statue from all over the city."

"Rio de Janeiro. Yes. I see the statue now, his arms outstretched and—" Swift gasped. "One of his hands has six fingers."

"No, it doesn't," I said.

"What I see isn't literal," Swift said. "It's a metaphor, a symbol of some kind, meant to convey a message. I think what Trudy is trying to tell us is that the man you seek is in Brazil."

Monk rose to his feet. "Thank you."

Swift stood up and so did I. "Good luck, Mr. Monk. I hope you find your answers."

I looked Swift in the eye. "Are we going to be reading about this conversation in tomorrow's newspapers?"

"This is between us," Swift said. "You have my word."

He saw us to the door. As soon as we were outside, I whispered to Monk, "Are you all right, Mr. Monk?"

"Why wouldn't I be?"

"He dredged up a lot of painful feelings."

"They are never very far from the surface," Monk said.

"I'm just surprised you answered his questions."

"I didn't tell him anything he couldn't learn on his own," Monk said. "Or that he didn't already know."

"What about your feelings?"

"I only told him what anybody would expect me to feel about Trudy's murder."

"But everything you said was true."

"It's easier than lying."

We walked to our bungalow. I unlocked the door and we went inside.

"So what do you think about what he told you?" I asked.

"I'm curious why he wants me on the next plane to Brazil."

"That's easy. Because Swift knows you're pissed about how he took advantage of you to publicize himself," I said. "He's afraid you're going to expose him as a fraud."

"Oh, I am," Monk said. "I just wonder if that's the only reason he wants me gone."

"Isn't that enough?"

Monk shrugged and looked up at the ceiling fans. "Do they look like they're moving at the same rate to you?"

23

Mr. Monk Goes to the Luau

The secluded luau garden was illuminated by torches around its perimeter and candles that had been placed on the long mats—woven from lauhala leaves—that were spread out on the grass like rugs. Each mat had a large centerpiece made of native flowers, ferns, and ti leaves. Young Hawaiian women wearing leis, grass skirts, seashell anklets, and bikini tops made of coconut shells were setting down on the mats, wooden calabash bowls full of poi, sweet potatoes, tropical fruit, and some kind of meat.

Onstage, there was a band of shirtless Hawaiian men in grass skirts with *maile* leis around their heads, playing music and singing in Hawaiian. Whatever the song was, it was sleepy and slow, the musical equivalent of lying in a hammock and being gently rocked by the breeze.

We were among the hundred or so hotel guests who'd been ushered by our hostess, another Hawaiian woman in a grass skirt and coconut bra, into a loose circle in front of a mound of sand in front of the stage.

Monk's attention was on the mats and the bowls of food the women were setting out. "Where are the tables and chairs?"

"There aren't any," I said.

"Where are we supposed to eat?"

"The food is being served on the mats."

"So we have to bend down each time we want to take a bite? That doesn't make a lot of sense."

"We're sitting on the ground, Mr. Monk."

He studied my face to see if I was kidding or not. *"You'll* be sitting. *I'll* be standing."

"Fine," I said.

"I don't see any silverware."

"I'm sure it's coming," I said.

Our hostess stepped into the center of the circle. She had long black hair and a stomach as flat as the mats we were going to be eating from. I absently touched my own stomach and then noticed that all the women there over the age of eighteen were doing the same thing.

"Welcome to the Grand Kiahuna Poipu," she said. "My name is Kiki, and I'm going to be your guide to the luau and the story of the history of Hawaii that we will tell in song and dance."

She went on to explain that luaus began as feasts the ancient Hawaiians held to celebrate major events and to communicate with their gods. They were originally known as *aha'ainas* until 150 years ago, when a European guest at one of the feasts mistook "luau," the name for a dish made of coconut milk, taro leaves, and chicken, for what the event itself was called. The mistake stuck.

Monk raised his hand, and I had a flashback to the last time I was standing in the luau garden, which was for Candace's wedding. I comforted myself with the fact that no matter what he did tonight, he couldn't possibly embarrass me as much as he did before.

I should have known better.

"Excuse me, Kiki," he said. "Speaking of food, there's this silly rumor going around that we're going to be sitting on the ground to eat."

"That's correct, sir. This is a traditional luau. You will sit on the ground at the lauhala mats and be served authentic Hawaiian dishes like poke." She pointed to the bowl of meat and said, "which is raw, marinated fish."

"Raw?" Monk choked out the word.

Kiki smiled. "It's quite delicious, I assure you. But I have to confess, we aren't being entirely authentic this evening. If this luau were being held in 1778, when Captain Cook visited the islands, we'd have Hawaiian priests on hand who would offer to chew your meat for you first."

Monk gave me a stricken look, much like the one he had had on his face at the T-shirt shop, as if to tell me, *I told you so.* He turned back to Kiki.

"Where's the silverware?"

"Like the extravagant and merry luaus enjoyed by King Kamehameha the Second and his honored guests, you'll be eating with your hands," Kiki said. "All the better to enjoy our famous two-finger poi."

"It's a good thing I came prepared," Monk whispered to me, reaching into his pocket and showing me a Ziploc bag containing a set of utensils.

"You brought those from the bungalow?"

Monk shook his head. "From home."

Two Hawaiian men in traditional dress, which is

to say virtually no clothes at all, joined Kiki in the center of the circle. They were carrying shovels.

"The main entrée tonight will be kalua pig, which has been cooking in this imu for the last nine hours." Kiki pointed to the ground behind her.

"She's pointing at the ground," Monk said.

"Yes, Mr. Monk. I know."

The Hawaiian men began digging up the sand behind Kiki as she spoke. Smoke rose from the hot sand, and almost immediately the men began to sweat from the heat.

"Hot rocks are placed in a six-foot-deep pit that's lined with banana leaves. An entire pig is salted and placed in the hole, covered with banana leaves to preserve the heat, and buried."

"Buried?" Monk said loudly, stepping into the center of the circle and addressing the other tourists. "We're supposed to eat something they've *buried* in dirt? With our *hands*? Do they think we're savages?"

"Mr. Monk, please," I said, pulling him back. "You're creating a scene."

"Wait until the health department hears about this," Monk said to Kiki. "They'll shut this place down."

"We've been doing this for centuries," Kiki said with amusement, her smile never wavering.

"And it ends tonight. I'm dropping the dime on you, lady."

"I can assure you, sir, you have nothing to fear from kalua pig."

At that instant, a woman in the crowd screamed in terror. We turned to see an elderly woman staggering back, her wide eyes fixed on the imu behind Kiki. Everyone followed her gaze.

The two Hawaiian men, as wide-eyed as the old lady, dropped their shovels and backed away from the hole they were digging to reveal a human hand, gnarled and cooked a deep red, sticking up from beneath the smoking sand.

I felt an irrational pang of fear in my chest and an instinctive desire to run. Apparently I wasn't alone. As the horrified guests scrambled out of the garden, Monk stood fast, unperturbed. In fact, he didn't seem surprised at all.

He looked at me and sighed. "I told you they were cannibals."

To Lieutenant Kealoha's credit, he wasn't offended by Monk's suggestion that Hawaiians were cannibals.

"I don't think anyone intended to serve the man for dinner," Kealoha said. "If they did, they probably would have seasoned him and undressed him first. At least, that's what we usually do when we eat people."

The police had roped off the luau garden in yellow caution tape, and crime scene techs were digging up the body, careful to preserve the sand around the corpse to retain any possible forensic evidence.

The dead man was dressed in upscale aloha wear, but his face was cooked beyond recognition. The medical examiner told Kealoha that preliminary evidence indicated that the victim was killed by a blow to the head with a blunt object.

One of the techs retrieved a wallet from the victim's pocket and brought it to Kealoha in a bag.

"His name is Martin Kamakele," the tech said.

"He's the operations manager of the hotel," Monk said.

"We found dried blood and brain matter on one of the shovels," the tech said. "It's a safe bet that's the murder weapon."

"Thanks." Kealoha sighed and looked at Monk. "Two murders in one week at one hotel. Hell of a coincidence."

"I don't believe in coincidences," Monk said.

"You think this is related to Helen Gruber's murder?"

"It has to be," Monk said.

"How?" I asked. "Lance killed Helen for her money. What possible involvement could Kamakele have with that?"

Monk shook his head. "I don't know."

"I'll have Roxanne Shaw picked up and brought in for questioning," Kealoha said. "But I'd be surprised if she did it. I've had an officer staking out her place all day."

"You suspected she might do something?" I said.

Kealoha shrugged. "I figured it couldn't hurt to keep an eye on her. I certainly didn't think she'd whack somebody with a shovel."

"This wasn't a premeditated crime," Monk said. "This was an act of anger."

"Why do you say that?" Kealoha asked.

"The pig was buried nine hours ago, and the body was buried on top of it. So the killing happened in broad daylight. The killer didn't bring a weapon; he used one that was at hand, probably just lying on the ground. And he didn't try to dispose of the body, only to hide it temporarily to delay its discovery. Who would plan a murder that way?"

"No one," Kealoha conceded.

"Lance did," I said. "He made it look like Helen

was killed in broad daylight by someone who hit her
with a coconut.''

"So you're saying Kamakele was killed last night,
stuck in a refrigerator, and buried here this morning
so the killer would have a kick-ass alibi?"

"No, I'm just noting the similarities," I said. "Two
murders in broad daylight where the killer found
something on the ground and clobbered somebody
with it. I think it's kind of eerie, that's all."

Monk cocked his head and looked at me strangely,
as if he'd suddenly noticed I had three nostrils instead of two.

"What? Why are you looking at me that way?"

"Because you've just solved half the mystery,"
Monk said. "Now all I have to do is figure out the
other half and we'll have a murderer."

24

Mr. Monk Mails a Letter

I couldn't help wondering what Monk meant when he said that I'd solved half the crime. I couldn't see how that was true.

One of the most irritating things about Adrian Monk, above and beyond the obvious, is that he makes statements like that and then doesn't explain himself.

After making that remarkable declaration, he just turned and walked out of the garden, too lost in thought even to say good-bye.

It was frustrating for me, but even more so for Kealoha, who couldn't understand why Monk would leave him dangling like that.

"He's doing this to torture me, isn't he?" Kealoha asked me.

"He does it to everybody," I said. "He won't tell us who the killer is until he knows he can prove it."

"If he tells us who he *thinks* it is, maybe we can help him."

"That may not be the half he knows."

"Then I'll just have to plod along the same way I would if Mr. Monk weren't here. I'll see if Martin Kamakele had any enemies and find out what Roxanne Shaw had been doing today."

"Let us know, okay?"

Kealoha nodded and I headed back to the bungalow. After seeing that cooked corpse, I had lost my appetite for dinner and had doubts I'd ever be able to eat meat again.

When I got there, Monk was sitting at the kitchen table playing a solo game of peanuts, taking apart the pieces and putting them back together again.

I didn't disturb him. I figured the game was helping him think. So I took a swim in our private pool, called Julie from my bedroom afterward to catch up on things at home, and then went out to say good night to Monk.

He was sitting in the living room in the dark, facing the patio and listening to the surf. His back was very straight and he was looking into the darkness as if he saw something there.

"What are you thinking about?" I asked.

"When Trudy was a baby, her grandmother knitted her a yellow blanket. Trudy was swaddled in the blanket when she was an infant, sucked on the corners when she was teething, and became so attached to it when she was a toddler that she couldn't sleep without it."

"It was her security blanket. Every kid has one. Mine was a stuffed fox I called Foxy."

"Trudy called the blanket her 'night-night.' As she got older, the blanket got more and more tattered and frayed. Her parents tried to wean her off of it by having her grandmother knit her a smaller, identical one that was pocket-sized. But Trudy wouldn't accept it. There was no substitute for her night-night."

"When did she finally let go of it?" I asked.

"She never did," Monk said. "She was still sleeping with her night-night when I met her and for all the years we were married. I buried the night-night with her so she'd always be comforted and safe."

"What made you think of it now?"

"Because that's still how Trudy makes me feel. She's my night-night." Monk sighed, not with sadness, but with contentment. "I've never told anybody about her blanket and that I buried it with her."

"I'm glad you told me." I put my hand on his shoulder and gave it a squeeze. "Good night, Mr. Monk."

"Good night, Natalie."

I went to bed, leaving Monk alone with his memories and his dreams.

I didn't know what to expect the next morning. We had only one full day left in Hawaii, and I was hoping to spend it relaxing. But I knew Monk wouldn't rest until he found Kamakele's killer and exposed Dylan Swift as a fraud, which meant I wouldn't be resting either.

I found Monk at the kitchen table, where he was carefully folding in half a letter that was covered with his typewriter-perfect handwriting. He stuck it in his inside coat pocket.

"Good morning, Natalie. Did you sleep well?"

"Like I was hibernating," I said. "You?"

"I wrote a letter," Monk said.

It took him twenty minutes to sign his name on a credit card receipt, so I had no doubt it took him most of the night to write an entire letter.

"To whom?"

"Captain Stottlemeyer," Monk said.

"That's nice," I said. "I'm sure he'll appreciate it."

"I'd like to stop and get it notarized on our way to breakfast," he said. "You think they have a notary on staff?"

"I don't know," I said. "But I'm sure a stamp is all that's necessary."

"I'd rather have it metered," he said, and we headed for the door.

"What's on the agenda for today?" I asked with some reluctance.

"Enjoying Hawaii," he said.

"What about the murder investigation?"

"It's half-solved," he said.

"What about the other half?"

He dismissed it with a wave. "In due time."

I was stunned. He'd never been so laid-back about a case before.

"What about Swift?" I said. "Aren't you going to expose him as a fraud?"

"I'll get around to it."

It wasn't like I wanted to talk him into further investigations, but it was such a radical change in his personality that it made me uneasy.

"How can you be so relaxed about things?"

"Isn't that the whole point of a vacation? You should try it."

"You didn't take one of those pills again, did you?"

"Why would I? Besides, I'm saving it for the flight home."

I decided not to question my good fortune any further and to enjoy the day to the fullest.

On our way to the restaurant, we stopped at the front desk, where Tetsuo greeted us. The entire staff, he said, was still in shock about what had happened to their boss, Martin Kamakele. There was talk about permanently canceling the hotel's luau.

"I think that's a good idea," Monk said. "Next you should consider folding your towels instead of rolling them. Turn your back on barbarism once and for all."

Monk asked if they had a notary on staff. They did, and it was Tetsuo. So while Monk and Tetsuo went into the office to notarize the letter, I went ahead to the breakfast buffet. On my way there I glanced out front and saw Dylan Swift stepping into a limousine that I presumed was taking him to the airport. He smiled and gave me a little wave. I acknowledged his greeting with a nod of my head.

He was getting away easy. Swift probably didn't even realize just how close he had come to career ruin. By his heading back to San Francisco and staying out of our sight, there was a possibility that Monk might forget all about him.

Monk was in such a relaxed mood that he didn't even lecture me, or the restaurant staff, about the horrors of buffet dining. On the other hand, after the aborted luau last night, it probably seemed sanitary and civilized to Monk by comparison—or at least like a step in the right direction.

He ate his Wheat Chex and milk while I indulged in an island breakfast of kiwi, pineapple, macadamia-nut pancakes with coconut syrup, and a cup of fresh Kona coffee.

After breakfast we went back to the bungalow,

where I changed into my bikini. My back was sun-burned, but not my front, so I slathered on some sun-tan lotion and settled down for some quality sunbathing.

Monk eagerly awaited the arrival of the maids. As soon as they got there, he hustled them into the living room for Housecleaning 101. With Kamakele dead, there was no one to object to his occupying the maids' time and attention. He began with "Vacuuming Theory."

"There are three steps to successful vacuuming," Monk told them. "Survey. Map. Vac. Survey the scene. Map a pattern of attack, and then vac, sticking to the plan despite whatever obstacles are in your path. Let me demonstrate . . . ."

I was able to tune him out until the vacuuming began forty-five minutes later and the noise drove me away from the bungalow. I put on a T-shirt and went for a walk.

My stroll took me past the Whaler's Hideaway, and I couldn't resist looking up at Roxanne Shaw's condo. She was there, sitting on her lanai, looking out at the ocean. Her neighbors were on their lanai, too, sunning themselves. I wondered if the swinging couple had invited her over for a friendly threesome yet.

I continued up the street, following the seawall, stopping once or twice to watch the big sea turtles swimming among the boulders and managing, some-how, not to get smashed against them by the pound-ing surf.

The street curved toward Koloa Landing, the point where the mouth of the river met the sea. Until the 1900s, that spot was Kauai's major port for whaling ships and all of the island's sea trade. The muddy, weedy landing was a popular spot for scuba divers and snorkelers. Where once there had been docks and warehouses, now there was a decrepit rental cabin made of lava rocks and, on the opposite shore, a modest condo complex hugging the edge of the rocky point.

I kept walking, crossing the concrete bridge over the tiny river and heading north in the general direction of Spouting Horn, the geyserlike natural phenomenon up the road, though I had no intention of going that far in my flip-flops. I passed a lot of homes, bed-and-breakfast inns, and condos along the jagged shoreline. There was no beach here, but there were other benefits to make up for it—views that seemed to stretch across the sea into infinity, and the dramatic show of the surf crashing against the rocks in explosions of frothy ocean spray.

I went as far as Prince Kuhio Park, looked at the well-tended grass, the muddy fish pond, and the tidy lava-stone foundations of Ho'ai Heiau, the ruins of a temple. This park was the birthplace of Prince Jonah Kuhio Kalaniana'ole, the last royal heir to the Hawaiian throne, who died in 1922. I tried to imagine what the place looked like a hundred years ago when he was born, but the shabby condo complex adjacent to the park, and the surfers drinking beer and whooping it up on their lanais, killed the mood.

I headed back the way I came, going much slower this time. Whatever exuberant energy had propelled me this far was used up. I was hot and tired, my back itched, and my feet hurt.

Roxanne Shaw was sitting on the seawall across

from the Whaler's Hideaway and facing my direction. I got the feeling she'd been waiting for me to come back.

I walked up and sat down beside her on the wall. I saw the unmarked police car parked at the corner, the sweaty detective in the loud aloha shirt making no effort to disguise the fact that he was watching us.

"I'm under de facto house arrest," Roxanne said bitterly. I bet that was the first time in her life that she'd ever used the term "de facto" in conversation.

"Could be worse," I said. "You could be sharing a cell with your lover."

"He didn't do anything wrong."

"Yeah, he's Mr. Innocent. He doesn't kill women; he just marries them for their money and waits for them to die."

"So we aren't perfect," she said. "But we aren't evil. The old ladies got something out of it. You don't think they loved having a buff boy toy of their own?"

"We've been over this already. You didn't wait here to tell me again about what humanitarians you two are."

"Monk is wrong. Lance didn't kill Helen and stage everything in such an elaborate way to create an alibi. He's not that smart."

"That's the first thing you've said that I believe. Maybe you're the brains."

She shook her head. "I get by on my great rack and perfect ass, not my intellect."

"Hey, that's good. Tell that to the jury," I said. "I'm sure it will go over big. Don't forget to flash some cleavage while you're at it to really sell the point."

"You have to help us," she said imploringly.

"Give me a reason. You could start by telling me who killed Martin Kamakele."

She shrugged. "I never heard of him until yesterday, when the detectives came to question me again. All I know is that Kamakele brought Helen and Lance some champagne on the day they arrived."

I got up. "If I were you, I'd start looking for the rich old geezer you're going to marry and the young stud you're going to have on the side."

"I'm not a whore."

"That's right, you're not. It's your lover who is. You're the pimp with the great rack and perfect ass."

I turned my back on her and walked away. By the time I returned to our bungalow, the maids were gone and Monk looked very happy with himself.

"Did you have a good time?" I asked.

He nodded. "I feel like I'm really contributing something useful to the people here and, in my own humble way, stoking the flames of the cultural revolution that will sweep this backward country and bring it into the modern age."

"Hawaii isn't another country, Mr. Monk; it's part of the United States."

"Are we sure about that?"

"Yes," I said.

"Kealoha called while you were gone. He discovered that Kamakele gambled heavily on island cockfighting and was deeply in debt. Kealoha's working theory is that Kamakele was killed for not paying the loan sharks."

"Do you believe that's what happened?"

"A dead man can't pay his debts. He was more valuable to them alive."

"So this gambling thing isn't the other half of the mystery you were talking about."

Monk shook his head.

"Are you going to tell me what it is?"

"You'll know when I solve the case," he said.

"Why not tell me now? What are you waiting for?"

"The right moment."

"Which is?" I asked.

"The moment when I solve the case," he said.

25

Mr. Monk Finds a Stain

Although we had our own private pool, I didn't want to hang around the bungalow for the rest of the afternoon. I wanted the energy that comes from being in a crowd and to enjoy the fun of people-watching.

So I put on another coat of suntan lotion, grabbed one of the paperbacks I brought, and left to lounge by the big pool. On my way out the door, I saw Monk carefully removing the artwork from one of the walls.

"The maids were just here, Mr. Monk."

"They were cleaning," he said. "I am straightening up."

I knew from experience that he meant that literally.

"We're leaving tomorrow. Do you really intend to spend your last day in Hawaii inside this bungalow making sure all the pictures and paintings are even, centered, and straight?"

"I'm allowed to have fun, aren't I?"

"What's wrong with getting a little sun?"

"Take a look at your back."

"Mr. Monk, this is Hawaii, one of the most beautiful places on earth. Most people consider it paradise."

"They don't know about the reptiles crawling all over the restaurants, the mud shirts, or people exhuming dead pigs from the ground and ripping them apart with their bare hands."

The phone rang. Since I was standing by it, I picked it up. It was Kealoha. They'd found our stolen rental car in the parking lot of the Kukio Grove mall in Lihue. I relayed the news to Monk.

"I want to see it," he said.

Kealoha had heard Monk. "I figured he would, which is why there's a patrol car outside your bungalow waiting to bring you here."

Kukio Grove was the beginning of the end for Kauai—a deadly cancer that had already metastasized. The open-air mall, anchored by a Macy's on one end and a Kmart on the other, could have been anywhere else in America. There was nothing about the shopping center that fit in with the local environment or culture. Over the years, other bland, homogenous franchises and box stores had been built around it in an ever-widening radius. Burger King and Borders. Home Depot and Wal-Mart. I was glad I had the chance to see the island before it became a Los Angeles suburb.

The Mustang was parked in a far corner of the lot, closer to the street than to the mall. The only other cop around besides Kealoha was the officer who picked us up at the hotel. This was not a major crime scene.

"The car was spotted by mall security because it was parked here overnight," Kealoha told us. "When they called us to have it cited and towed, we ran the vehicle's license plate and it came up as stolen."

Monk walked around the Mustang, peering at it from every angle as if it were a meteor instead of an automobile. The car looked like every other Mustang on the island to me. I couldn't have said whether it was our rental car or not.

"This is definitely our car," Monk said.

"As I said, we matched the plates."

"Someone could have switched the plates and put them on another car. But they didn't. I remember the vehicle identification number."

"You *do*?" Kealoha said. "Why would you memorize that?"

"It's the first thing you do when you rent a car," Monk said. "It's no different from learning your room number at a hotel. Everybody knows that."

"I guess I don't travel enough."

"If you're going to be an effective investigator, you need to become more of a man of the world," Monk said.

"Like you," I said.

"Let's not create a goal that's completely out of his reach," Monk said. "People only strive for what they think is possible to achieve."

"That's good to know," I said.

"I guess I can stop dreaming of being a jockey," Kealoha said, and gestured to the car. "The Mustang obviously wasn't stripped, so I figure some kids were looking for a slick ride for the day at the expense of some haole tourist."

Monk pressed his face as close to the driver's-side window of the car as he could without making physical contact with the glass.

"The seats are stained," he said. "They weren't stained before."

"If we catch the kids," Kealoha said, "we'll charge them with grand theft auto and make them wash the car, too."

"I've seen these stains before," Monk said. "They were in the car that Brian rented."

"I'm not surprised," I said. "I'm sure a lot of cars here have the same kind of stains."

"No, you don't understand," Monk said. "These *are* Brian's stains."

"Who is this slob Brian?" Kealoha asked. "And why would he steal your car?"

I explained to Kealoha that we'd come to Kauai for my friend Candace's aborted wedding, that Brian was her jerk of an ex-fiancé, that his rental car had been vandalized, and that he'd left the island days ago.

"I'm confused," Kealoha said.

"So am I," I said. "How could these stains be the stains from Brian's car?"

We both looked at Monk.

He looked back at us. "Let's rent another car."

Monk didn't bother to explain himself. He insisted that we take him to the nearest car-rental agency, preferably one we hadn't rented from before.

I argued that we had only one more night left on the island and that it was insane to rent another car now. But Monk didn't care.

Kealoha gave us a ride to AutoPlanet, the one big rental company left that didn't know us. He waited around while Monk put the attendant through the ordeal of finding him a convertible that was as close to factory fresh as possible.

We ended up with another Mustang, identical to the ones we had before.

"Where to now, Mr. Monk?" I asked after all the papers were signed and all the insurance options had been accepted.

"The police station," Monk said.

"You didn't need a rental car for that," Kealoha said. "I could have taken you there. What do you want at the station?"

"A knife," Monk said. "The sharpest one you have."

We followed Kealoha back to the police station and parked in the lot. Kealoha went inside and came back out holding one of those ugly blades Rambo used to carry around. It was so sharp, I was afraid I could get cut just looking at it.

"We took this off a drunken marine in Kapaa," Kealoha said, showing us the knife as we got out of the car. "He never came back to claim it."

"You could cut a tree down with that thing," I said.

"He said he used it for slicing apples."

Monk motioned to me for a wipe and I gave him one.

"If you will recall, someone smashed the wind-shield and tore the soft-top of Brian's car." Monk took the knife from Kealoha and thoroughly cleaned the handle with the wipe as he spoke. "When it came back from the body shop, not only were the windshield and soft-top fixed, but the seats were replaced, too."

"Yeah," I said. "So?"

"But the carpets were still dirty. I thought it was odd. Now I don't."

He gave me the dirty wipe, opened the driver's-side door of the car, and slashed the seat with his knife.

"Mr. Monk!" I ran up beside him. "What's the matter with you? You can't do that!"

He looked up at me. "You took the insurance, didn't you?"

"It doesn't cover you for this!"

Monk shrugged and continued slashing the seat cushions as if nothing had been said about it.

"Is this your way of removing difficult stains?" I asked, not bothering to hide my exasperation.

Kealoha joined us. "I'd like to know, too, since technically I'm witnessing a crime here."

"Brian's rental car was brand-new, just off the boat," Monk said as he slashed. "When we went to the rental company for the first time, a couple was there returning a brand-new Mustang that had been damaged in an accident. The next day our car was stolen."

"Yes, I know all that," I said. "What I don't get is why you're ripping up these seats."

He stopped slashing and looked at his handiwork. He'd shredded the upholstery, exposing the stuffing and the springs. Hacked-up bits of foam padding were all over the floor.

"After our car was stolen, we rented another new Mustang. A few hours later someone sideswiped us," Monk walked around to the other side of the car.

"You're cursed," Kealoha said. "And, if I may say so, a little crazy."

"That may be." Monk opened the passenger-side door, leaned inside, and began slashing the seats again. He acted as if it were the most normal thing in the world to be doing. "But that's not the reason our first car was stolen or why a truck crashed into our second one. In fact, all these car accidents, thefts, and acts of vandalism have one thing in common: Each rental car involved was just off the boat."

Monk leaned back and smiled. I recognized it as the smile he gets when everything fits and order is restored, like when he organizes the items in a grocery store dairy case by expiration date. Or when he solves a murder.

Kealoha and I walked around the car and peered inside. The back cushion of the passenger seat was torn apart. Monk had cut away the vinyl and padding to reveal that the seat was stuffed tight with bags of white powder.

I had a hunch it wasn't sugar.

"I figured it would be drugs," Monk said. "I think you'll find that the rate of car thefts and accidents increases considerably after a new fleet of cars arrives on the island and are distributed among the rental agencies."

"How did you know the cars were being used to smuggle cocaine?" Kealoha asked.

"I didn't until I saw Brian's stained seats in our stolen car. Then I remembered something you said—that virtually everything on the island, from cars to peanuts, has to be shipped in. I figured that fact of life must also apply to illegal goods as well."

"So they're smuggling cocaine onto the island by

hiding it in the seats of new rental cars," Kealoha said. "They have inside men at the rental agencies who let them know when the cars are rolling off the lot and with whom. Then they vandalize, crash, or steal the cars so they can remove the hidden drugs."

"Those were Brian's seats in our stolen car. Because all the seats look alike, they just swapped out the ones with the drugs," Monk said. "They put Brian's seats, now emptied of drugs, into the next drug-laden car that came in."

"Why not just break into the cars while they are on the lot?" I asked. "Why wait until they are rented?"

"To avoid getting caught in the act and to draw less attention," Monk explained. "The lots are under constant surveillance and there are people around them twenty-four hours a day. Not only that, but if they always hit the newest cars on the lot, it would be noticed right away. But when it's seemingly random accidents and thefts of rental cars out on the road all over the island, something that happens every day here, neither the rental agencies nor the police are likely to make the connection."

"He's right," Kealoha said. "And there's one body shop in Kapaa that gets most of the rental car repair work."

I remembered the rental agent at the Grand Kiahuna Poipu telling us that. Now it all made sense.

Monk handed Kealoha the knife. "Something tells me that car repair is not their primary business."

"I wonder how many years this has been going on right under our noses?" Kealoha shook his head in amazement. "I'll bust the shop tonight. You wanna come along?"

Monk glanced at me. "I don't think so. This is our

last night in Hawaii, and a drug bust doesn't seem like the right way to spend it."

I smiled at Monk. "Thank you."

He shrugged.

"I'm gonna miss you, Mr. Monk. You are one hell of a detective," Kealoha said. "How come you aren't on the SFPD anymore?"

"Creative differences," I said.

"You ought to move here," Kealoha said. "We'd hire you in a heartbeat."

"Really?" I said.

"With him on the payroll, we could lay off half the force," Kealoha said. "We'd save a fortune on manpower, not to mention lowering the crime rate by half."

Monk did one of his full-body shivers. "As appealing as that job offer is, I'll pass."

"Excuse us a moment." I pulled Monk aside so we were out of earshot of Kealoha. "You really should seriously consider this, Mr. Monk. He's offering you your dream. Don't you want a badge again?"

"I have no desire to be the sheriff of hell," Monk said.

"What if I moved here with you?"

"You'd do that for me?"

"I'd do it for myself and Julie. If someone paid me to live here, I'd jump at the chance. It would be an adventure in paradise."

"You'd live someplace where your daughter had to wear mud shirts and eat food off the ground?" Monk said. "Who are you kidding? I would never expect you and Julie to endure that kind of hardship just so I could be a cop again."

"It wouldn't be a hardship; it—"

He interrupted me. "That's very kind of you, Natalie, and I'm touched. But come on, look at this place."

Before I could argue, he turned back to Lieutenant Kealoha. "It was a nice offer, Lieutenant. But my life is in San Francisco."

"Well, I hope you'll come back to visit us soon," he said.

"I certainly will," Monk said, and then added in a whisper that only I could hear, "when dogs start using restrooms."

26

Mr. Monk Goes Home

The two of us had dinner together again at the Royal Hawaiian. Afterward Monk returned to the bungalow to finish straightening up, and I went to the hotel's beachfront bar to sample some more of their tropical drinks.

The bar was lit by torches and moonlight. There was a band, some hula dancers, and a warm breeze off the water. The drinks were smooth, sweet, and plentiful. Best of all, since the patrons were mostly couples, I was left alone to enjoy the night without getting hit on by anybody.

I missed Julie but I would have gladly stayed another week if given the opportunity. With all the things that had happened since we'd arrived, I'd hardly had any time to enjoy the resort or explore the island. And yet I was certainly relaxed, more so than when I arrived. Between the night air, the music, and all the drinks, I could have been poured into bed that night. As it was, I returned to our bungalow after an hour at the bar and went to bed content.

I was awakened early on our last morning by the sound of splashing in our pool. Since I was the only resident of the bungalow who swam, I figured either a seal had found its way into our backyard or we had an intruder swimming laps. I put on my bathrobe and went out barefoot to see what was up.

I was surprised to see Monk doing a pretty decent backstroke across the pool. He smiled when he saw me.

"Dive in and I'll race you," he said.

It was the first time I'd seen Monk shirtless. And if he was aware of me looking at his nakedness, he certainly wasn't bashful about it.

"We're leaving here in two hours," I said. "Don't you have to pack?"

"How hard is that? You just throw everything into a suitcase and zip it up."

Now I understood what was going on. Monk was high. He must have taken his preflight dose of the anti-OCD drug Dioxynl already.

"Are you hungry?" he asked.

"I don't know yet. I just got up."

"I'm starving." He climbed out of the pool. "The buffet opens in five minutes. Let's go before there's a line."

He looked around a moment before he realized he didn't have a towel.

"Wait here," I said. "I'll get you a towel."

"Forget about it," he said, and started walking toward the living room.

"You'll drip water all over the house."

He waved off my concern. "It's water, not acid. It'll be dry in five minutes. You have to learn to relax, babe."

Monk was lucky I wasn't holding a heavy object.

I showered, got dressed, and finished my packing. When I came out of my room, I found Monk waiting for me in his freshly laundered golf clothes, his suitcases by the front door, ready to go.

We left our bags with the bellhop and went to the buffet. There was already a short line, but it moved fast. Monk grabbed a plate and piled it high with scrambled eggs, white rice, sausage, hash browns, bacon, ham, melon, and pineapple, all mixed together.

"You don't have to take all your food at once," I said when he came to the table. "You can go back for more as often as you like."

"Cool," Monk said.

He set down his plate and went back to the buffet for another one, which he filled up with an omelet, pastries, pancakes, smoked fish, bagels, crepes, and Grape-Nuts cereal.

"Are you sure you have enough food?" I said.

"I have a high metabolism."

"If you eat all of that, you'll be ready to go into hibernation for the winter."

Monk devoured his breakfast, taking each bite from a different item. He was channel surfing, only with food. He didn't care if his lox was mixed with his Grape-Nuts or his pancakes with his pastries. He washed it all down with four cups of Kona coffee, jacking himself up on caffeine on top of his mind-altering Dioxynl high.

I was so caught up in watching the spectacle that I almost forgot to eat my own modest breakfast of pancakes, pineapple, and yogurt.

We'd finished eating and were about to go to the lobby and check out of the hotel when Lieutenant Kealoha strode up to our table.

"I was hoping I'd catch you before you left," Kealoha said.

"Not to be rude," I said, "but haven't we said goodbyes to each other twice already?"

"I wanted to give you the good news personally. We raided the body shop last night. The truck that hit you was there, and so was the man with the goatee that you described. We found millions of dollars' worth of cocaine."

"All right!" Monk yelled, raising his fists in the air in victory and dancing around the table. "That's the way, uh-huh, uh-huh, I like it. Oh, yeah!"

Kealoha stared at him as he danced. "Not only that, but we discovered a crop of marijuana in the field behind the shop. It's the biggest drug arrest in Kauai history. There's already talk around the station that I'm going to be promoted to captain."

"Give me five." Monk held up his hand. Kealoha slapped it. Monk slapped back. "You deserve it, man."

"Maybe if I solve Martin Kamakele's murder, they'll make me chief."

"Wish I could help you there, bruddah, but the Monk doesn't know who killed him. What would you like from the buffet?"

"Nothing, thanks."

"I'll get some more food and you can eat it off my plate. They'll never know."

"Really, I'm fine," Kealoha said.

"You'll change your mind when you see the grub."
Monk got up and hurried to the buffet, piling his
plate high with bacon.

Kealoha looked at me. "Is he on drugs?"

I nodded.

"Have a nice flight," Kealoha said, and walked
away.

I won't torture you with the details of our flight
home. It might not be torture for you to hear, but it
would be for me to recall it. The horror began when
we were in the security line and Monk started pulling out the bacon and pastries he'd stuffed into his
pockets at breakfast. Things only got worse and more
embarrassing from there. Let's just say that Monk
isn't welcome to fly on Hawaiian Airlines again.

After five hours in the air with Monk, I was glad
to be home. Julie loved her Red Dirt shirt, although
my mom found it almost as disgusting as Monk did.

My mother had heard all about what happened at
Candace's wedding. Apparently the news had spread
throughout the high society of Monterey and San
Francisco. I felt terrible for Candace.

"When will you learn not to take Monk to wed-
dings?" my mother said.

"Would it have been better if Candace married a
married man?"

"I'm sure the situation would have resolved itself
more quietly, and with more dignity, than what happened at the wedding."

"You mean it would have ended up being just as
disastrous, if not worse for poor Candace, but at least
it could have been kept quiet."

"Her parents may never come back from safari," my mother said.

Julie gave me a fashion show that night of all the clothes my mother had bought her while I was gone. By the time it was over, I was so exhausted that I could barely keep my eyes open. I kissed Julie and Mom good night and went to bed.

I was awakened by the phone at nine A.M. sharp. I knocked the phone over reaching for the receiver and nearly fell out of bed trying to pick it up off the floor.

"What?" I snapped into the receiver.

"Where are you?" It was Monk.

"Obviously I'm at home. You just called me here. Some detective you are." I'm surly when I'm tired and still half-asleep.

"Why aren't you here?"

"It's my first day back," I said. "I assumed I had the day off."

"You just had a week's vacation in Hawaii. How much more rest could you possibly need?"

"I'm recovering from the flight," I said.

"You were sitting the whole time. I don't see what's so difficult about that."

I restrained myself. My job was difficult, but I wanted to keep it.

"I'll stop by this afternoon," I said.

"That's too late. I need you now. I have work to do."

"You have a case already?"

"Of course," Monk said. "I have to expose Dylan Swift as a fraud."

"Can't you expose him tomorrow?"

"He's taping his show today at eleven at the Belmont Hotel, and I want to be there," Monk said. "And then there's Martin Kamakele's murder to deal with."

"What can you do about it from here?"

"I can solve it," Monk said. "Today, in fact, if you can drag yourself out of bed."

The low-lying fog over San Francisco swallowed the buildings of the Financial District, obscuring the upper floors from view and blotting out the sun, leaving the streets windy, cold, and gray.

But San Franciscans like me were used to mornings like this and never lost hope that before the day was out, either winds off the Pacific would blow the fog away or the sun would burn it off. If neither happened, so be it. The fog gave the city—and, by extension, all of us who lived there—character. Character meant more to San Franciscans than sunlight anyway.

The Belmont Hotel had plenty of character. It was one of the oldest hotels in the city and a Victorian masterpiece right in the heart of Union Square. It was as much a part of San Francisco as the Golden Gate, Fisherman's Wharf, cable cars, and foggy mornings.

On our last wedding anniversary before Mitch was sent overseas, we dropped off Julie with my parents in Monterey and spent a wonderful night in a nineteenth floor room at the Belmont. We stayed in the old tower, the one that dates back to the 1920s, not the new one they built in the 1970s, which I guess isn't so new unless you compare it to the old one.

Mitch and I never left our bed except to look out the window at our view, at the sliver of the Bay Bridge we could see between the clustered skyscrapers of the Financial District. We didn't even sleep. We held each other close and listened to the music of the street: the clanking of cable car bells, the raplike rantings of a sidewalk preacher, the wail of distant police sirens, someone playing a harmonica, the honking of cars trying to inch up Powell Street, the drums and clatter of Hare Krishnas marching down Geary.

It's a memory I cherish. And for that reason, I was very uncomfortable about going to the Belmont with Monk to see Dylan Swift.

I can understand how my apprehension might not make a lot of sense to you. But the Belmont is a place that has a lot of emotional resonance for me because of the time I spent there with Mitch. If Swift and I were both at the Belmont, and Swift really could talk to the dead, I was sure to hear from Mitch again. In the same way the Grand Kiahuna Poipu, by virtue of its placement as the jumping-off point for souls, might give Swift a foot in the door to the great beyond, I figured the Belmont would be crackling with psychic energy as far as Mitch and I were concerned.

I'd finally reached a sort of peace with my grief back in Hawaii. But it was a fragile peace. Another message from Mitch, real or not, could shatter it. So I was very uneasy as we approached the ballroom where Swift's show was shot.

Monk was as excited as a kid on his way to Disneyland, though you'd have to know him well to recognize it. To the casual observer, Monk appeared as tightly wound as ever. But I saw the intensity in his eyes, the slight curl of a smile at the edges of his mouth, and the way he kept rolling his shoulders.

There was an enormous line of people waiting to get inside, hundreds at least, jamming the hallway in carefully roped-off lanes that snaked the line back on itself several times in the corridor. Even so, the line stretched down the corridor and out of sight around the corner.

"We'll never get in," I said.

"Stay here," Monk said.

He went to the head of the line and said something to the beefy security guard there. The guard mumbled into his radio, listened to the reply, then motioned Monk into the ballroom. Monk waved me up.

"What did you say?" I asked as we were moved to the front of the line and admitted into the ballroom, which was already rapidly filling up with people.

"I told him I was Adrian Monk and that Mr. Swift would be very upset if he knew we stopped by and were turned away. The security guard checked. Apparently I was right."

There were several minibleachers, with only three rows each, arranged in a half circle facing a stage. The ballroom was lit by the harsh glare of enormous movie lights mounted on scaffolding that stretched over the stage and bleachers. Cameras that pivoted on the ends of telescoping crane arms were positioned in each corner of the room. Several flat-screen monitors hung from the scaffolding so we could see ourselves on TV.

"Mr. Monk, the only reason Swift would let you in is if he intends to take advantage of you."

"I know," Monk said, scanning the audience for two empty seats.

"He's in his element here and in complete control of what happens. He'll reveal your most intimate secrets and fears on national television."

"I'm counting on it," Monk said.

"Or he will reveal mine," I said, revealing my true fear.

"I won't let him do that, Natalie."

"You don't have any control over what happens here, Mr. Monk. This is his show."

He smiled enigmatically. "Not today."

27

Mr. Monk Talks to the Dead

We found two unoccupied front-row seats next to two familiar faces—Captain Stottlemeyer and Lieutenant Disher were sitting in the audience waiting for us. Stottlemeyer looked grumpy and uncomfortable, but Disher was wide-eyed and exuberant.

"What are you doing here?" I said as we took our seats beside them.

"Ask Monk," Stottlemeyer said. "He insisted we show up for this freak show."

"It's gonna be great," Disher said. "This guy Swift can talk to the dead."

"No, he can't," Stottlemeyer said. "Because dead people don't talk. You want to know why they don't talk? *Because they're dead.*"

"I'm looking forward to introducing you to my uncle Morty," Disher said.

"He came down here today, too?"

"He died ten years ago," Disher said. "But if Dylan Swift makes a connection to the beyond, I guarantee you my uncle Morty will grab the phone."

Stottlemeyer groaned. "You'd better have a damn good reason for dragging us down here, Monk."

"Did you get my letter?" Monk asked.

Stottlemeyer patted his breast pocket. "It's right here in my pocket. Unopened and unread, just like you told me. If I give it to you now, can I leave?"

But as Stottlemeyer spoke the doors closed and an assistant director, a young woman wearing a headset microphone, stepped onto the stage.

"I'm Abigail Donovan, the first assistant director, and I want to thank you all for coming today to be a part of the Dylan Swift show."

The audience applauded. Why, I don't know, but we joined in because it seemed to be the thing to do. Donovan smiled, pleased with the response.

"That's great; we love an enthusiastic audience. Your positive energy is very, very important to the show. We're assuming you came here to talk to a loved one who has passed on. If not, we ask that you give up your seat to one of the hundreds of people outside who are anxious for a reading."

Monk whispered to me. "She's making sure Swift has a receptive audience, people eager to help him when he starts fishing for information under the guise of hearing from the dead."

"Remember that this is a dialogue between you and your departed loved ones, with Dylan in the middle," she said. "He needs your cooperation to interpret the messages he's relaying, so don't be shy."

"In other words, if he gets it wrong, tell him the right answer," Monk whispered to Stottlemeyer. "It's the audience that's doing all the work, not Swift."

"The best suckers are the people who want to be suckered," Stottlemeyer replied in a whisper.

"You could be on camera at any moment during the program," Abigail Donovan said, "and we want your friends at home to know you're having fun. React to what he is saying."

"So Swift will know if he's scored with one of his guesses," Monk whispered to me.

"This show is produced live on tape, so we'll be shooting in real time, pausing only for the commercial breaks."

I didn't listen to the rest of the technical stuff she had to say; I was still trying to figure out what she meant by "live on tape," which sounded like a contradiction to me.

When she stepped off the stage, the show's theme music blared from several speakers and the main title sequence played on the monitors. The main title was comprised of shots of Dylan Swift talking to people who were either amazed at his powers or overwhelmed and sobbing with joy.

The instant the main titles ended Swift bounded out from between two bleachers onto the stage with a big smile on his tanned face.

"Hello, my friends!"

The audience applauded uproariously, many of them rising to their feet. I could feel their excitement and anticipation as palpably as the heat from the TV lights.

Swift's gaze panned the bleachers, settling for just an instant on Monk and me, but long enough for me to be sure he'd seen us in the audience.

"What happens or doesn't happen today depends largely on you. My ability to communicate with your loved ones on the other side requires that you be receptive, open, and willing to receive their messages.

You know your loved ones better than I do, and I may not always understand the messages I'm receiving. It's up to you to interpret them."

Monk whispered to Stottlemeyer, "In other words, if his guesses are all wrong, it's not because he's a fraud; it's because you weren't receptive enough."

"I'd like to arrest him right now," Stottlemeyer said.

Swift closed his eyes and held his hands out in front of him, palms up, as if feeling the heat from a campfire. "I'm sensing blue and the letter *M*."

Disher's hand shot up. "Me! Me!"

Stottlemeyer yanked Disher's arm down, but it was too late. Swift had opened his eyes and was on his way over.

"What's your name?"

Disher stood up. "Randy Disher."

"How do you know this spirit is calling out for you, Randy?"

"Because my uncle Morty loved to fish at Loon Lake," Disher said. "And his favorite color was blue."

"Yes, I see him now," Swift said. "He's an older man, not exactly fat, but not thin, either."

"That's him! He had a beer gut." Disher turned to Stottlemeyer. "Isn't this amazing?"

"That's one word for it," Stottlemeyer said.

"I see a very special place on the lake. It's his favorite fishing hole, the one he never told anybody about," Swift said. "You know the one I mean, his secret spot."

"In the bay, by the swimming dock in front of the little red cabins?"

"The secret is out now," Stottlemeyer said.

"That's the one. He wants you to know that his

spirit is there and the fish are still biting." Swift put his hand on Disher's shoulder. "Go park your boat in front of the little red cabins when you want to be close to him and you will be."

Disher nodded, all choked up, and looked to the ceiling. "I love you, Uncle Morty."

"He loves you, too," Swift said, then turned and regarded Monk.

"Hello, Mr. Swift," Monk said.

"This, ladies and gentlemen, is Adrian Monk, the great detective," Swift said. "If you watched me on *Larry King Live* last night, you know that Adrian and I worked together with the spirit of a murdered woman to find her killer and bring him to justice. You can read the whole story in my next book."

The audience *ooh*ed and *aah*ed. I noticed that Swift was calling Monk by his first name now, like they were old buddies, something even I didn't feel comfortable doing. Stottlemeyer was Monk's oldest friend and he didn't call him by his first name, either. The fact that Swift was assuming such familiarity must have been particularly galling to Monk. But if it was, Monk hid it well.

Swift smiled warmly at him. "It's good to see you, my friend. How are you?"

"Troubled," Monk said.

"Is it about your wife, Trudy?"

Monk nodded.

Stottlemeyer stared at Monk, obviously surprised that he'd disclosed something so personal on television—or at all.

Swift faced the audience in the other bleachers. "Adrian's wife was killed a few years ago, and her murder was never solved. You should know that I've relayed some messages from Trudy to Adrian before, but beyond that, we've had no subsequent contact." Swift faced Monk again. "Isn't that true?"

"Yes, it is. I'm here now because I believe there's more she has to tell me. I can feel it."

"I'm sure you can, Adrian. Your connection to your wife is very strong. What you're feeling is her effort to communicate with you. And she *has* reached you, but you lack the gift to receive more from her than that vague sense that compelled you to see me again. She wanted you to seek me out today because there *is* more she wants to tell you."

The audience fell silent, staring in rapt attention at Swift and Monk.

"But I have the gift. I can feel her concern for you. Trudy knows you're in pain. She wants you to be at peace."

Swift closed his eyes and began to tremble all over. The entire room became eerily silent, as if everyone were holding their breath, waiting for whatever powerful revelation would surely come.

His trembling stopped and his eyes opened. He met Monk's gaze and spoke to him as if the two men were all alone.

"I'm sensing something, Adrian. It's an object of some kind. It feels soft and it makes her warm. It's like being cuddled. Do you know what it is?"

Monk shook his head.

"Help me here, Adrian. It's something very important to her. It's something she's had all of her life and has even now in the afterlife. I'm sensing the letter *N* very strongly," Swift said. "I'm sensing it so strongly, it's almost like there are two of them. Yes, definitely two Ns. And I see the night sky. What does this image mean?"

I got a shiver down my spine. I knew the answer. And I was certain Monk knew it, too. It gave me the creeps.

"Her night-night," Monk said. "It was what she called her security blanket."

Stottlemeyer and Disher shared a look of true astonishment. I'm sure I had the same expression on my face, too. Until the other night in Hawaii, Monk had never shared that information with anyone else. There was only one way Swift could have known it.

"Yes, her night-night," Swift said. "I feel it around her as a baby. I sense her sucking on the corners when she was teething. She couldn't sleep without it, even when she was an adult. So you buried her with it, didn't you, Adrian?"

Monk nodded. "So she would always be comforted by it."

People in the audience were so touched by the story that several were beginning to cry. To be honest, my eyes were tearing up, too.

"It worked, Adrian," Swift said. "It keeps her warm and safe in her eternal sleep. It cuddles her the way you used to."

Monk broke into a smile, but not one of happiness. It was one of victory. "You've just helped me solve another murder."

"Your wife's?" Swift said.

"No, the murder of Martin Kamakele, the operations manager at the Grand Kiahuna Poipu."

"And you've solved it here, on my show, thanks to that message from your wife?"

"I couldn't have done it without you."

"Incredible," Swift said.

The audience applauded, and Swift basked in their admiration for a long moment before motioning them to stop.

"I don't deserve that," Swift said. "It's the spirits who are doing the work. I am just their messenger and Adrian Monk their agent of justice. Tell us, Adrian, what the spirits have helped you discover."

Monk stood up and motioned to Stottlemeyer. "I'd like you to meet Capt. Leland Stottlemeyer of the San Francisco Police Department."

Stottlemeyer stood up and Swift shook his hand.

"It's a pleasure, Captain," Swift said.

"A few days ago, I sent Captain Stottlemeyer a notarized letter from Hawaii that he hasn't opened," Monk said. "Captain, would you please take out that letter now and show us the postmark?"

Stottlemeyer stood up, took out the letter, and held it up. On the monitor, I saw the camera zoom in on the Hawaii postmark from two days ago.

"Would you please open the letter and read it?" Monk asked.

"Gladly," Stottlemeyer said.

Swift shifted his weight nervously, a forced smile on his face, as Stottlemeyer tore open the envelope and removed the letter.

"It's a handwritten letter from you that's been signed, dated, and witnessed by a notary," Stottlemeyer said, and held up the letter. The camera cut away from Swift to a tight shot of the notary's seal, then back to Stottlemeyer as he began to read.

" 'Last night in our bungalow at the Grand Kiahuna Poipu, in the presence of my assistant, Natalie

Teeger, and no one else, I shared a story about my wife, Trudy, and her security blanket, which I called a night-night. I said that Trudy was swaddled in it as a child, teethed on the edges, and couldn't sleep without it. I said that she carried the blanket with her all her life and that, unknown to anyone but me, I'd buried it with her.' "

Stottlemeyer paused for a moment, glanced up at Swift, and broke into a grin before he read the rest. " 'That story, which Dylan Swift has told you today, never happened. It's a lie that I came up with last night.' "

There were gasps of shock throughout the audience. Swift looked as if he'd been slapped. He was wide-eyed, his cheeks reddening. He shook his head in denial. I remembered the emotion Monk showed when he told me that story. I believed it. Even now, hearing the content of that letter, I still did.

"The story is true; it's that letter that is the lie," Swift said. "I know what I am sensing. Trudy had a night-night and she is holding it now. I see it very clearly. What does this have to do with Martin Kamakele's murder?"

"It shows why you killed him," Monk said. "It also explains why you murdered Helen Gruber and framed her husband, Lance, for the crime."

"Okay, that's enough," Swift said, turning to face the nearest camera. "We're ending this taping now."

"I don't care whether you end the taping or not," Stottlemeyer said. "But you aren't going anywhere."

"You're a con man and a fake," Monk said. "You rely on 'cold reading,' an old-fashioned grifter's trick, to make people think you are communicating with spirits when, in fact, the sucker is giving you all the information. Like you did with Lieutenant Disher a few moments ago."

"*Lieutenant* Disher?" Swift said.

Disher flashed his badge at Swift. "That's right, pal, I'm a cop."

I looked up at the monitors. The cameras were still rolling, holding on a two-shot of Monk and Swift. Somebody in the production booth must have realized this film could end up being very valuable.

"You said you were sensing a color and a letter, and you waited for an eager mark in the audience to show himself," Monk said. "The mark, Lieutenant Disher, gave you the significance of the color and the man's name, identifying the spirit as his uncle. You said he wasn't fat but he wasn't thin, a nondescription, and waited, once again, for Lieutenant Disher to give you the rest."

"I was totally onto you," Disher said. "I was just playing the dupe to set the trap."

"You were lulling him into a false sense of superiority, is that it?" Stottlemeyer said.

"Exactly," Disher said, though his face was bright red with embarrassment.

"But cold reading isn't the only trickery you use," Monk said to Swift. "You tape your shows at hotels, knowing that many of your guests will stay there. That's important, because all their rooms are bugged with listening devices."

This news moved through the audience like a wave. People rustled in their seats, whispering to one another and shaking their heads in shock and anger. The cameras panned over them, capturing it all on-screen.

"That's not true," Swift said.

"Here's what happened. Kamakele was the manager of hotel operations here at the Belmont and planted the devices for you. He also supervised the remodeling of the Grand Kiahuna Poipu and made sure the rooms there were bugged, too," Monk said. "Your scheme was going smoothly until an elderly woman named Helen Gruber rented the bungalow next to yours. She complained to the hotel staff that she was hearing voices. They thought she was delusional, but you knew the truth. You knew that her hearing aids were picking up the transmissions from the listening devices. Like this one I found in the bungalow."

Monk reached into his pocket and pulled out a tiny transmitter about the size of an M&M. So that was what Monk was doing on our last day on Kauai. He wasn't straightening up; he was searching for the bugs.

The listening devices explained how Swift knew all about my trip to Mexico with Mitch and the details about my husband's death in Kosovo. He'd overheard me tell Monk about it in my hotel room.

"You couldn't take the chance that Helen would figure out what she was hearing. You were already planning to kill her when you saw me at the hotel. That's when you realized you could capitalize on her killing by helping me solve her murder. But you'd have to frame somebody else for it first. You'd overheard everything that had been said in Helen's bungalow, so you knew all about Lance's affair. He made the perfect fall guy. You waited until Lance went snorkeling; then you crept into their bungalow. You hit Helen over the head with a coconut and stuffed her in the refrigerator for a few moments to leave enough forensic clues behind to create the impression that she'd been kept inside all night. You then put her in the hot tub and carefully staged a scene you knew I'd recognize was faked."

"Why did he kill Martin Kamakele?" I asked.

"Because when the news broke about Swift's involvement in solving the murder, Kamakele figured out what really happened," Monk said. "He met with Swift in the luau garden and blackmailed him. Swift was outraged, grabbed the shovel, and killed him, then buried him with the roasting pig. That's how Swift got the blister that's healing on his hand."

"This is all absurd speculation and completely false," Swift said. "You can't prove any of it."

"I don't have to. You proved it for me," Monk said. "Since you can't speak to the dead, the only way you could have known the things you told me and Lieutenant Kealoha was if you committed the murder yourself. The Kauai police will find the listening devices and the recording equipment in your bungalow. They will test Helen Gruber's hearing aids and discover they pick up the transmissions. That should be enough for a jury."

"They'll never believe it," Swift said.

"Are you kidding?" Stottlemeyer said. "There are people who believed you could talk to the dead with far less evidence than this. I'm not worried. But you should be. Look at your audience."

Swift glanced at the people in the bleachers and saw the anger, betrayal, and disgust on their faces. And for an instant, I saw on his face his horrifying realization that Stottlemeyer was absolutely right.

Lieutenant Disher stepped forward, taking out his

handcuffs. "Dylan Swift, you're under arrest for the murders of Helen Gruber and Martin Kamakele."

The producers of Dylan Swift's show, realizing they were now out of a job, sold the footage to the local and national media within minutes of his arrest. A little over an hour later, people from San Francisco to Bangladesh, from Walla Walla to the Galapagos Islands, saw Swift's humiliating ruination.

Stottlemeyer wasn't thrilled about it, and neither was the district attorney, because the wide exposure of the tape was going to make it difficult to find an unbiased jury anywhere on the planet.

Lance Vaughan was released from jail, and the last I heard, he and Roxanne Shaw had sold the book rights to their story to Penguin Group (USA), and a movie version was in the works at HBO. The couple sued the Kauai Police Department for false arrest, defamation, and a host of other indignities. The case is still in litigation, and probably will be for years to come, but as a result, Lieutenant Kealoha didn't get his promotion.

None of that really mattered to me or to Monk. He'd figured out the puzzle, righted the wrongs, and accomplished what he'd set out to do. Order was restored, and that was what he cared about most.

But I'm getting ahead of myself.

In the immediate aftermath of the show, something was still nagging me about the case.

We slipped out the back exit of the hotel before the press showed up, and walked back to my car, which was in a parking structure a few blocks away.

"I believed that story you told about the night-night," I said as we strolled along.

"If I didn't convince you, I never would have been able to convince him. I knew he was listening to everything we said."

"I still believe that story."

"Even though it's a lie?"

"I don't think it is," I said. "You told it with too much emotion, and you aren't that good an actor."

Monk was quiet for a long time. "It wasn't Trudy who had the night-night. It was my mother."

"You buried her with it, didn't you?"

"Yes," Monk said. "But I had it dry-cleaned first."

Of course he did.

Read on for an excerpt from the next
book starring Adrian Monk, the brilliant
investigator who always knows when
something's out of place . . .

Mr. Monk and the Blue Flu

Coming in January 2007

The San Francisco city hall was built not long after the 1906 earthquake to scream to the world that the city was back, bigger, stronger, and more opulent than ever.

The building's Beaux-Arts flourishes, Doric columns, and Grand Baroque copper dome inspired by St. Peter's Basilica in Rome meant you'd never mistake it for anything but a capitol of some kind. As if the grand dome weren't grand enough, it's topped with an ornate steeple and a torch that lights up at night when the City Council is meeting.

The building always struck me as garish and pompous rather than majestic and imposing. I guess that's fitting for a place that houses mostly politicians and bureaucrats.

But standing in Mayor Smitrovich's office, I felt like I was in an aquarium. There were tarpon, swordfish, and Dorados mounted on the walls, their mouths agape, forever twisting in midthrash. A pair of window cleaners worked outside, peering in at us from the other side of the glass behind the mayor. All that was missing to make the effect complete were a ceramic mermaid and a castle for us to swim around.

"It's a real pleasure to finally meet you, Mr. Monk," Smitrovich said, coming around the desk and shaking Monk's hand. "I'm a big fan."

I handed Monk a moist towelette.

"Really?" Monk said, wiping his hand.

"I truly appreciate your tireless efforts on behalf of this city."

"That's such a relief. I was beginning to think you were ignoring all my letters," Monk said. "It's about time someone in authority ended our city's shame and turned Lombard from the world's crookedest street to the straightest."

"You want to *straighten* Lombard?" the mayor said.

"Whoever approved that street should have been beaten with his T-square," Monk said. "It's a good thing he was stopped before every street in the city looked like Lombard. It's astonishing to me that nobody has ever bothered to correct it."

"You know how it is, Mr. Monk," the mayor said. "There are so many other pressing issues that demand our attention."

"What could be more important than that?"

"Actually," the mayor said, "that's why I asked you here today."

"You're not straightening Lombard?"

"Not just yet."

"I know you'll face some opposition from a wacko minority of hippies and beatniks. But I'll back you one hundred percent."

"That's reassuring, because I truly need your support," the mayor said. "It's clear to me that we both share a deep and abiding love for this great city."

"It can't be great as long as the world's crookedest street is here," Monk said. "What would be great is a city with the world's *straightest* street. Just think of all the tourists who would come here to see it."

"Millions of tourists *do* come to see Lombard Street," the mayor said.

"To ridicule us," Monk said. "Where do you think the phrase 'those crazy Americans' came from? Lombard Street. Fix the street and they'll never say it again."

"Right now, I'm more concerned about the lack of police officers reporting to work. Most of the patrol officers are on the job; it's the detectives and supervisory personnel who aren't showing up," the mayor said. "It's creating a serious public safety issue. We don't have the manpower to investigate major felonies. You know how important the first forty-eight hours are in an investigation. Tracks are getting cold. Something must be done about this, especially with this strangler on the loose. They couldn't have picked a worse time to pull this crap."

"You could drop your demands for big cuts in police salaries and benefits," I said. "I bet that would bring the detectives back to work."

"Sure, I could give the police officers what they want," the mayor said, shooting me an angry look before shifting his gaze back to Monk, "but then where would the money come from to straighten Lombard street?"

Monk glanced at me. "He has a point."

"No, he doesn't," I said. "With all due respect, Mr. Smitrovich, these people lay their lives on the line for us. We owe them a decent wage, affordable medical care, and a comfortable retirement."

"And what should I tell the sewer workers, the schoolteachers, and the firefighters who aren't enjoying the same benefits, Miss Teeger? And what do I tell the citizens who want new schools and cleaner, safer, *straighter* streets?"

The last bit was clearly for Monk's benefit, but Monk wasn't paying attention. He was tipping this way and that, trying to peer around the mayor.

The mayor looked over his shoulder to see what was distracting Monk. All he saw were two window cleaners running their blades across the glass, wiping away the soap.

"You didn't invite Mr. Monk down here to give him the city's party line on the labor negotiations," I said. "You want something from him."

"That's true, I do," the mayor said, addressing Monk. "I'd like your help solving the city's homicides."

But Monk was busy waving at the window cleaners. They waved back. Monk waved again. They waved back. Monk waved again and they ignored him.

"Mr. Monk consults for the police because of his special relationship with Captain Stottlemeyer," I said. "He's not going to work for another detective."

I looked at Monk for confirmation, but now he was wiping the air with his hand palm-out in front of him. The window cleaners finally understood and soaped the window again. Monk smiled approvingly as they wiped it again with their blades.

"I don't want him to work for any other detectives," the mayor said. "I want *them* to work for *him*."

"I don't understand," I said.

"I want to reinstate him in the San Francisco Police Department," the mayor said. "And promote him to captain of the Homicide Division."

"Is this some kind of joke?" I said. "Because if it is, it's cruel."

"I'm completely serious," the mayor said.

Monk marched over to the window and tapped on the glass. "You missed a spot."

The window cleaners shrugged. They couldn't hear him. He mimed spraying the window and wiping the glass in front of him again. They shook their heads no.

I looked at the mayor. "Now I know you're joking."

"He's got a better solve rate than all the detectives in the homicide department put together, and at a fraction of the cost. With Monk at the helm, the homicide department could do the same job or better than they've been doing, with half as many men. Besides, I think he's ready for command."

"Are we talking about the same man?" I said. "Look at him."

Monk shook his head at the cleaners and pointed to the spot they had just cleaned. The two cleaners started hoisting their platform up to the next floor. Monk banged on the glass.

"Get back down here," Monk yelled.

The mayor smiled. "I see a man with an incredible eye for detail and a commitment to sticking with a task until it's done right.

Monk turned to me. I hoped he'd finally say something about the mayor's outrageous offer.

"I need a wipe," Monk said.

"Excuse us for a moment," I said to the mayor, then went over to Monk and handed him a wipe. "Did you hear what the mayor just said?"

Monk tore open the packet, took out the wipe, and began scrubbing the glass with it.

"What are you doing?" I asked.

Monk looked at his wipe and shook his head. "Silly me, the stain was inside." He turned to the mayor and held up the wipe. "Crisis solved. You can relax now."

"Then you'll take the job?" the mayor said.

"What job?" Monk asked.

"Captain of the Homicide Division," the mayor said.

Monk looked at the wipe in astonishment, then at me. "This was all I had to do? All these years I've been working to get back in, and it comes down to this?"

"Mr. Monk," I said quietly, so the mayor couldn't hear me. "He's taking advantage of you. He's using you as a ploy to break the strike. You'll be a scab."

Monk winced with revulsion. "A scab? That sounds disgusting."

"They are," I said. "You'd be relieving some of the pressure on the city and undermining the officers' efforts to get a better contract."

"But he's offering me my badge," Monk said.

"He's offering you Captain Stottlemeyer's job," I said.

Monk handed me the dirty wipe, then faced the mayor. "I want the job, but not at the captain's expense."

"You'd just be filling in until this labor situation is resolved, commanding a handful of other reinstated detectives who, for various reasons, had to leave the department," the mayor said. "But if you do a good job, and I know you will, this temporary assignment could become a permanent position at another division. I know you want to support the captain, but think about all those crimes going unsolved. Do you want people getting away with murder?"

Monk looked at me. "How can I say no?"

"Repeat after me," I said. "*No.*"

Monk considered for a minute, then turned to the mayor. "I'll do it."